Forgive Me If I've Told You This Before

FORGIVE ME IF I'VE TOLD YOU THIS BEFORE

Karelia Stetz-Waters

Forgive Me If I've Told You This Before
© 2014 Karelia Stetz-Waters

ISBN 978-1-932010-73-2

Ooligan Press
Portland State University
Post Office Box 751, Portland, Oregon 97207
503.725.9748
ooligan@ooliganpress.pdx.edu
www.ooligan.pdx.edu

Full credits located on page 300.

Library of Congress Cataloging-in-Publication Data

Stetz-Waters, Karelia.
  Forgive me if I've told you this before / Karelia Stetz-Waters.
    pages cm
  Summary: At high school beginning in 1989, shy, intelligent Triinu comes to realize that she is a lesbian—and in love—just as her home state of Oregon is debating Measure 9, which would allow discrimination against gay people.
  ISBN 978-1-932010-73-2
  [1. Lesbians—Fiction. 2. Gay rights—Fiction. 3. Toleration—Fiction. 4. High schools—Fiction. 5. Schools—Fiction. 6. Family life—Oregon—Fiction. 7. Coming out (Sexual orientation)—Fiction. 8. Oregon—History—20th century—Fiction.] I. Title. II. Title: Forgive me if I have told you this before.
  PZ7.S8426For 2014
  [Fic]—dc23
                                    2014023156

Cover design by Robyn Best
Interior design by Riley Kennysmith

Printed in the United States of America

For queer kids everywhere. Hang in there.

The Dome of God

Half-orphaned Isabel Avila sat beside me on the bench in the Camp Luther Grove dining hall, her dark hair pulled into a high side ponytail. "It wasn't Triinu's fault," she said. "Jared is like one of those rednecks who drives around with a big antenna on his truck listening to the police scanner because he can't get into the police school because he's, like, a pervert or something. He's like that … only for God."

Pastor Brown looked at Isabel. He was probably thinking about her father who had died last year, just after Isabel turned thirteen. Then he looked back to me, probably thinking about my mother (president of the altar guild) and my father (church council member for three terms running). He sighed, probably thinking about Jared Pinter, the volunteer interim youth minister I had not-really stabbed in the groin with a Bic pen.

"You know you're in high school now," he began.

That too was technically incorrect. We were going into high school at the beginning of September. That was why we were at Camp Luther Grove for summer "Fun in the Son."

Jared had brought it on himself, really. Every summer, shortly before school resumed, the whole Avila family and I would pile into their bumper-stickered van and head out to Camp Luther Grove. Waiting for us at the end of a dusty road were cabins, tents, pop-up trailers, and kids camping on blue tarps. Children, grandmothers, and teenagers alike wandered the grounds, occasionally popping into the rec room to fashion a macramé bracelet. Isabel and I had always had the same agenda: eat as much candy as possible, talk to as few adults as we could, and spend absolutely every free minute in the creek. It was 1989, and it was still okay for children to be feral. We knew how to swim and there were no poisonous snakes, so the adults let us be. I had never stabbed anyone. I had never even used the Lord's name in vain.

Then this year, one evening at about twilight, when Isabel and I had been heading down to the creek to put our toes in the water and talk about which of the New Kids on the Block we were going to marry, Jared shot out of a cabin like a Ken doll in a slingshot.

"Hello fellow Christians!" he called out. "Isn't it a great night to be godly?"

Pastor Brown was right; we were growing up. A year earlier, we would have simply run into the night, shrieking. As it was, we stopped and dropped our heads.

"Isn't God grrreat?" Jared said, imitating Tony the Tiger and punctuating the statement with a finger pointed skyward, as though God was a big blimp hanging directly over Camp Luther Grove. "Why don't you come in with the rest of the group and learn an awesome new church song?"

It was my fault. Isabel had the guts to say no, but I hedged. Always the apologist, I said, "Well, maybe we should go in and all. I mean, it's just one night." And before I knew it we were inside the cabin surrounded by older teenagers. It smelled like damp socks, and there was no candy.

"Okay," Jared said. "Let's hit this." He made some ridiculous chuffing sound into his hands and the group began to chant.

"I believe in God. That guy is almighty, and he has a son. That guy's the cool one. It's Jesus! It's Jesus!"

Jared drummed on an imaginary drum set.

"He frees us!" the group chanted.

"Come on girls," Jared said. "You should know the words by now. He frees us!"

We were not used to this. Church belonged to adults like my parents. Sometimes the adults would spat over the propriety of talking in the sanctuary before church or how frequently to serve communion.

Occasionally Isabel and I would bicker over our own differences. She hated going to church. I liked being an acolyte. Every Sunday, the altar guild tucked me into the red-and-white acolyte robes. Thus transformed, I followed Pastor Brown through the ancient movement of the liturgy. I felt called. Isabel thought it was all a bunch of baloney, but then I might have thought that, too, if God decided to give my father cancer and make him die. So we didn't talk about it.

One thing was clear, though: God belonged to the adult world, and youth belonged to us. God never used slang, and He certainly did not want to hear the Righteousness Rap for a third time.

Isabel put a finger to her forehead and pulled an imaginary trigger.

When the group finally stopped chanting, Jared took out his Bible. "So kids, what passage do you want to talk about today?" Without waiting for an answer he said, "How about Leviticus 20:13." He opened his Bible. "Who wants to read?"

A girl with aggressively permed bangs waved her hand as though it was on fire. "Me! Me!" she said, and began to read: "'If a man has sexual relations with a man as one does with a woman, both of them have done what is detestable. They are to be put to death; their blood will be on their own heads.'"

I looked at Isabel and furrowed my brow.

"What the fuck?" she mouthed.

Forbearing Emmanuel Lutherans did not talk about

damnation; they talked about salmon bakes. Agape love. The Mother-Daughter Fashion Show. My mother said that there was a hell, but there was no one in it. No one got blood on their heads.

"What does this passage mean to you?" Jared asked.

The room was quiet for a long time.

"Fine," Jared said. "I'm going to give you all a piece of paper and a pen, and we're going to write down some of our thoughts. I want you all to ask yourselves if God will save the ho-mo-sex-uals." He pronounced each syllable separately. "Then write your answer on the paper."

Isabel took a pen and wrote on her paper, "What's for dinner?" I shook my head. She wrote, "Jesus!" We had an ongoing joke about Jesus. As far as we could tell, every Sunday school question could be answered with the word "Jesus." I pretended to focus on my own paper, but out of the corner of my eye I saw her write a few more lines and push the paper back to me: "What causes gravity? Jesus! Who won the Super Bowl? Jesus!"

I really didn't understand why everyone was so fond of Jesus. Now that my mother was taking Pastor Brown's adult Bible study class, she referred sometimes to the "historical Jesus." I held nothing against that man. Poor Jesus, with his dusty sandals and his wild ideals. I wanted to follow him to Gethsemane and put my hand over his praying palms. "Stop, Jesus," I would have said. "God will forgive our sins without all this mess."

But the historical Jesus was not the Jesus served up during Sunday school. The Sunday school Jesus had risen from the pages of a Christian coloring book and would not return to his tomb. He was like Isabel's older brother: jovial and bossy, with thick ankles and freshly scrubbed hair. Jesus loved us and forgave us, but he counted the change in our offering envelopes as though we might cheat the pastor of his quarters.

A few minutes later, Jared told us to stop writing. "So," he said. "Will God save the ho-mo-sexuals?"

"Jesus," Isabel said meditatively.

I could not look at her. Even if I could keep a straight face, I feared my spleen might start giggling as Jared solemnly agreed, "You are so right, Isabel. He's the answer to all questions, isn't He? So, will Jesus save the homosexuals?"

Ursula Benson, whom I recognized as an occasional Sunday school student from the other side of town, raised her hand. Isabel and I rolled our eyes at each other. The last time Ursula had been fun was the day she got kicked out of Mrs. La Farge's sixth-grade Sunday school class for not sitting like a lady. Now she just liked to talk.

"Why are you even asking us?" Ursula demanded from beneath plum-colored bangs. She must have been commandeered by Jared's surprise slingshot attack. She would never have come to something like this on her own.

Jared folded his hands on his lap and nodded with regretful concern. "I am asking because you can be the arm of God's salvation through Jesus Christ our savior."

"You want me to tell my gay friends they're going to hell?"

I giggled. No one had gay friends.

"How do you know the homosexuals are going to hell? Show me where it says it in the Bible." Ursula pushed her bangs out of her eye.

"Leviticus 20:13." Jared snapped his Bible closed.

"That's what some ancient civilization, like, a million years ago thought. They probably thought safe sex meant not sleeping with your mother."

"Ursula!"

Ursula jabbed a finger at her Bible. "Isn't there a bunch of stuff in here that says women shouldn't cut their hair and we shouldn't eat shellfish?"

"Cutting hair is a whole lot different from being a pedophile."

Ursula folded her arms. "What does Jesus say about gays?"

Jared leafed through his Bible again.

"Well?"

An interesting pattern of red blotches appeared on Jared's neck, and Isabel wrote me a quick note: "I see the face of Elvis on Jared's neck." I wrote back, "No, it's Jesus."

The girl with the curly bangs wiggled in her seat, but her hair did not move. It had been sprayed to a crisp. "Ursula ... let's just pray, okay?" she said. Isabel and I rolled our eyes.

"I think that is a great idea. Let's pray to the great dude in the heavens," Jared said. The prayer went on for several lifetimes, during which time I was fairly certain I identified the source of the sock smell: a boy with glasses who was one grade ahead of us and who always looked slightly damp, as though life was so embarrassing it made him perspire constantly. I generally sympathized, but not when it meant smelling his sock feet.

Finally Jared said, "Amen." I thought that was the end of it. Then he yelled, "Reverence Round-Up!" so loudly I jumped in my seat. "On the count of three, everyone run around the camp and gather as many people as you can for a prayer circle. Ready, set, go!"

Isabel was first out of the door, but we were separated by a group of cheering teenage girls. I was just about to exit when I felt a hand clamp around my wrist. "Not you, Triinu."

I froze. Jared held my wrist in his hand. I looked at him. He was very muscular and very blond. Even his chest hair was blond. I could see because he wore a tank top with thin straps that revealed the tops of his pecs.

"That's a very pretty name—Triinu. Does it come from Estonia like your mom?"

I nodded.

"Is it short for anything?"

"Katariina."

"Ka-ta-rii-na." He drew out the syllables. "Come here and sit next to me."

I still clutched the pen and paper on which I had written, "Who thinks Jared Pinter is full of shit? Jesus!" Reluctantly, I sat down. He sat next to me, leaned over, and looked under the veil of my hair as you might look at a child under a tablecloth.

"Talk much?" he asked. Shy people can't answer that question, with its innuendoes and un-statements, even though the answer is simply no. Then he touched my leg and murmured, "Your leg is so soft." No boy had ever touched me, let alone a man who all the high school girls at church said was so handsome he could be a televangelist or a male model.

Now here I was, alone with Jared. He stroked my leg again. "It's like silk. Do you know what silk is?"

I tried to open my mouth and say, "Shove off, dickweed, of course I know what silk is!" but I couldn't. I couldn't say anything. That was why I liked church camp. I didn't have to talk to anyone except Isabel. In middle school, Isabel and I had been teased by every kid a grade above us and a grade below us, but the church kids left us alone, especially now that Isabel's father had died. We moved in and out of Luther Grove's rooms without permission, but we were never reprimanded. Everyone assumed I was comforting Isabel in her grief, although I never did, and she never talked about her father. Still, it was a wonderful cover, and we used it to avoid all kinds of unpleasant activities.

Jared had not gotten the memo. He had separated us. Now

he was touching my leg and saying, "You're a very pretty girl. You should talk more." I felt at a loss without Isabel. If she were there, she would have made some blunt excuse and we would have left, but she wasn't there, and Jared stood up and locked the door. "Do you have a boyfriend?" he asked.

I noticed that he had actually braided the hair beneath his armpits. He was like some pale, blond foreigner with ways unlike our own. A stranger. A savage. I thought maybe we had seen a video about this in social studies. The lesson was not to judge. Other cultures were different and possibly inferior, but it wasn't their fault.

"Because you're definitely pretty enough."

Or maybe this was a scene from the *Stranger Danger* film we were shown in school, the one where the kidnapper read the little girl's name on her T-shirt. He called her by name, and she thought he knew her. Then the screen faded to black.

Jared ran his thumb along the frayed edge of my cutoffs. "Are you a senior? You seem very mature for your age."

Or maybe this was what I had been waiting for. I had a whole Trapper Keeper notebook full of poems I had written to my imaginary boyfriend. Maybe I wanted this.

Suddenly I was on my feet. "I need to find Isabel. She's gonna wonder where I am."

At that exact moment, there was a pounding on the door. "Triinu!"

"There she is now. See you soon, gotta run!"

It was in that moment of haste that Jared grabbed my hand. It really was his fault. I tried to yank my hand from his grip, so he also stuck out a leg to stop my progress. I was already in motion, and I tripped and fell toward him. In my effort not to fall *on* him, I stuck out my arm, forgetting the Bic pen that I had been clutching. Then I did fall, and the pen slipped from my grasp as

14

it lodged in Jared's thigh. He let out a bellow much louder than the one he used to call for the Reverence Round-Up.

I flew to the door and opened it. All I could see was Isabel, a sea of faces behind her, the result of the Round-Up, presumably. I didn't need to tell her to run.

I had known Isabel forever. She was the first stranger to emerge from the milky scent of childhood. At age five, I had recognized my mother, my father, and poor Crystal, a classmate at school who had been badly burned when her house caught fire, but the other children were a blur. Then, suddenly, I was running toward Isabel's turquoise coat on the playground. Our hands clasped and we were off. And, almost as soon as we started to run, we heard hoofbeats. Behind us was a stampede of phosphorescent horses. We never had to say, "Let's pretend we have magic horses." We simply turned around and there they were. "I hear the horses coming," Isabel would say, and we would mount them, their glittering shoulders carrying us over the roots and rocks that tangled our woodland lots, our sneakers riding high above their sharp hooves.

I heard that thunder of hooves as we raced for the maze of deer trails that laced the woods beyond the camp. Into the star-speckled darkness. Into the ferns and the cattails. Into the moon that filtered past the jagged edges of fir branches. I didn't know if I was running from Jared or from the fear of punishment or simply from the inanity of treating God like some made-to-order buddy when I had read the Bible. I knew what happened when God visited the earth. We cowered in fear. We crucified. And sometimes we walked blindly by, like dumb animals stunned by a bright light, saying, "Why is the tomb so empty?" I knew one thing. It was never simple, and there was more of God in the darkness of our flight than in Jared's musty cabin.

Sadly, even God's soldiers must eat, and several hours later we had returned to the dining hall, lured by the promise of Rice Krispies treats. Just as we were about to enter the hall, Pastor Brown appeared and apprehended us.

Isabel explained the story as I had related it to her. I kept my head bowed. "He touched her leg!" Isabel exclaimed for the hundredth time.

"I know." Pastor Brown sighed. "I know. He shouldn't have done that. I've talked to him. But Triinu, you shouldn't have stabbed him with a pen."

"It was an accident," I whispered.

"She should have stabbed him in the eye," Isabel said.

"I'm sorry," I whispered.

"You're a young woman now," Pastor Brown said. "If someone does something you don't like, you have a right to just say no. You didn't have to stay with Jared, but you shouldn't have stuck him with your pen."

"Jared locked the door," Isabel pointed out.

"Triinu?"

I was aware of the pastor's eyes boring into the top of my head.

"Do you understand, Triinu?"

I nodded. I couldn't explain that it wasn't the lock that held me in that cabin but the dawning realization that I was supposed to be happy with Jared. *He could be a male model.*

"Triinu thinks he's a slug," Isabel said. "A big, fat, slimy slug." Actually, I liked slugs better.

Pastor Brown sighed again. "Okay. Stay out of trouble, girls."

Released, we headed down to the creek and lay on one of the sandy shoals and put our toes in the water. The summer before, Isabel had given me a wooden boat with the name *Corazón Fiel* stenciled on its side.

Her mother had taken the children on an ill-fated trip to Guatemala right after their father died. Mrs. Avila had wanted to experience her late husband's Guatemala, the Guatemala of native women cooking over open fires and colorful celebrations that did not sell T-shirts on their sidelines. She had been willing to sleep on plank beds, travel in hot busses, and eat from roadside stands to feel a connection with her husband again.

Sensing a dearth of shopping opportunities, Isabel had bought me the boat early in the trip. The boat was not particularly beautiful. A mast rose from its body, adorned with turquoise and pink sails, and its name, written on one side of the hull, looked like it had been written hastily in bleeding marker. The construction was light, but it was large and impossible to disassemble.

Isabel had written to me from every post office she could find in Guatemala, and I felt that the wrath of her letters had been directed more at the God who let her father die than at her mother or the boat:

> I bought you this fucking boat and you better like it because I've dragged it all over Guatemala! You will be in so much trouble if you don't keep this present till you DIE, because I think I'm going to DIE hauling it on these fucking busses with my mother who wants the fucking authentic Guatemalan experience. Why can't we just go to Disneyland?

Now the *Corazón Fiel* floated in an eddy, tied to the shore by a string. Above our heads, we could see not only a million stars, but also a band of pale light where the stars seemed to concentrate.

"It's the Milky Way," I said. Then I added, "Maybe God is like a big dome." I hadn't thought of this before I spoke, but as I spoke, I saw the dome clearly. It was like the night sky, dark and star-specked, except the stars were windows. At these windows, separated from each other by great distances, people sat watching. Isabel was at her window, my mother at hers, my father at his, and I was at mine. Maybe there was even a window for Jared. And millions and millions of strangers, peering through, were looking into the dome at God, for God was in the dome. He was also in the intergalactic darkness behind the dome, and in a way He was the dome. But the way we looked at Him was by sitting at our windows, and because our windows were all in different places, we all saw Him from different angles.

I tried to explain this. The image had occurred to me instantly, and it seemed utterly true. "Everyone has a window in the dome," I said. "It's like the planetarium, only we're on the roof, looking in, only it's not really a roof. And we're all looking at the same thing, but just at different angles. Maybe people from one church, like Mormons, all have their windows in the same area, so things *kind of* look the same to them." I rambled on. "And then also, sometimes, people look in the dome and see someone else's window, far away. Then they think that person is part of God too. Or maybe, if I was on Earth looking up, I'd see everybody else looking at God, and they'd look like stars. But it's always the same God."

"Maybe," Isabel said. Isabel, who usually called me a dork-weed when I talked "all poet-y." Isabel, whose father had just died. Isabel, who ate only cheese and nutritional yeast because her mother was grieving and couldn't go grocery shopping. Isabel, whom I had known since childhood.

Isabel said only, "Maybe. Maybe it's all true."

18

The Perfect Prick

The last weekend before the start of high school passed like the golden globe of an egg yolk tipped back and forth between the halves of its shell and then dropped into a bowl, beautiful and then quickly gone. "We lived," as my mother would say, translating an idiom from her native Estonian, "in the old way." That weekend, like every weekend, my mother tidied her gray hair and drove into town to do the grocery shopping. She passed through the same farms, each claiming their acreage in the Grass Seed Capital of the World. She cooked a potpie. As always, my father emptied the household trash cans into a black garbage sack, quoting as he went, "I am the old leech-gatherer." Every weekend, every year, every sack. The malamute threw her steel bowl up and down the deck stairs at dinnertime. I walked in the forest and read novels in my pajamas. Then summer ended like the end of the world.

My father woke me at six on the morning of the first day of high school. It was still dark. The house did not look much different than one of the larger cabins at Camp Luther Grove. We lived in the forest outside of town, and the A-frame house was built entirely out of cedar. Two-story windows on the south and east side of the house revealed the dark arms of oak trees, the feathery branches of firs. On the back porch, the malamute slept, content in her swaddle of fur.

Unlike the church cabins, every horizontal surface in our house was piled with books. So too were the shelves built against every perpendicular wall. My mother had stashed books—Greek tragedy, British poetry, paperback science fiction—three tiers deep on every shelf.

In the kitchen, my mother sat with her long silver hair loose around her shoulders. In her furry white robe, she looked like a gentle, sleepy bear or a wizard. My father minded the stove, flipping an egg. "Plasticized," he said, delivering it to me on a plate. He was on a mission to create the perfect over-hard egg. No brown skin. No *munavalge*, as the Estonians called the runny white.

"I don't want to go," I said.

Isabel had promised that high school could not possibly be worse than middle school. I believed her on that account. But I wanted to stay home. I wanted to follow my mother around as she cleaned the house. I wanted to throw bread crusts to the dog. I wanted to curl up in my bed beneath the sloping cedar wall of my room and read about Frodo and Samwise and their journey to Mordor. I wanted to finish the epic poem I had been writing about how terribly misunderstood I was. It was up to 102 rhyming couplets. I did not want to go to high school and actually be misunderstood.

"They're all cretins," my father said. "They're mongrel hordes."

"I want to stay home," I said.

"*Paljugi mis me tahaksime*," my mother said kindly. *There are many things one might want.*

The Estonians knew. After the Soviet invasion, some had gone into hiding in the woods, waiting for the Americans to rescue them. The Forest Brothers, they were called. My mother's cousin died of appendicitis, lying in a dirt bunker carved into the forest floor, waiting for the Americans. They never came.

"I won't learn anything you couldn't teach me," I added.

My parents nodded.

My mother had been the best UC Berkeley graduate student of her generation. A medievalist, she could translate Latin,

German, French, and Old English. My father was a physics professor at the local university. On the weekends, when it was too rainy to garden, he folded himself into a desk chair and wrote chapters for a textbook on an obscure subset of physics called Lie groups. My parents viewed public school with the same distaste I did. School was an obligation forced on the truly educated to waste their time. But my parents were also scrupulously law-abiding. The clock edged toward six-thirty.

"You've got to get dressed," my father urged. "Let's 'smite the sounding furrows.'" He was an inveterate quoter. Lyrics from operas and bits of poetry sprinkled his talk like the idioms of an obscure, well-educated nation. "'Ask not for whom the bell tolls—it tolls for you,'" he added.

My mother kissed me on the top of my head. "It's 'never send to know for whom the bell tolls.'"

"Ah yes!" my father said. "Send not."

My father drove me to school through the low-hanging fog that was so localized I could mark the exact moment we entered the valley's marshes. Each time we passed through a patch of fog I made a wish, silent and pleading: *Not me, not me. Let it be some other girl who goes to high school and carries a pink backpack and eats lunch with Isabel. Let me live in the woods and drink rainwater.*

We arrived before the car had even warmed up. "Today is the first day of the rest of your life," my father said. I glowered at him but gave him a quick hug before I got out of the car. He called after me. "'We who are about to die salute you!'"

Middleton High School was built like a fortress by people who clearly thought teenagers were evil. The walls were cinder block. The lockers were industrial-strength steel. The carpets were a coarse blue material that seemed designed to repel blood. The only windows in the entire structure, those in the front foyer, were covered with posters depicting car crashes and needles. "Only You Can Say No to Drugs" was emblazoned across them. And every inch of hall space was filled with people. But there was hope, because there in the middle of the freshman hall stood Isabel, her hair in its characteristic side ponytail. She wore a shirt reading "Pow! Bang! Shazam!" in iridescent red lettering.

"Isabel!" I called, my voice shrill and nasal and desperate. "Issy. Iz! Hey, Isabel, wait up!"

Somewhere in the distance I heard someone mimic me. "'Issy. Issy.'"

I didn't care. She had heard me. I was not alone. I flew to her, although I did not hug her. We had never been that kind of friends.

Over the loudspeaker, a voice interrupted our reunion. "This is Principal Pinn. I want to welcome you all to the first day of the year. Here are a few rules to remember." The list went on forever.

Isabel rolled her eyes. "Don't breathe. Don't look at anyone. Blah blah blah," she said.

"I know." I tried to affect a blasé cool I did not feel. "Don't do drugs. Don't touch yourself."

Isabel laughed.

"And now here's a little song you may have heard. I think this sums up what a lot of you are feeling right now," Principal Pinn said. The tinny PA system cut to "Summer of '69," with its sentimental depiction of country porches and the promise that these years were the best of our lives.

"Shoot me," Isabel said. "If these are the best years of my life, just shoot me. Back of the head. Make it painless."

22

I raised a finger to her forehead and pretended to pull the trigger.

"Thanks," she said, then added, "Oh, God!"

Coming down the hall, headed straight toward us, was the person I loathed most in the world: Pip Weston.

Three years before, early in sixth grade, Pip had slammed my locker door closed, nearly taking off my fingers. "Retard!" he had yelled as he loped off down the hallway. I had never seen him before in my life, and I had thought this was an aberration. He must have mistaken me for someone else, but he was back at lunch, and then at passing time, and then after school. I could barely get the locker door open before he banged it shut again. "Retard!"

What had made it worse was that his attention seemed to bring on the scorn of other kids at school. "Your fly's undone, retard," Pip would whisper as he bumped past me on his way to the back of the classroom. "Oh look, she thinks someone will fuck her if she leaves the barn door open." Behind me a whole row of boys would chuckle and high five.

"Maybe she can fuck a retarded sheep."

I always stayed mute.

Isabel's approach had been bolder. Pip teased her too, but she tried to insult him back. It never worked. Whatever insult she slung at him, he would just wrinkle up his nose and repeat it in a nasal voice until all his friends started chanting it along with him. At first it seemed that Isabel failed because her insults were too tame. "Dorkweed" and "pond scum" didn't pack a punch, but soon she was lobbing "motherfucker" and "asswipe." To no avail, though. Indeed, if she had told Pip she wanted to sodomize his first born with a tire iron, he probably would have just wrinkled up his nose and repeated it back in a fake soprano.

"'I want to sodomize your first born with a tire iron. I want to sodomize your first born with a tire iron.'"

There would always be another round of laughter, another crowd of boys led by Pip. It was like the inverse of one of Pastor Brown's Bible stories. Instead of the people of God populating the earth, it was Pip who multiplied. He was in every hallway, outside every bathroom door. His friends were the pack of coyotes Isabel's brother had told us would surround a person and eat them if they stayed still for too long in the fields. I could hear their teeth gnashing.

I had hoped Pip could not find me here amongst this multitude of students. I could barely keep Isabel in my sight, despite her remarkably shiny T-shirt. But there he was, coming directly toward us. There was nothing we could do. I thought, *Not me, not me.*

Then God seemingly intervened. On the other side of the hall, two older boys had been roughhousing, pretending to tackle each other over a Nerf football. One of them threw the ball, and it hit a locker near my head. The other boy lunged for it, knocking Pip out of the way. Then the bell rang, and we raced for our homeroom class.

During first period, I replayed the scene in my mind, though in my daydream one of the older boys walked over and rested his hand on the locker above my head. "That jerk bothering you? 'Cause you don't have to worry. You're in high school now. I'll take care of you."

I looked for the boy from my daydream when I was released for morning break, even though I could not really remember his face, and I knew enough to recognize his letterman jacket as a sign that he probably would not like me.

"Who are you looking for?" Isabel asked at lunch when I was still scanning the passing crowd.

"No one."

"Yeah. Who do we know here?" She was right. We knew no one. We were defenseless.

"Pip Weston is an asshole dickweed," I said.

"Yeah. He's an asshole," Isabel said.

"He's an asshole, dickweed, poop sniffer, booger eater."

We went on like this for a while, but I could tell that Isabel did not really think we were funny. The more I tried to make her laugh with my outrageous insults, the more juvenile I sounded. There were no words for how much I hated Pip. There was no way that one fumbled Nerf football could save me.

I knew what was wrong with me. I had known ever since the field trip in middle school to the Oregon Coast Aquarium, where I had seen the flounder. The larval fish, I had read on a plaque, began life with eyes on both sides of its head. As the fish matured, one eye migrated until both eyes were situated on the upward-facing side of the body. The flounder then spent the remainder of its life on the ocean floor, submerged in sand, its pigmented body changing colors to match its surroundings.

The tank illustrated this nicely. Some flounders rested in black gravel. Some flounders rested in white gravel. Black on black. White on white. All with the requisite eyes on top. Still, none of them looked fully finished. The relocated eyes were cocked at an off-angle. The fins from the flattened side jutted out like deformed, stunted limbs. They had had other plans before their eyes moved. They had planned glamorous upright lives, swimming in schools with other symmetrical fish. Perhaps they would have swum up to the surface of the ocean and turned the color of sunlight.

It was happening to me, too. It had started in the sixth grade. My eye was moving. It was the vital second part of the "When You Get Your Period" lecture, the part where my health teacher explained that my eye was slowly crawling around my head. "Of course you look funny. Your eye is behind your ear. Yes, you'll stay that way. No, it's not entirely your fault."

Isabel was just as bad off, but she seemed to care less. At least she did things—like the high side ponytail and the wardrobe of shiny synthetic fibers—that seemed to make her feel better.

I was alone after math class, waiting for the bell to ring so that I could hurry to my last class, when Pip finally cornered me near the girls' bathroom. I tried to dart away without looking at him. When I stepped to the right, he stepped right. When I moved left, he moved left. Finally, he had me backed against an empty trophy case.

"I heard you tried to cut a man's dick off at church camp," he said. He managed to make it sound pathetic, like I had wet the bed. On the other side of the hall, a girl in a long black dress and an exorbitant amount of white face makeup leaned up against the wall and watched us. She chuckled. Then she pulled a cigarette from behind her ear and tapped it on the heel of her hand.

"It was an accident," I whispered.

"'It was an accident. It was an accident,'" Pip mocked.

Down the hall, Principal Pinn—whom I recognized by his wide, toothy grin—was chatting with another adult. I caught his eye and mouthed "Help." I did not say it out loud because that would have branded me a tattletale and a fink. Principal Pinn noticed me and strode toward us. For a moment, I was relieved. Then he clapped his hand on Pip's shoulder.

"This girl bothering you?" He winked at me, as though I ought to think it was clever that he was coming to Pip's aid instead of mine. "Looks like she's got a bit of a crush on you," he added.

"Does not!" Pip said, stepping away from me.

"Really? Looks like she was trying to kiss you. Is that why you were standing so close?"

"No way." Pip wiped his mouth with the back of his hand. "Yuck!"

"I don't know." Principal Pinn grinned. His teeth were like corn kernels that had been overfertilized and left too long on the cob. "When a girl and a boy pay this much attention to each other, it can only mean one thing." He clapped Pip's shoulder again. "You go get her, tiger." Then he walked away, humming loudly, as if to say, "I'm not listening."

In the privacy of the principal's hum, Pip lunged toward me. "If you tell anyone I have a crush on you, I'll fucking kill you, you fucking *dyke*." He wedged his knee between my legs. "Is that why you did it?" He pitched his voice higher, a mockery of a girl's voice. "'Oh, I'm so scared of your big dick.'"

"Let me go!" I protested.

"'Let me go. Let me go. I'm so scared of your big dick. I'm gonna cut it off because I'm a *dyke*.'"

"Stop!" I tried to shove him, but he pressed his forearm against my chest. I could smell his breath—peanut butter. He had a clump of something white stuck between his front teeth.

"'My name is Triinu, and I like pussy,'" he wheedled.

The girl on the other side of the hall covered her smile.

"I never did anything to you, Pip."

"'I never did anything to you, Pip,'" he repeated, then added in his own voice, "You just suck. I just have to look at your ugly fucking face every day."

27

I was wearing a brand new pair of jeans and a white blouse my mother had ironed for me. She had plaited my hair in a French braid and told me that my hair was the color of honey. She had even let me wear the silver bracelet her brother, Paulus, had given her the year before he died. Everyone knew he died because he couldn't bear what had happened in Estonia, so it was Estonia's bracelet, and hers, and his, and she loved me. Somehow that made it all so much harder because I could not tell her what Pip did. I could not tell her that I was a flounder and that my eye was moving across my head. Deep down, I knew I deserved what Pip was dishing out. I knew the footballers in the hall would never save me. The only guy who would ever like me was Jared, and he braided his armpit hair, and it was probably *his* socks that made the whole cabin smell like wet dog. Isabel said he was a pedophile. And I had had this little, tiny bit of hope that something would get better, but nothing ever got better. Then, if regular life wasn't bad enough, your father could get cancer, and it didn't matter how much you prayed about it, he would still die, and then no one would ever talk about him ever again. I started to cry.

On the other side of the hall, the girl in the black dress sighed audibly and pushed herself off the wall. "Jesus Christ," she said, as though everything in life was an utter trial but, unlike me, she was simply bored by it.

Then, before I realized what she was doing, she strode across the hall. I thought for a moment she had come to mock me too. Instead she grabbed the back of Pip's head by the hair and yanked him away from me like a rag doll. He grabbed his head and tried to free himself, but her black fingernails were tightly clawed in his hair.

She was much bigger than him. She was like a grown-up, and he suddenly looked like a kid. "This jerk bothering you?"

She was wearing boots that came up to her knees and were adorned with a dozen heavy buckles. Now she kicked Pip in the shin.

"Hey! Mr. Pinn!" Pip yelled. "She's picking on me!"

The principal glanced back. "Let him go. I'm warning you."

The girl kicked Pip again before releasing him.

"Ow!" Pip rubbed the back of his head indignantly. "You … you …" Even as he spoke, he backed away. "You freak."

"No shit." The girl grimaced. She raised her voice a little bit louder. "Prick!" Then she strode off without saying another word.

I watched her all the way down the hall, the way her dress swirled around her boots, the way her hips swayed beneath the black material, the way her fingers tapped the side of her leg as though waiting to punch. The crowd parted for her, and I was sorry when it closed again because she was perfect. It was perfect the way she delivered the jibe—*prick*—with just the right blend of venom and disinterest. Isabel and I were like bees: when we stung, we died. She was a yellow jacket, her barb a cruel black hook with a little sack of poison trembling on its tip.

The Benefits of Smoking

We all got to hold the smoker's lung in a jar for one minute.

"Really look at it," pleaded Miss Charm, our health teacher. "Think about what you'd be doing to your body if you started smoking." It was her first term teaching, which she had been foolish enough to tell us. Now every boy in the class took it upon himself to ask her how to spell "testicles" while the bolder girls asked if they could get pregnant if a boy farted on them. Then they would all giggle as Miss Charm said, "We're not studying sex ed until next term. Next term!"

"But I'm gonna bang my girlfriend tonight. I gotta know," a boy named Ben Sprig called out. Behind me, a girl named Pru-Ann Ramsden giggled.

"Just look at the lung." Miss Charm looked near tears. "Somebody give Ben the lung!"

When we weren't holding the lung and considering our mortality, we were supposed to fill out a worksheet titled "Tobacco: A Death Sentence."

"What's the answer to number thirteen?" Pru-Ann poked me in the head with her pencil.

"Mouth cancer," I whispered without turning around.

"And number fourteen?" I tried to ignore her. She poked me again. "Fourteen!"

"Tracheotomy."

"Fifteen?"

"You're not even doing the worksheet at all." I turned around. Pru-Ann had a tiny mouth and big blue eyes that bugged out slightly. She looked a bit like a friendly fly.

"Please. I don't want to do it. You're doing it."

"No."

She made a kissing sound. "Come on. You're so smart."

In the front of the room, Miss Charm fluttered around the jar. "This was a real human being," she told popular Tori Schmidt, who was busy combing her hair with an enormous pink brush.

"It's just gross," Tori said. "I'd get a lung transplant."

"It's not even real," another boy added. "It's just a turkey breast. I know. My brother is a senior."

"It's a human being who suffered and died because of tobacco." Miss Charm sounded like me when I tried to fend off Pip. On the other side of the room, Ben coughed loudly, except he wasn't really coughing. He was saying the word "penis." Miss Charm jumped at the sound.

"What's number sixteen?" Pru-Ann asked.

I gave up.

"Sixteen is precancerous polyp. Seventeen is carbon monoxide." I started reading the answers off. Class was almost over. I couldn't decide whether I hoped the lung would reach me or not. I didn't want to look, but I wanted to tell Isabel about it. It was the perfect lunch table conversation topic. I'd wait for her to take a big bite of turkey sandwich, and then I'd say, "You know what that reminds me of?"

On the other side of the room, Ben coughed the word "balls."

Miss Charm jumped again.

"I'm sorry, I have a cold," Ben said with feigned innocence.

"That's enough, Ben. Now everyone is going to be quiet until the end of the class. That's ten minutes. Do you all think you can be quiet for ten minutes?"

Miss Charm was walking the lung to the back of the room, where Pru-Ann and I had yet to see it. Just as she passed Ben's table, he took a deep breath, leaning his head all the way back. I saw it as if in slow motion. His mouth opened. Miss Charm's lip trembled. The jar was in her hands, coming toward me. It might have been turkey. It probably wasn't.

Then Ben sneezed, a nuclear explosion of a sneeze in which he projected the word *"scrotum!"* Miss Charm jumped as though a gun had gone off. The jar slid from her hands. The lung of the unknown smoker hung suspended in the air for one millisecond, as though the rest of the body still existed but had become invisible. Then it crashed to the floor in a spray of glass and formaldehyde, and Miss Charm finally got the attentive silence she had been waiting for. For several seconds, we all just stared.

Then someone said, "Dude!"

Ben said, "Hardcore."

And then everyone was talking at once, crowding forward, trying to get a look at the lung that was so much more interesting on the floor than it had been in a jar.

"Back! Everyone back," Miss Charm yelled. "Did anyone get glass on them? Ben, you have detention for the month. Don't touch it."

Pru-Ann poked me in the arm with a skinny finger. Then she pulled a plastic pencil case out of her bag and pushed it at me.

"What?"

"Look," she opened the plastic box. Inside was one slightly rumpled cigarette. "I bummed it off a guy in my math class."

I gasped like an after-school special. "Smoking causes cancer!"

"Yeah?" she said, her blue bug eyes opening especially wide. "So? You don't have to smoke. Just come with me."

"You smoke?"

She said yes in a way that made me think the answer was actually no. I tried to square Pru-Ann's bright eyes and Mickey Mouse sweatshirt with the death stick in her pencil box. It was slightly dirty, as though the first haze of cancer was already darkening its skin. I knew what I was supposed to do. I was supposed to tell a teacher before Pru-Ann got mouth cancer, emphysema, and precancerous polyps.

Miss Charm was fluttering her hands and calling for a broom. In a shriller voice she yelled, "Don't step on it, Tori!" She seemed preoccupied. Plus Pru-Ann was already dragging me by the wrist. I had never skipped school, not even the last five minutes before lunch, but now I found myself escaping the classroom under the cover of Miss Charm's panic.

"Come on," said Pru-Ann. "Let's go to the smoking section."

The smoking section was just a spot of concrete beneath an overhang outside the gym. In this minimal shelter, one trash can and a picnic bench marked the place where students eighteen and older were allowed to smoke.

I approached with caution.

A few students leaned against the wall of the gym, shrugging against the rain. It was already mid-November, and nothing would dispel the stratus clouds that hulked over the foothills. Everything was gray. The high school buildings were gray. The sky was gray. Even the smokers were gray, as though they had been photographed in black and white.

They were talking softly. Passing a cigarette box around their small group, a white girl with dreadlocks murmured, "Look here. It's an advertising thing. Can you see his dick? In the camel." A boy with duct-taped sneakers took the pack from her. "Look. In the front leg of the camel. Here's his head, his feet, his arms like this ..." She leaned close to her friend.

Then I saw *her*: the girl who had saved me from Pip. She sat on the top of the weather-beaten picnic bench, looking like one of the herons that stalked the wetlands around the school, a shadowy figure with draping, tattered clothes. Ragged. Elegant. Predatory.

"Who's that?" I whispered, trying to indicate my savior without actually looking at her.

"Who?" Pru-Ann said loudly.

"Over there."

"Her name's Deidre Thom. She's a senior."

A senior. No span of years was as insurmountable as the three years between new freshman and freshly minted senior. I wanted to hide. I wanted to take her picture and study it the way I studied the landscapes printed on the front of the Sunday service bulletin at Forbearing Emmanuel. I wanted to run back to the cafeteria, to find Isabel, to tell her … but what could I say?

Pru-Ann stepped toward the girl with the dreads and squealed, "Hiya! Whatcha lookin' at? Do you have a light? 'Cause I was, like, totally jonesing for a cigarette, and I asked my friend to give me a cigarette, and then this popular guy was, like, 'Oh, do you smoke?' and I was like, 'What's it to you …'"

For a very long time, the smokers just looked at her. Then my savior held out a lighter—not to Pru-Ann's cigarette, just in the air before her so that Pru-Ann had to take another step and bend down to touch the flame.

In health class videos, smokers sidled up to innocent non-smokers and said, "You wanna cigarette? Come on. Be cool. Live a little." When, finally beguiled, the nonsmoker put the cigarette to his lips and sucked in and choked, the smokers congratulated him. "You're one of us now."

That did not happen.

Pru-Ann pulled on the cigarette, pursing her lips in an O, and then released an untroubled stream of smoke. By the time she had taken two drags off the wilted cigarette, the band had dispersed, their backs to us. She handed the cigarette to me, and I took a tentative drag.

"What do you think?" Pru-Ann asked.

I waited to feel my throat constrict as a layer of cancerous cells lined the soft palate and the larynx. They didn't. "It's okay." I handed it back. "Not really my thing."

"Yeah," Pru-Ann said. "That kind of sucked."

She started to walk away. I followed, thinking I had come to the end of my smoking section adventures. But as we left, two girls wearing neon windbreakers and a boy wearing a bright sweatshirt that was a size too small turned the corner of the gym.

One of the girls was saying, "Well gosh darn it, second cousin ain't nothing. I say he's cuter than a pig in shit."

"You fuckin' slut," the other girl said. Her bangs were as stiff as a Brillo pad and stood three inches tall.

"Americaaaa …" the boy sang, "God shed his grace on meeee!" It was clear this threesome did not fit in with the smoking section crowd. They were loud when the others were quiet, colorful in their pinks and blues while the rest of the smokers wore black and army green.

My savior perched on the edge of her picnic table, gazing impassively at the performance. The girl with the dreads glanced at the boy in duct-taped sneakers and widened her eyes. No one said anything until they left. Then, when the three misfits were clearly out of earshot, the boy in duct-taped sneakers whispered, "Dude. Her hair."

His friend nodded, holding her hand up in front of her forehead in a clawlike imitation of the girl's bangs. "I thought it was gonna come get me."

35

That was all. I was waiting for someone to yell, "Hey retard, why are you such a snatch?" but no one said anything. That was why, when Pru-Ann invited me to the smoking section the following day at lunch, I followed.

I knew I should eat with Isabel. I should have waited for her at her locker. I should have walked her to the cafeteria. We would have shared a table in the corner, eaten our lunches, and suffered. "However I with thee have fixed my lot …" Even if I had gone home sick, I would have left a note in her locker. A warning. *You're alone. I can't save you.*

Instead, I hid in the bathroom until I was sure she would have left the freshman hall in search of me. Then I emerged, like Peter, like Judas, and ran to the end of the hall where Pru-Ann was waiting for me.

I knew what I did to Isabel. I knew she would stand alone in the cafeteria with no place to go, seconds passing. She would be wearing her favorite shiny red stretch pants and a silver Mylar scrunchie in her hair. Then Pip would spot her. "Hey, it's the big red tomato. Fucking *spic*! Does your daddy have another wife in Mexico?"

Isabel was Guatemalan.

Her father was dead.

She had given me the *Corazón Fiel*.

"Let's go this way." I directed Pru-Ann toward the sophomore hall.

I could not risk passing the cafeteria where I knew Isabel would be looking for me.

When I saw her after school, I said, "Oh, Isabel, were you waiting for me? I didn't see you. Try looking in the smoking section if you need to find me."

Where and for how long one girl waits for another, those hallway machinations—they probably did not look like much to

Principal Pinn. But those lunchtime betrayals were complicated, and they were real.

Isabel said, "What's so great about Pru-Ann?" but she meant, "*Et tu, Brute?*"

I said, "I'm allowed to have other friends," but I meant, "I have not heard of the man named Jesus, King of the Jews."

Like the freshman hallway, the smoking section had its own hierarchy, but it was more like the species chart in biology than a caste system. There were four species: real smokers, punks, skaters, and goths.

The real smokers came to the section because they *actually* smoked. They smelled of smoke, and they lived in trailers, and they stole their mothers' cigarettes. The rest of them came because it was their natural habitat. Sure, some of the skaters and most of the punks smoked. Pru-Ann smoked. Occasionally Deidre would light a black Djarum cigarette and exhale a cloud of clove-scented smoke, but they didn't *come* to smoke. They came because it was better than the cafeteria or the pep rally.

"This is so much better than fucking Taco Tuesday," Pru-Ann's new friend Brent Macintosh said one day, waving vaguely toward the cafeteria. The smell of meat grease wafted toward us.

"What do you think it is, anyways?" he added. "Beef? Really?"

Pru-Ann giggled explosively.

"Nutria," I said, deadpan.

Brent chuckled.

Brent was a straight edge punk, meaning he didn't do drugs or hadn't had the chance to. He drew black Xs on the backs of his hands to indicate his status. There were also clean punks, like the girl with the dreads, and crusty punks who had dirty fingernails, muddy boots, and safety pins skewered through pustulous holes in their ears.

"Yeah, this is like, ten times better than anyplace else in the whole school. Like, seriously!" Pru-Ann effused.

On the far end of the section, the skaters clattered on and off a low curb with the single-minded attention of dogs gnawing bones. Some stayed there for the entire school day. Brent and I watched while Pru-Ann talked.

Derek Potter, a boy so thin I could see the striations of muscle in his face when he chewed gum, made a daring jump from the picnic bench, over the trash can, and to the curb. He was supposed to ride the bottom of his board for a few feet before jumping off. Instead he fell, landing on his shoulder with a bone-jarring crack. Rising, he said only, "Sick."

His friends looked on, assessing the damage.

"Dude."

"Dude."

The skaters were always falling. They were always scuffed. They were always bruised. They were mended with duct tape. It was their *raison d'être*.

"I could never do that," Brent said.

"I could totally be a skater if I, like, tried," Pru-Ann said. "But there are no girl skaters."

"You're kind of goth," Brent volunteered. It was a compliment she didn't really deserve.

As Pru-Ann and I had spent more time in the smoking section, the spectrum of our wardrobes had shifted toward black. She got rid of her acid-washed jeans and took to wearing the same black Metallica T-shirt every day. I had bought a black karate *gi* and called it an overcoat, but it wasn't really goth.

There were only two real goths at the school: Brooke Keppinger and Deidre, the girl who had rescued me from Pip. They were beautiful like antique photographs. They wore gowns and elbow-length gloves. They painted their faces white and added dark eye shadow to make their eye sockets into holes. And everything they wore was black.

"They're so cool," Brent said gazing over at them. "It's like they're from another planet."

From somewhere at the far end of the smoking section, Derek yelled, "Pinn!"

Every couple of days, Principal Pinn would decide that patting Pip on the back and discussing "family values" with the other teachers was not the full extent of his job. He would put on a coat and trudge across the quad to check IDs.

Derek and the clean punk with the dreadlocks tossed their lit cigarettes into the trash can. Pru-Ann hid a pack of Marlboro Lights in a drain spout. I had nothing to hide. I wasn't in it for the precancerous polyps—just the company.

Still, Principal Pinn's approach filled me with dread. Maybe he would make me go back to the freshman hall. Maybe he would produce Pip, like a jack-in-the-box. "Look who wants to kiss Triinu Hoffman. Wow, what a lucky girl. Sure wish we had more kids like good ol' Pip!" I ducked behind a cement column.

Deidre remained perched on her moldy park bench, a long, black cigarette held loosely between her fingers. She took a drag.

Principal Pinn arrived, a little out of breath from his walk. "I know for a fact you're not eighteen yet." He put his toothy grin as close to Deidre's face as her cigarette would allow. "And you're smoking! That's suspension. And do you know what that means for a senior? Are you applying to colleges? Because I can call any one of them and tell them you were caught on campus *breaking the law*." I could see his spittle hit her black gown.

She readjusted the cigarette between her lips, drew in a breath, and let the smoke out in his face. The clove smoke was thick, like the fog that blanketed the valley in winter, and it smelled wonderful. Then, like a magician pulling the ace of hearts out of thin air, Deidre flicked her fingers and produced a driver's license. Principal Pinn snatched it, glared at it.

She smiled a wry, little smile that said, "Doesn't it just suck to be alive and be you?"

"I'm watching you, missy," he barked. Then he stomped away without interrogating the other section dwellers.

"Happy birthday," one of the skaters said.

And I knew what I wanted to be when I grew up.

I combed the Goodwill racks for satin gowns. I painted spider webs on my cheeks, lined my lips in black, and turned my face white with an off-brand face powder that could have been used in Kabuki theatre. I dusted gray eye shadow under my collarbones and along my sternum. I bought the biggest, heaviest black boots I could find in the army surplus section at Pirate's Cove Antiques.

My father stood in the door of my bedroom like an awkward suitor and asked me if I was on drugs. He told me that he loved me. My mother loved me. I could tell them anything.

"They're just clothes, Dad." I groaned with indignation, wrapping a black shawl around me. "They're just clothes. Why don't you *trust* me?"

"You seem unhappy," he said.

"Just because I wear black doesn't mean I'm unhappy, Dad. It's just cool."

"What do you mean by cool?" my father asked gently, professorially. "What makes it cool?"

"You just know … I don't know … it's just cool. I just … why can't you leave me alone? Dad, it's my room!" I didn't really want him to leave, but I couldn't possibly explain that when Brent and Pru-Ann met in the hallway, they pretended to orgasm ecstatically. Seeing Pru-Ann coming toward him through the crush of sophomore cheerleaders, Brent would holler, "Oh my God! Yes! Yes! Yeeeeeees!"

Pru-Ann would yodel back, "Fuck! Uh. Uh. Uh. Fuuuuuuck!"

What could Pip say to that? "Hey retard, were you faking orgasms in the hall?" What could he say to my clothes? "Hey retard, are those combat boots?" They were combat boots.

In part, I knew it was all artifice. I was tall and thin, and this was something to do with all that length. I had always slouched. I had a gangly, loose-limbed, hunchbacked way of standing that made my blouses wrinkle and my sweaters sag—until I became goth.

Now I lounged in pools of black velvet. I slouched toward Bethlehem in black lace and long gloves. On rainy days, when I cut across the campus lawns, my hems soaked up water. Inside, I left a snail's trail of dew on the polished linoleum, like the slippery leavings of something half-risen from the dead. My gown caressed the hallway, and I was not of this world. I would never be prom queen. I would never be popular Tori Schmidt's friend. I would never be Principal Pinn's special helper. And why would I want that? I was not a girl among girls. I was not *Sassy* magazine's Teen of the Month. I was a dark acolyte. I was the death's-head gliding past the couples kissing in the hall.

All the while, I missed Isabel. She confronted me a few times, and I defended myself with indignant truisms. "I'm allowed to have two friends," I'd retort. "I didn't realize I had to spend every waking minute with you."

"Do you even like Pru-Ann?" she asked one day while we stood by our lockers. "What do you guys talk about?"

We didn't talk. Pru-Ann talked. She talked about boys and getting cigarettes. She called me Triinu-Wiinu for absolutely no reason and made me do her homework for her. "What do you and I talk about, Isabel?" I shot back. *"Nothing!"*

That was true. Isabel and I hadn't really talked much since her father died. When I went over to her house, I would sit on the floor by her bed and look out her window at the grass seed fields. I had spent my whole life watching those fields change with the seasons. Green, gold, brown, and gray, except for the year the farmer planted a crop of flax and it bloomed so yellow it made the sky bluer. And we were silent—the great, deep silence of children. She let me be. She never said, as Pru-Ann did, that I needed to wax my legs, pluck my eyebrows, and get laid before I turned sixteen. When I had sat with Isabel watching the fields, God had rested in our silence. Long after we stopped playing with our imaginary horses, the magic of their hoofbeats echoed in that quiet.

What Pru-Ann offered was not companionship. She offered protection. She sold me my freedom. The price was Isabel's heart.

Let's Get It On

Miss Charm rallied over winter break. When we returned in January, she still had the same bouffant of blonde curls. She wore the same cotton turtlenecks printed with flowers, but now there was something hard in her eyes. "This term we are going to study sexual health."

Ben opened his mouth.

"And I don't want to hear *any* chatter, because this is serious." She handed each of us a permission slip to give to our parents.

"Is this going to be like *Your Changing Body*?" Tori asked. "'Cause we saw that video, like, fifty times in middle school."

"Oh no," Miss Charm said. "This isn't anything like *Your Changing Body*." I saw a wicked gleam in her eye. After school, I hurried to give my mother the permission slip. Two weeks later, Miss Charm introduced us to the STD slideshow, a prolonged presentation on the various lesions and discharges brought on by venereal disease. "This material is very disturbing," Miss Charm said. "But it is best to be prepared and to know the risks of unprotected sex." She clicked the first slide into place. An enormous penis filled the screen.

In the front row Tori whispered, "Oh, my God! Gross!"

Behind me, Ben whispered, "That's my dick. Fuck yeah, man. Six-footer!"

In retrospect, the slideshow was well intentioned. All the patients who allowed their miserable bodies to be photographed for the slide show were all trying to save us from that one forgettable afternoon that could ruin our life, that one afternoon when we pulled down our underwear because it was easier than explaining that we were shy and would rather ride bikes in the country than have sex. There were other children whose parents simply told them to "stay on first base" and "don't give the milk away for free when you can make him buy the cow." How easy would it be to forget a lesson like that? It was much harder to forget gonorrheal lesions projected on a six-foot screen.

The problem was that even the healthy organs looked diseased when photographed at close range and blown up to huge sizes. Miss Charm arrived at the syphilitic penis, and I couldn't tell the difference between the diseased member and its healthy precursor. Then, when the slide show ended, Miss Charm reminded us that "many infections are asymptomatic. This means the person may be infected without even knowing it."

My hand flew up. "Miss Charm, why did we see the slideshow if the diseases can be asymptomatic?"

Miss Charm liked me. I never giggled when Ben coughed the word "testicles," and I kept my eyes on my own paper, even if I did let Pru-Ann cheat off me. Miss Charm looked disappointed. "Triinu, I think you know the answer to that question."

I really didn't. Somehow I failed to grasp that the slideshow was a scare tactic. I thought it was a diagnostic tool. I thought we were supposed to memorize the lesions so that we could check our partners, surreptitiously, before sex.

I expected a video might follow. In the video, a chipper couple would check each other's genitals for lesions and warts. "Why can't we just check ourselves with a mirror?" the girl would ask her boyfriend.

"Well, Laura," the boy would say in a disturbingly paternal voice, "you should always check your partner, because some people lie about what they find down there."

"Really, Fred?"

"Really, Laura. I know it's hard to believe, but it's true. No matter how much you trust me, you shouldn't take my word for it. Come on. Have a look."

Then the couple would metamorphose into a crude, two-color cartoon, and we would be privy to their STD check. "No lesions. No warts. No discharge." Their voices would be cheerful and carefree.

"Gee, Fred, I sure feel better now we've done that."

"Thanks, Laura. Thanks for loving me enough to respect yourself."

I wished that I was still talking to Isabel. The possibility for hilarity was enormous. When I joked about the slide show to Pru-Ann she just laughed and said, "I'm so horny!"

I didn't really know what that meant, and it seemed like she was speaking to a gallery of distant observers, not to me. "I'd just die if I was still a virgin at sixteen," Pru-Ann added, looking around the smoking section to see who was listening.

That night, haunted by the fact that Pru-Ann wanted to lose her virginity within the next eleven months and I had never even used a tampon, I locked myself in the bathroom. I sat down on the toilet and unwrapped one of my mother's tampons. Then I opened my Bonne Bell compact mirror so that I could take a look before I proceeded. One girl in health class had been very concerned about "putting it up your pee-pee hole," and, although the class had laughed at her, I didn't want to make any mistakes. I spread my legs and bent over the mirror.

It was awful.

The curly, brown hair around my pubis was familiar. The skin beneath it was not repulsive. It was soft and crinkly, neither wet nor dry. However, as I gingerly pulled apart the folds,

45

I saw—my stomach seizing in dread—that I was grotesquely deformed.

Health class pictured the female genitals as a symmetrical set: one dot, two holes, two matching inner flaps, two matching outer flaps. The minora and the majora. I had labeled them in pencil on a photocopied worksheet. What I saw in my mirror was different. I had one inner flap on the left, and it wasn't "minora," as I had written on my worksheet. It was enormous, a wide, flapping sail. It should have come off a model ship. It was a tent, a bed sheet, the wing of a huge, wrinkly butterfly. And on the other side: nothing! Just a little ridge.

I snapped my compact shut and pulled on my pants. After all the indignities of adolescence, I almost expected this. What made me think my body would be whole and beautiful when I had seen the slides on the screen? I knew what lived down there.

Apparently the fear of *down there* did not affect other people as keenly as it affected me. I thought eleven months was optimistic. Really, who would want to sleep with Pru-Ann? She talked liked a seven-year-old hyped up on candy, and she smelled like cigarettes and Debbie Gibson perfume.

I was wrong. Apparently it was easy to give the milk away for free. A week after the STD slideshow Pru-Ann called me from the waterfront, yelling over the noise of traffic, "I did it! I did it!"

I knew what she meant, but I said, "What?"

"*It!*" Pru-Ann squealed.

I could tell by the tone of her voice I was supposed to say, "Oh my God, Pru-Ann, this is enormous!" She wanted to giggle some quip about how it was enormous. Then I was supposed to say, "You're *too* much. Tell me everything!" But I was thinking about the slideshow. "Who was it?" I asked.

His name was Matt-something. He was one of the real smokers, a handsome junior with tight jeans. He had never talked to Pru-Ann until he asked her to meet him on the tennis courts after school. When he was done, he gave her a ride to the waterfront, and she called me from a payphone. "My friend Penny saw me, and she gave me a high five before I even *told* her. She could tell I was different. And before we did it, I was just like, 'Come on baby, let's get it on.' It was amazing."

"Hmmm," I said.

"And now you can do it too! I'll help. We'll find someone."

I wondered how flounders had sex. Did they just flop around on the bottom of the ocean? Perhaps the female deposited her eggs in the sand, and then the male came by a day or two later and fertilized them. That would be nice.

I didn't want to have sex. I didn't like boys standing close to me. Most of them smelled, not foul, but like other people's houses, the fact of their bodies lingering in the air. Those who did not smell—Brent, Derek with his blue eyes and ink-black hair—were too marvelous to bear. They stood near me and I thought I would faint. Still, I was afraid that I would grow tired of Pru-Ann mocking, "Sweet fifteen and never been kissed!" I was afraid I would yearn for a postcoital high five on the waterfront. I was afraid that I would smile and say yes. Some boy would say, "Come on baby. Let's get it on," and I wouldn't be able to force the word "no" out of my mouth. At the crucial moment, with the sky filling my head and the rough rubber tennis court scraping my back, I wouldn't see, and I wouldn't stop, and I wouldn't recognize anything Miss Charm had warned me about.

Pru-Ann was no help. She was eager to see me deflowered. Getting me laid was a small favor she could do for a friend. She soon had someone specific in mind.

Shortly after having sex with Matt-something, Pru-Ann started dating a twenty-one-year-old named Tom Ryland. He spent most of his afternoons at the waterfront or sitting in the darkened studio apartment of his friend Ralph Camp. She thought Ralph would be perfect for me. "Would I like him?" I asked.

Pru-Ann opened her eyes wide, her mouth an indignant circle. "Of course you'll like him! You're both tall and skinny and weird, and you can date him, and I can date Tom, and we can do everything together, and you can get laid, and it'll be perfect."

I sighed and glanced across the smoking section at Deidre, who stood shaking out the tangle of her dark hair.

"Will you do it? Are you listening to me? This is the most exciting thing that has ever happened to us." Pru-Ann bounced up and down, her sweater pulling where her thumbs stuck through holes in the cuffs. "You can be alone with Ralph ra-ra-ra-*Ralph*." She stopped singing for a moment and fixed her large eyes on me. "Will you do it?"

"Yeah, baby. Let's get it on." I was joking.

"Really, you'll do it!"

"No, I won't do it," I said. "I don't even know him."

But somehow that did not matter. I found myself inexorably drawn to the waterfront.

Because I was fifteen.

Because I had betrayed Isabel.

Because I was a flounder, and perhaps this was my one chance to be deflowered.

Because someone had put me in a little go-kart at the top of a hill, and the brakes were faulty, and this was what the world wanted.

The waterfront was little more than an alley behind a row of factories. It was labeled as a park on the town map, but it was just a sidewalk running along the sluggish river. There, boys named Snig and Leech and Brian Anarchy gathered to skateboard. Girls with dreadlocks played hearts and held strands of their hair over lighters, watching the filaments bend and blacken. A homeless man named Little Pete greeted everyone saying, "It's just another day in paradise." Every few hours, the police drove by and handed out tickets for skateboarding, but they never crawled down the bank of the river to the muddy niches where Little Pete slept and the skaters smoked pot and looked up at the trees.

We sat on the waterfront for almost an hour. It seemed as though no one made plans here. They simply waited or showed up. Eventually Tom and Ralph arrived, appearing as silhouettes in the distance and slowly coming into focus.

Pru-Ann squealed. "Tom! Tommy!"

When they drew closer, she leapt up and kissed Tom on the lips with a smack. Tom kissed her back while pulling the cigarettes out of her breast pocket. "Ha!" he said, holding them over his head. "You shouldn't smoke. It'll kill ya."

Pru-Ann jumped for the cigarettes. He grabbed her wrist and twisted it backwards. "Ow. Hey! Those are mine. Fuck you." Pru-Ann sat back down on the bench and crossed her arms over her chest. "That hurt."

Tom took out a cigarette and held the pack out to his friend. "Who's this?" Tom nodded toward me.

"That's Triinu. She's a virgin."

I would have been more embarrassed if I had been sure that it was me sitting beside Pru-Ann, etching an anarchy symbol in the park bench with a pocketknife. I had had that pocketknife

49

since I was eight. When a family with teenage boys moved into the house south of mine, Isabel and I had spotted them: tall boys in canvas pants sliding down a sandy embankment on sheets of cardboard. "Let's take the pocketknife," Isabel had whispered before we went outside, "in case we see the boys." I had nodded solemnly.

What was I doing on the waterfront with these people?

Tom pointed a thumb at his friend. "That's Ralph."

"Gee Tom," Pru-Ann said. "I think we should go *over there for a long time*." They left conspicuously, groping each other as they moved to a bench twenty feet away.

"Girls don't get me if they're stupid," Ralph muttered, looking down at his shoes. "Pru-Ann says you're not stupid." He had grayish-blond hair and yellowed spectacles like the wings of an amber moth.

Ralph opened his wallet and took out a folded piece of paper. He had drawn a cartoon of a woman dressed in a white night gown being carried—or was it raped?—by an alien with large, almond-shaped eyes. "That's my mother. You know what that means? My IQ is classified."

Pru-Ann glanced over and mouthed, "He's perfect!"

Ralph thought he was an extraterrestrial. He thought his mother had been impregnated by aliens and that he was their progeny. He thought the Holocaust was a hoax. He thought his CB radio tuned in to frequencies from outer space. He was a thin, frayed shadow of a man, holed up in a one-room apartment with a hot plate. But to me he was no stranger than the STD slideshow.

Ralph talked for a long time. I stared at the moss growing on the sidewalk. Finally he stood up, holding out his hand to me.

From across the stretch of cement that passed for a park, Pru-Ann mouthed, "Go, go, go!"

No one was going to save me. Ralph's hand felt cold and large in mine. A man's hand.

"Hey, baby. Let's get it on," I said, except that it wasn't my voice.

He led me down a wide street with low-fenced houses. It was fall, and there were still nasturtiums and a few late blooming roses rusting in the yards. Beneath one, a cat crouched skeptically.

I had once picked up a stray cat from the side of the road. I remembered that as we walked. The pregnant Siamese had pleaded with me to take her home, and I, in turn, had pleaded with my father. Once inside, the cat gave birth in my mother's towel cupboard. My parents let me keep the best kitten for myself. At that moment, that kitten—now the best cat—was sleeping on my bed.

Ralph grumbled, "Girls. Fuckin' girls don't get me!" We hurried past the quiet houses.

Eventually the houses gave way to weedy lots, then to train tracks. Beyond the tracks lay a large field and, beyond it, a series of small buildings, their wan lights already fighting with the twilight. Weeds tangled around my feet. I noticed the debris in the field: a candy wrapper, a beer bottle, a white pump inexplicably wrapped in a man's shirt.

Finally, we arrived at the bunkerlike houses. The cinderblock structures resembled a compound of two-car garages refitted for meager human occupation. Ralph opened one door. Through the door, I could see a small room with a single mattress on the floor and a *Rocky II* poster on the wall. He pushed me in and closed the door. Through the small window I could see a light on in one of the university buildings: one last professor, one anxious graduate student leaning over his books. Ralph stroked the back of my hand with one yellowed thumbnail, watching me through his amber spectacles.

The light in the university building switched off. Ralph edged closer and placed his lips on my neck. He smelled of beer, cigarettes, and something else, clammy and familiar. He ran his tongue up and down my neck. I waited to feel something. I had read romance novels. I knew the flower of my womanhood should open its dewy petals. I should sigh as the fire of longing seized my heated core.

He smelled like old cold cuts. That's what it was. I knew I recognized the smell.

He licked my neck for a long time. Finally, he said, "So ... Pru-Ann said ..."

I knew what Pru-Ann said.

Outside, the sky was fading from twilight to night. Soon it would be Christmas. Pastor Brown would tell us how our hope and our salvation lay in a manger lined with straw, wrapped in rough cloth, such a small babe to save us all. And my mother would remind me that the stable was bigger on the inside than the out. I said, "I've got to go."

"But Pru-Ann said you liked me."

"No." I paused in the doorway. "She was wrong."

It felt good to walk into that crisp darkness.

Pru-Ann would have done the same thing if her parents had given her the best kitten. If her mother had leaned in the archway between the kitchen and the living room, listening to her play the piano and sing, *"Dance, then, wherever you may be ..."* If her parents loved the sound of her bare feet on the kitchen floor, she might have told Ralph, "I'm sorry that your whole life is in this room, that your grim body cries out, and that you think I am holding a small basket into which you will put all your pain. I am holding nothing for you."

The kitten. The forest home. The light from the well-stocked refrigerator shining on my toes. Those were the reasons why I left Ralph's apartment and did not go back. But there was also one other reason.

The day Deidre Thom had rescued me from Pip Weston, I had found myself watching her move through the busy hallway. The sound of locker doors had slammed off the walls, and someone had stumbled into a trash can, and a boy had yelled, "Seniors rule!" Deidre had walked, neither jostling nor yielding, just letting the crowd carry her along. I had watched her body, thicker than the whippet girls who brushed past her. I had examined the spread of her hips, the curve of her ass, the weight of her step as she marched through the hall.

And nothing had happened. I had not stopped in my tracks. I had not felt sex wake in my womb. I had seen the slope of her back drop into her hip, and I had thought she was beautiful. I hadn't needed Pru-Ann to persuade me or *Tiger Beat* to declare her "everyone's fave cutie." I had simply looked at her and wanted to breathe the air that passed over her body. And some plan that the world had for me had been foiled. Nothing could have made me love Ralph Camp, but I might have hesitated for a moment had a part of me felt that we were—whether I liked it or not—fitted pieces, our bodies a question and an answer, our differences a kind of symmetry. But Ralph and I were only strangers, and I hurried out of his room and into the bright twilight.

The next day I called Pru-Ann to confess my sin of omission.

"Pru-Ann's not going to be able to talk to you," her father growled.

"Okay," I said. Her father scared me.

"She's not going to be back for a while."

Pru-Ann's mother came on the line, her voice shrill and teary. "Triinu, we sent Pru-Ann to an outdoor camp."

53

For a moment, I thought she meant something like Camp Luther Grove, but no one went to church camp during the school year.

"We … we found out that she's been smoking," Pru-Ann's mother said.

"Smoking pot and drinking," her father added.

"It's a wilderness program for teens with substance problems," her mother said. "We don't know when she'll be back. We don't have any contact with her while she's away."

"Can I say goodbye?" I asked.

"She's already gone," her father said.

My only other answer was the sound of the dial tone.

Mission Trip

As a goth, I was still allowed to like a few trappings from my life at Forbearing Emmanuel. Candles were goth. White lilies were goth. Ash Wednesday, Good Friday, and anything related to tombs were goth. I still balked every Sunday when I had to go to church, but if I had been punk I would have been required to run outside in my long underwear yelling, "An-ar-chy! An-ar-chy!" However, the summer mission trip posed a problem. I wanted to go, but it was decidedly un-goth.

If there was a schism in our Lutheran church it was between the high-communion faction, like my mother, and the Fun in the Son faction, like Jared Pinter. Youth group mission trips were run by practitioners of Fun in the Son. These well-meaning twenty-somethings tried to relate to us by talking about Jesus, the groovy dude. My God is a funky God.

I cringed. I didn't think Jesus was "totally tubular." God was not my "buddy from the Bible." I had read the scriptures. I knew. God could whisper in the darkness, "Breathe," and make the world begin, but he could also strike you down or simply turn away.

I wanted God to smite us all before we chanted "Hip Hop Hallelujah" again, but I had a problem. I could not wait for the end of school, to be released from the windowless freshman hallway where I no longer had Pru-Ann's protection. At the same time, I was afraid of that ubiquitous summer question, posed, in my imagination, by a horde of nameless, sneering teenagers: "Whatcha been up to?"

Nothing. I'd be up to nothing. Doing nothing. Going nowhere. Seeing no one. Being no one. Nothing. Nothing. Nothing.

In fact, I was lucky. My parents did not believe in summer jobs. They did not believe that picking strawberries or cleaning dormitories would develop my character. Or perhaps they *did* believe that a summer plunging condoms out of clogged toilets would turn me into a sharp-eyed entrepreneur, and they wanted none of it. I could look forward to a summer spent walking in the forest during the day and sitting on the deck in the evenings, listening to my father read Yeats, above us a coruscation of stars.

But I was fifteen. This rare chance at leisure looked, to me, like failure. "Whatcha been up to?" someone would ask. I would know the right answers—partying, hanging out with my boyfriend—but they would be lies.

A mission trip was a solution to this problem. True, it wasn't the same as "partying" and "hanging out with my boyfriend." True, I was goth now, and goths definitely did *not* go around saying they loved Jesus. But the trip was one way to occupy ten days in the summer, and if anyone called me on its inherent ungothicness, I could always sigh and say, "I know, but I had to get out of this fucking town."

If my parents were pleased about this renewed interest in the church, they were clever and kept their enthusiasm behind their eyes. "It'll be a bunch of Christian folk singers," my father said dryly.

"Yeah. And they'll say they 'trust us to follow the rules because we're all Christians.' What does that have to do with anything?" I said.

My father winked.

One Tuesday before the end of school, my mother drove me to Forbearing Emmanuel. It felt strange being in church on a weekday evening; the halls were empty and everything felt familiar but lonely, like a house left empty over a long holiday. A single light glimmered in the church office, and although the adjacent Fireside Room was well lit, the room missed the milling coffee drinkers who filled it to capacity on Sunday mornings.

A few teenagers and their parents sat in a circle. I recognized Ursula Benson, Jared Pinter's antagonist, the girl who had asked what Jesus said about the homosexuals.

There were two high schools in town. I went to Middleton High. Ursula went to South High. I only ever saw her across the crowded sanctuary. Up close, I noticed that she had dyed her hair burgundy with black stripes in the bangs. It was longer than it had been at Camp Luther Grove and made a striking contrast against her blue sundress, which she paired with heavy, black knee-high boots and a slash of violently orange lipstick. Beside her chair, her lumpy knit purse bore buttons reading "Keep Your Laws off My Body," "Meat Is Murder," and "A Woman without a Man Is like a Fish without a Bicycle."

I smiled at her, and to my surprise, she came over and sat down next to me. Pulling her chair close, she leaned toward me. "I heard about what happened at camp," she whispered.

I could smell her perfume, a blend between cloves and lemon. It was a bright, crisp, autumnal smell. I breathed it in as I tried to formulate my response.

Now that I was goth, I recognized Ursula. She was cool. She was one of those kids who had been cool since middle school. She had made the critical shift from pink track suits to eighteen-hole Doc Martens at another school, another age, another life. I was still trying to outrun my former self. She had jumped a train and left her childhood in another zip code.

"It was kind of an accident," I mumbled.

She placed her hand on mine. "You don't have to say that."

57

Her eyes scanned the circle of Lutheran youth and their parents. "You did what you had to do. You know Jared was dating Stacy Gillman. She's only *fourteen*!" My eyes must have registered a question because Ursula added, "He's twenty-one."

Ralph Camp was twenty-one. I just shook my head and said, "I know. He's so old."

"He thought he could just take advantage of you." *Take advantage*. It sounded like something a parent would say. "And you stopped him." Ursula squeezed my hand. "You stopped him from ever doing that to another girl."

"I don't know," I said.

"You did. My brother said the knife went right through his penis!"

The knife? His penis?

"He said the doctors reattached it, but he'll never have any feeling." She dropped her voice lower. "And you know that's what girls have to do. We've got to fight for ourselves because no one is going to fight for us. I mean, they let him be a youth minister. It's like letting a pit bull loose in a pen full of kittens."

I tried to piece the story together. I had castrated Jared with a knife because I was like a pen full of kittens. "I . . ."

"It's okay if you don't want to talk about it. It must have been traumatic." Ursula stroked the back of my hand.

I was too shy to touch my friends. When Isabel and I had still been friends, I would sometimes braid her hair. I could do a perfect French braid without ever brushing her scalp with my fingers. On the rare occasion when we had hugged, we were like trees bending in the wind, barely touching. When Pru-Ann tried to squeeze me, I slid out of her grasp with a drop-and-twist motion I had learned in a self-defense class. But I liked the way Ursula touched me, and it made me feel like I had been very lonely before she took my hand.

"It was hard," I said. "I'm still not really sure how it all happened. I just did what I needed to do."

"I think that was really brave."

At the front of the room, Pastor Brown called the group to order. This year's mission trip, he said, would be the most ambitious yet. The youth group got to decide between three prepackaged trips: one to San Francisco, one to Santa Clara, one to Mexico. Missions in a nutshell. "I don't know what these other people are going to say," Ursula whispered to me. "But we've got to say 'Mexico,' okay? Mexico would be so cool. We would have such a great time." She looked at me intently. "Have you ever been?"

I shook my head.

"Me neither," she whispered as though it was a secret. "I mean, wouldn't that be great? Mexico! You and me, going to a whole new country."

When I was five years old, I went to kindergarten and met Isabel. From a great distance above our heads a voice called out, "I want everyone seated on their *own* carpet square. I'm going to count down from ten." I slid into place on a blue square, and Isabel slid into place beside me. I hadn't noticed her before, but the next thing I knew, it was recess and we were racing across the playground together, hoofbeats in our heels. "Don't look back or you'll fall over the cliff," Isabel yelled. So I ran with her, my eyes fixed on the horizon, and we were friends.

There was some of that first magic in the Fellowship Hall that evening. It was like a single note that hangs true in the air, like the first intimation of dawn when the sky is still black. When Ursula sat down next to me and said, "I don't know what these *other* people are going to say, but we've got to say 'Mexico,' okay?" I liked her simply. I liked the smell of her perfume, and it seemed, suddenly, inexplicably, that the world had always been divided between *us* and those *other* people.

On the morning of the mission trip, I packed and repacked my suitcase three times. I thought about calling Isabel and telling her I was leaving. It felt monumental. Mexico. With Ursula. I wanted to leave a message for Isabel: "If I don't come back, I just wanted to say ..." But I could not form the words "I'm sorry," and the only other thing I could think to say was "I love you," which Isabel and I had never said to each other before, so I zipped the suitcase, hopped in my mother's station wagon, and forgot that Isabel had ever existed. I was so excited I felt like singing.

When my mother dropped me off, Ursula was already sitting in the enormous blue van that would ferry us to Mexico with Ursula's mother at the helm. "Triinu, sit here." Ursula shifted a bag to the floor. "I don't want to hurt anyone's feelings, but we have definitely got to sit together on this trip."

Of course we did.

After all the youth missionaries were accounted for, we got on the road. There was me, Ursula, five other kids, and Mrs. Benson, who knew how much she could trust us, regardless of whether or not we were Christians. One girl sat in the front seat with her feet on the dashboard. Four boys sat behind her, leaning in their seatbelts, waving intermittently at drivers in the passing vehicles. Ursula and I sat in the very back, whispering.

When we stepped out of the van at the end of the day, the landscape had changed. We lived in the Willamette Valley, the self-proclaimed Grass Seed Capital of the World, a land of lush floodplains dotted with blue-green pines. But after only one day of driving south, everything was brown: the grass, the trees, the smoggy sunset fading above an expanse of crouching rooftops. We stayed at a host church in a basement Sunday school room covered with butcher-paper artwork. The boys suggested we stay up all night, and everyone agreed. But minutes later, the rest of them were asleep.

In the privacy of their slumber, Ursula and I talked and talked. At first, the substance of our conversation would have filled only a thimble. I told her I had a pack of NoDoz in my bag. She told me that she had six clove cigarettes in a red leather pouch in her purse. I told her I had read a book on Satanism. She told me she had paid twenty-four dollars for Susan Faludi's *Backlash*.

She told me she thought Derek Potter had the cutest butt in the world.

I told her I wanted a garter belt.

She told me she wanted to be a politician.

I told her Pru-Ann had been sent to wilderness camp.

She told me her best friend, Chloe Lombardi, was boy crazy.

She asked, "So what else are you doing this summer?"

I said, "Not much. Parties. Hanging out on the waterfront."

Ursula scooted her sleeping bag closer to mine and whispered, "My mom always said I'd like you. Don't you hate how your parents are always right?"

I said, "My mom always said I'd like you too," although that wasn't true. My mother said that Ursula dyed her hair garish colors and that she was probably troubled, but I was still pretty sure my mother would have picked Ursula over Pru-Ann if she had the chance. "I thought you were so serious," I added. "I thought all you did was argue with our Sunday school teachers. I never thought you'd do anything silly like look at guys' butts."

"No butts about it!"

We laughed, but then Ursula grew serious. "We do need to argue with our Sunday school teachers, though."

"Of course," I said. "What would they do without us?"

"No, I mean it. You know, there's a group who wants people to vote on whether or not it's legal to be gay. Have you heard of Save the Children?"

"Yeah. They try to feed children in Africa and stuff."

"This is different. This is in America. It's this group that fights against gays. They say gays can't reproduce so they have to recruit. They say that gays go around molesting children so that they'll turn out gay. They tried to pass a ballot measure that would have fired all the gay school teachers in California."

"Are they Lutherans?"

"I don't think so, but they're Christians. They say they're Christians. There's another group like that—the Oregon Citizens Alliance. They're trying to gather signatures for a ballot measure like that in Oregon. Forbearing Emmanuel is having a discussion about it. Can you believe that?"

"Wow."

I might have had more to say on the subject, but Ursula shivered in her sleeping bag and said, "It's so cold."

"We're sleeping on the floor of a basement."

"Thanks." Ursula elbowed me gently.

"It will be warmer in Mexico."

"Not helpful."

"What do you want me to do about it?"

"Come here." She tugged on the edge of my sleeping bag. "Zip up with me."

My hands trembled as I unzipped my sleeping bag and zipped it onto hers. I lay back down, careful not to touch any part of her body. She lay down too, but she pressed her side against mine and wrapped her arm through my arm and clasped my hand to her chest. For a terrifying moment, I thought she was going to kiss me. I closed my eyes. *Don't, don't, don't,* I prayed.

Our companions were lying only a few feet away. What would happen if they woke up and found me and Ursula kissing in the same sleeping bag? Mrs. Benson would send me back to Oregon. I might have to ride on a Greyhound bus. Hopefully she wouldn't just leave me in a basement in California. Still, Ursula said that Christians were voting about the gays. *Against* the gays.

I held my breath. But Ursula did not kiss me; she just kept talking. Finally I relaxed as she chatted on about Derek and the skaters at her school and the book she had read on the beauty industry. Eventually I chimed in with my thoughts about Pru-Ann and the smoking section. Whenever there was a lull in our conversation, one of us would say, "Don't say anything. We're going to sleep now," until it became a joke.

"I'm sleeping. Are you sleeping?"

"I'm sleeping."

"Okay. Shhh. We're sleeping," I giggled, covering my mouth. Mirth and the effort it took not to chortle and wake our companions filled me until my eyes bulged.

Ursula whispered, "Breathe! Breathe!"

We stayed up until the sky in the small basement window changed from purple to gold. Just as the first sharp finger of sunlight edged its way into the room, I took a deep breath and said, "I haven't been honest with you, Ursula."

"Oh?"

I closed my eyes. "I really didn't cut Jared with a knife." I waited, but Ursula did not say anything. "I just slipped. I was holding a Bic pen, and when I fell, it just kind of stabbed him in the thigh. I don't think there was really any blood or anything. I think he just pulled it out."

I waited for her disappointment, her condemnation. I had misled her. I wasn't a knife-wielding feminist. I had not saved countless young girls from sexual assault by castrating a pedophilic youth minister. I was just so remarkably clumsy that I managed to stick my pen in Jared's leg in my effort to flee into the wilderness.

"That's okay," Ursula said. "If you had really stabbed him, you'd have been arrested, and then we would never have gotten to go to Mexico together."

"Really?" I asked.

"Yeah, really," she said, as though forgiveness was the easiest thing in the world.

Sensing that our companions were waking, I unzipped my sleeping bag and rolled away from Ursula. One of the boys stirred and said, "Are you up already?"

Up already? We were *still* up.

Over the course of our stay in Mexico, we did various charitable works, although it quickly became clear that the trip was more for our benefit than for the benefit of any Mexican heathens. We traveled to a bleak building site where we planted a dozen anemic-looking saplings that wouldn't survive the week. We visited a neighborhood of low apartments that looked like windowless sheds. We were supposed to paint there, but dozens of children rushed from the apartments and took over the work, plunging their hands in the paint and casting it on the walls while we stood in the shade of a tin awning. We traveled to a nursing home and sat with the residents, repeating a few hastily acquired Spanish phrases, even though we couldn't understand the residents' answers. Later, in a clinic, surrounded by a sea of tarps and plywood structures, we listened to a nurse explain that they did not have medicine for simple infections.

I saw it all: the poverty, the dust, the matted plastic bags stuffed into flimsy walls. I saw children in dirty shorts. I saw teenagers on laden bikes. I saw old people sitting on cardboard, staring up at us, without any trace of the cheek-pinching affection of my American grandmother. I saw it all, and I did not see anything.

We climbed a hill behind the clinic to survey the slum extending to the horizon, and I asked Ursula to take my picture. I felt windblown and happy. I might as well have been wearing a visor and an "I ♥ Mexico" T-shirt. I could have been in Cancún.

Back at the camp, I shared a picnic table with Ursula and one of the other missionaries, a lanky brunette from Fresno. The girl spoke Spanish, and Ursula pressed her to teach us some phrases. "It's a shame how few Americans speak Spanish. Everyone should learn it," the brunette said, stretching her leg along the bench. She was a runner.

"I agree," Ursula said. "I wish they taught an intensive program at my school. I'm going to go abroad junior year with the Rotary Club. I'd like to go to Spain or come back here."

"You should choose Mexico." The girl leaned over her other leg. "Americans don't realize how people live here. That was terrible what we saw today."

Ursula nodded. "We have so much. It bothers me that some people have so much less."

What bothered me was the way the runner continued talking while bending over her muscular leg. What bothered me was the way Ursula leaned toward her, chin in her hands, and repeated, "¿De dónde eres? Le invito a cenar," after her. What bothered me was the earnestness with which they exchanged addresses at the end of the trip; I was careful to avoid the brunette as we said our goodbyes.

On the way back from Mexico, we stopped at Disneyland and waited a hot hour for a rollercoaster ride. In line behind us, two boys hit each other with Mickey Mouse ears while their father entertained them by asking them how much they were going to puke on the next ride.

Ursula looked at me. "There's a pool at the hotel. You want to go swimming?" she asked, and linked her arm through mine, the smell of sweat and sun and perfume lifting off her shoulders. Then, arm in arm, Ursula and I ambled past the lines of people waiting. Waiting for snacks. Waiting for rides. Waiting to feel the laws of gravity buckle but not yield. We slipped through an inconspicuous exit and onto a street shadowed by high-rise hotels so tall they seem to fall, constantly, toward the earth. She lit a clove cigarette and, although I never smoked with Pru-Ann, I took a long drag when Ursula passed it to me, feeling the dampness of her lipstick on the filter.

A passing businessman frowned at us, and he was right to. We were fifteen, from good families, and we knew better. Our lipstick was too dark. Our clothes were too tight. We talked too loudly. We shouldn't have been smoking, and neither of us knew that you don't inhale clove cigarette smoke—you only swirl it in your mouth like cigar smoke. I breathed it in all the way, and it felt like smoking burnt sugar and swallowing a handful of whole cloves without water. My stomach spun, my head expanded, and my eyes watered. And I was so happy, I could have sung. *Dance, then, wherever you may be ...*

In the cool hush of our hotel room, Ursula changed into her swimsuit while I stared intently at the closed curtain. "You can turn around," she said. "We're both girls."

I turned to face her, now staring at the carpet.

"Are you going to change in the bathroom?" she asked me.

"Of course."

She laughed, perhaps at the earnest speed with which I answered. "Look at me," she said.

66

When I looked up, she had the straps of her bathing suit down at her elbows. Her breasts were much larger than mine. Her nipples hung down instead of pointing up and out, which seemed wrong, but I still thought she was beautiful. I liked the width of her hips, the thickness at her waist. I could have put my fingers in her belly like rising bread dough. My body had not changed much since I was ten. My belly was a bowl. My ribs were visible when I stood upright. My breasts were no more than a symbol etched on the surface of my chest. I looked away.

"Are you all right?" Ursula asked.

"I … um …"

She spread her arms wide. "It's just a body. It's not who I am. It's like a suitcase or something." Then she walked to the window of our hotel room and threw open the curtains. We were seven stories above the ground, but the next high-rise was less than a block away.

"Ursula! Someone's going to see you."

She stood there for a long time, staring out the window, her arms wide, the sunlight streaming in around her. Then she turned.

"Yes. You."

A few weeks after the mission trip, Ursula invited me to a town hall meeting. Her mother dropped us off in town, and we followed signs taped to the walls of city hall. I was excited to be out with Ursula, doing something important. She said young people didn't care about politics. *Young people*—as though we weren't them anymore. Still, the room looked boring before the meeting even began. There were no windows. The walls were painted an industrial beige. Folding metal chairs were packed in together like prisoners in a tight cell.

I motioned toward seats in the back row, but Ursula said we had to sit up close so we could hear what they were saying.

"But what if we want to leave?" I asked.

She shot me a look.

In front of the room sat a police officer, a man in a suit, and a woman in a handspun sweater that looked like the Guatemalan imports Mr. Avila used to wear. A moderator introduced the guests. "With us today we have Chief of Police Moore," the man began. "John Newman from the mayor's office, and Mrs. Alex Cleland from Tolerance Oregon."

"Ms.," the woman corrected.

The man proceeded without acknowledging her. "They're here today to talk about the recent incidents of graffiti."

The woman beside me raised her hand. "I don't think we should call this an incident. It's a hate crime. This is the *third* time!"

Another woman in a nearby row leaned over and whispered to her friend, "This is what they get for flaunting themselves."

"Why aren't you treating this like a hate crime?" the first woman asked.

The moderator looked to the police chief, who cleared his throat. "The law is very specific," the chief said. "Some groups of people are what we call a 'protected class.' Sexual preference is not a protected class."

"All the graffiti was on gay people's houses," Ursula whispered to me.

"Sexual preference is not a protected class any more than brunettes or felons or people who drive green cars," the chief went on. "Sexual preference is just that: an opinion, a choice."

"It's sexual orientation," someone called from the back. "And it's not a choice. Who would choose this kind of abuse?"

Among the assembled crowd, there was a long discussion of where the graffiti appeared, when it appeared, and what it said. Two men, who looked so similar they could have been brothers, argued at great length about whether the graffiti read "faggot" or whether it was an indiscernible scrawl. The police chief settled into his seat and exhaled a long breath that said this was a waste of his time.

I kept waiting for Ursula to lean over and ask me if I wanted to leave. It was the kind of thing Isabel would have rolled her eyes at, all those adults talking over each other, each one more self-righteous than the next, their questions all veiled statements.

"Don't you think we need to get perverts out of our community?"

"Isn't our country founded on equality?"

"Isn't it the police's job to protect all citizens?"

"Isn't it the police's job to protect decency?"

Somewhere to Ursula's left, a man stood. His voice broke over the monotonous drone of rhetorical questions. "I'm going to say what everyone else is thinking." He paused theatrically. The room quieted. "These people asked for it, and they deserved what they got. Plain. Simple."

I knew that voice. It blared through the PA system every morning. I glanced over.

"That's my principal," I whispered to Ursula. I was still craning my neck and pointing when he saw me. I expected him to give me his toothy way-to-go-kid grin, the one he shared with Pip whenever they crossed in the hall. After all, I was taking an interest in politics, unlike other young people. He just glared and continued speaking, staring directly at me without smiling.

"I am a principal at one of our high schools."

"Jail warden!" a man in a tie-dye shirt yelled. "Brainwasher!"

The moderator at the front of the room said, "Everyone will be quiet. We will listen to each speaker in turn. Mr. Pinn, please go ahead."

"They brought their disgusting ways into our community," Principal Pinn went on. "They're the ones lurking outside our schools. They're the reason we can't let our children play in the street anymore. We need to send them a message. We're not that kind of community. And I'm not afraid to say it."

The room exploded. The crowd roared, some in approval, some in disgust, all of them clamoring to be heard. Principal Pinn was still looking at me. Cold sweat ran down my side, beneath my velvet gown. "We shouldn't be here," I whispered to Ursula.

"It's fine," she said. She seemed excited.

The woman in front of us yelled, "He's right. They're sexual deviants!"

Someone else yelled, "It's indecent!"

Everyone was yelling. I looked behind us. They were regular people. Middle-aged women in floral prints and men with potbellies and mustaches like Mr. Benson, but their fists were raised. Their teeth were bared.

"We're going to take questions one at a time. If you cannot wait your turn and remain civil," the moderator pleaded, "We will close down the town hall meeting."

They didn't remain civil, but the discussion went on for almost two hours.

We stayed until the very end. When it ended, Ursula wanted to go up to the front and ask the police chief a question, but the crowd had surged around him. "Let's just go," I said. "No one's listening to anything."

"You're so right," Ursula said as we exited into the summer afternoon. "That's the problem. No one listens."

I was happy she thought I was clever. I was happier still to be out of the town hall and back in the sunlight. "Your mom's not coming to get us for another hour," I said. "Let's go down to the waterfront."

Ursula pursed her lips as though to say no, but then she nodded. On the waterfront we found a small patch of grass between concrete warehouses. Ursula was wearing her blue tank dress. I could still see the outline of her bathing suit, pale against her flushed skin, the fading sunburn peeling off her shoulders to leave mottled patches of red and tan.

We lay down and stared up at the clouds. The crown of her hair touched my shoulder. I could smell her shampoo, her perfume, the scent of cut grass. Above us, the sky was impossibly blue. I could hear music from somewhere far away.

Tom Ryland strolled past, walking a bicycle. He stopped and looked down at us. "Hey Triinu, you got a quarter?"

"She does," Ursula said, moving closer to me. "But she promised all her quarters to me."

"I promised all my quarters to her," I said, and Tom walked away, his bicycle rattling beside him.

"That's Pru-Ann's boyfriend," I said. "Or ex-boyfriend I guess, now that her parents sent her away to that wilderness thing. I doubt he's waiting for her faithfully."

"What did you think about all that stuff at the town hall?" Ursula asked.

I closed my eyes. I felt like there was a right answer, but I didn't know what it was. "I don't think it really has anything to do with us," I said, because I wanted that to be true.

Ursula stiffened. "How can you say that?"

"I mean, I know it does," I backpedaled. "Like mortgages and children and car loans and stuff. I know that it's *going* to matter." I plucked a dandelion puff from the grass beside me, and held it up to the sky, every feathered seed framed by blue. How could I tell her I just didn't want it to matter today? I blew on the dandelion, spreading its little parasols across the sky. I watched them float up.

I expected Ursula to chide me, to say, as my civics teacher always said, that "people who don't take an interest in politics don't have a right to be in the polis!" She didn't. She just shifted closer to me on the warm ground. "Maybe this is what matters," she said.

That same summer I took one other trip. Every year, my father and I went to Pennsylvania to visit his parents for one week. "Small Town Perfection," the welcome sign read, and everyone in town called my father "Rodge." I slept in my father's childhood bedroom, his old ham radio still positioned on the desk just as he had left it the last time he called out into the star-specked sky: "Roger two-four-five-four. Is anybody out there?" My own toys were tucked in the attic. I still felt the same childhood chill as I looked down into the dirt-floored canning cellar, such a contrast to the rose-patterned wallpaper in the kitchen.

As we walked through town, my father told me stories about his childhood. "Forgive me if I've told you this before ..." he began, and he told me about his best friend, Harold—how they used to collect arrowheads in the plowed fields, how Harold always found more because he combed the dark furrows so patiently. He told me about canoeing on the Susquehanna, rowing from island to island in the shallow river. I could almost see him roll up his trousers and lift his boat over the shallows, his pale feet steady on the rocks below.

One evening we went miniature golfing in the neighboring town. Teenagers in tight perms and Wranglers putted balls through the windmill and over the double dice. We had to wait for them to play, and I played slowly. It grew dark as we progressed, although I hardly noticed the twilight fade around the halogen lamps above the course. And everywhere there were mayflies, so thick they were like snow. They landed on the golf course, in the shrubbery, and in our hair. They only lived for one night, my father told me, because they were born without mouths, born to love each other and nothing else.

It seemed to them, as it did to me, that that night was very long. Everything important in the world was contained in that night: those lights, the sound of voices muffled by the damp heat, my father's lean shoulders as he bent over his club and ... *plunk*! The ball dropped into its white cup. But of course, the night was not long at all. It was so beautiful and so short.

A Ledger of Your Sins

"Usually," my father said, "you keep your crazy relatives in the attic."

"Not the basement," I added.

My mother set down the tray on which rested Vanaema Emi's dinner of boiled cod and potatoes. The cod jumped, and one of the potatoes hit the floor. The malamute gobbled it up.

"We talked about this, Roger," my mother said. "My mother can't live alone, and we're not going to be one of those families …" She broke off with a sharp intake of breath, like the reverse of a sigh.

Vanaema Emi—Grandmother Emi—had arrived earlier that month, preceded by a Bekins moving van packed with musty boxes. "I know, I know!" My father raised his hands. "I'm just saying, crazy relatives usually end up in the attic. It's easier to hide them when the meter reader comes around."

It was a joke, but I could tell he had gone too far. My mother was getting that glassy-eyed look she got just before she slammed something and rushed upstairs to their bedroom to cry. She had already slammed the cod.

"It's great to have Emi live with us," I said.

"Katariina, we're all happy to take care of her," my father added.

It was too late.

"Do you think I want to be my mother's nursemaid while you two go on with your lives? Do you think I want this? Do you think I want to wait on her hand and foot while you have a career? Do you think I want a daughter who dresses like a funeral director?"

I was going to argue that I dressed like I was at a funeral, and a very fine Victorian one at that. A real funeral director would probably wear a skirt suit and beige nylons. I kept my mouth shut.

"A veil. We're about to sit down to a nice dinner, and she's wearing a black veil." My mother nodded in my direction. "I don't even recognize her. What am I supposed to tell Emi?"

My father and I looked at each other. "Kids these days?" he offered.

"Well, I guess it doesn't matter. Too bad. We could have had a few good years with Emi, but I guess that's not important."

My mother reached for the tray, but I was faster. "I'll take it downstairs," I said with too much cheer. "I'd love to eat with Emi."

In fact, I did not like the pale, poached meals my mother prepared for my grandmother and, by extension, for all of us. Boiled leeks. Boiled onions. Boiled cod. All of it saltless because of my grandmother's weak kidneys. I thought that if my mother hated caring for Emi so much, she should fry her up a big plate of bacon and Cheetos. I wasn't advocating murder, just survival of the fittest. However, more than boiled cod, I hated the pained expression my mother got every time she mentioned Vanaema Emi, and I hated to hear my mother cry. She removed herself from us when she cried, but she hid in her bedroom, which was directly above mine. Every night for the last month, I had fallen asleep to muffled weeping, like ghosts haunting the air duct.

I walked the tray downstairs. "Emi, dinner," I called. "You should eat your cod. Mom made it for you. I could get you some salt."

Emi did not seem to hear. With a yellowed fingernail, she slit the packing tape on a large box. She opened the box and removed a small painting of birch trees. Between the birches ran a low, rustic fence. Vanaema Emi laid the painting on a box.

"Zees are zee old people," she said, her English sliding into a dialect of Zs. She pointed to some of the trees. "And zees are ze young people." She pointed to another stand of trees on the other side of the painting. "And zis ..." She pointed to the fence. "Zis is between zem. Zey can see each other, but zey can't ..." She shrugged. "Zey cannot come over."

Had it been my American grandmother, I would have crooned, "No, Grandma, I love you. We're family." Vanaema Emi didn't seem to need that kind of reassurance, and, indeed, I thought she was right. She was on one side of the fence, an eccentric, accented woman in a pillbox hat. I was on the other. And somewhere beneath the birch woods was the bunker where the Forest Brothers waited for the Americans to save them.

Back upstairs, I told my father about Vanaema Emi's pronouncement. "Ha," my father laughed. "You know how she got that painting, right?"

I shook my head.

"Your mother and I bought Vanaema Emi that painting. We thought the birch trees would remind her of the Estonian countryside. We had the painting shipped, and we waited for her to say something about it. Eventually we called her to ask about the painting. She said she had received a painting from the Republican Party. I asked her: why did she think the Republican Party would send her an oil painting? She said it was because she was an Estonian doctor. The Republican Party! An Estonian doctor!"

"Why *did* she think it was the Republican Party?" I asked.

"Oh. I don't know," my father sighed. "Vanaema Emi never

understood America. She was a Republican. They sent her pictures of the president and address labels. Why not an oil painting? Why not a car? She's crazy."

"Is that why Mom is so unhappy?"

"Your mother just wants something to be excited about, something that's *hers*."

"I'm so glad to get out of the house," I sighed as I plopped onto Ursula's bed later that week. "My grandmother's come to live with us, and my mom is miserable. I don't get it. Why did she invite her to live with us if she doesn't want her here?"

"Scoot," Ursula said, nudging me where I sat on the edge of her bed.

I slid off the bed onto the floor. "Not *off*, just *over*," she scolded, patting the bed next to her. I scrambled back up. She was holding something behind her back. "I have a surprise for you. Close your eyes."

I closed my eyes.

"Hold out your hands."

I held out my hands.

"Okay, look."

After that build up, I expected more than a soft cover library book.

"*Understanding Your Body: A Feminist's Guide*," I read from the front cover.

"Yes!" She touched the cover of the book reverently, then flipped it open on our laps.

For a moment, I thought this had something to do with Emi, so I was surprised when the book opened to a photograph of a naked infant, covered in slime and stuck between some woman's open legs. "Yuck!" I said.

"It's supposed to empower women to learn about their

bodies," Ursula said. "I got it from the library. I was so embarrassed. My mom's friend Mrs. Garst—she's married to this conservative asshole—she works at the library. She *totally* would've told my mom if she saw me check this out."

"What's in it?"

"Everything." Ursula turned the page. "Birth. Menstruation. Sex. See? They've got everything here. Masturbation. Orgasm. Loooooobricant." She stopped at a black and white photograph of a woman with a seventies haircut holding a mirror between her legs. "Have you ever?"

Ursula's bra showed beneath the thin cotton of her T-shirt; she wore cutoffs that exposed dimpled thighs. I pulled the collar of my turtleneck over my nose.

"You have? That's cool." Ursula put her arm around my shoulders and gave a quick squeeze. "It's not embarrassing."

"It *is* embarrassing," I whispered, although somehow I couldn't help smiling. "I'm deformed."

I hadn't meant to say it, but it was easy to tell Ursula my secrets. "How?" Ursula asked, reassuringly disbelieving. "Every woman is different. I read that."

I tapped the photograph in the general vicinity of the woman's vagina. "One … It's not …" I bit the top of my turtleneck. "Well … you know. They're supposed to be … symmetrical. It's *deformed*."

Ursula cocked her head. "You know, I think that anyone who's going to have sex with me had better like me the way I am. I'm not a skinny woman." She held her arms out. "But I'm curvy. I'm well proportioned. If some guy can't appreciate that, then fuck him … or *not!*" She patted the book. "I'm sure you're not deformed, but so what if you were? I don't think any guy is going to be thinking about *that* when you're doing it. Hey, maybe there's something in the index."

She flipped to the back of the book. "Labia. Page 143." She found the appropriate page and skimmed it for a while. Then she said brightly, "Here it is." She read out loud. "'It is not uncommon for the labia to develop at different rates, normalizing by the end of adolescence.' See, it's just like getting braces. There's an adjustment period."

Another indignity. "Of course you look funny, dear. Your eye is behind your ear, and your labia is normalizing," I said, mockingly.

"You look worried," Ursula said.

I was worried, and it wasn't because of my irregular labia. I was thinking about Deidre Thom's hips swaying in a black skirt. I was thinking about the night Ursula and I lay on the floor of a California church, and she held my hand, and I prayed she would not kiss me—because I had wanted her to. I was thinking of my parents in their gentle marriage; of cheerful Mrs. Benson patting Mr. Benson's butt and their children groaning, "Mom! Dad!"; of the homecoming court, the winter formal, the senior prom; of *Pretty in Pink*, *Sixteen Candles*, *The Little Mermaid*; of Adam and Eve, Mary and Joseph, Elizabeth and Zechariah. I was thinking that every toy I had ever loved as a child had been paired with an equally beloved companion: one mommy and one daddy. Only the imaginary horses I rode with Isabel were not mated. They had been ours alone, sexless and fierce, and they were gone now.

Could I tell Ursula all that? Could she laugh that off with a quick glance at the index?

That night after I went home, I clutched my diary to my chest and lay in the center of my bedroom floor. I couldn't bring myself to put the word on paper lest, like a magic spell, I conjured the reality by speaking its name. I was standing on the edge of a cliff, and there was no stepping back. Even if beautiful Derek Potter with the blue eyes and the jet-black hair turned and beckoned to me, it was too late. I did not want him. There was only forward and beneath me the unimaginable drop, the valley full of fog.

The next day at school I heard Pip Weston tell Ben Sprig a joke. "What do you call a faggot up to his neck in sand?"

Ben kicked a trash can for no reason. "Target practice?" he asked.

"Not enough sand!" Pip replied. They both laughed. When Pip caught sight of me, he rushed over. I tried to dodge into the humanities hallway, but he caught up to me before I could escape. "Here," he said. "Take it." He handed me a flier. "I think you need to see this." On the orange paper were heavily Xeroxed words: "God hates fags. Homosexuality is a sin. Save our families."

I dropped the flier. It drifted lazily to the floor. "You're an asshole," I said.

"'You're an asshole. You're an asshole,'" Pip mimicked in a falsetto. Then he turned to Tori Schmidt, who was walking down the hall. "Save our families?" he asked, handing her another copy of the flier.

She giggled. "Thanks, Pip."

"God bless you," he said, his voice suddenly serious and manly.

I was still thinking about his "God bless you" as I dressed for church on Sunday. I didn't want to go, but goth or not goth, church was required in our family, and confirmation class started that early September morning.

Ours was a small class and reputedly evil. I had always found the church kids friendly, or at least harmless, but some combination of Ursula's expulsion from sixth-grade Sunday school, my encounter with Jared, and Isabel's unrelenting surliness had given Pastor Brown the impression that we were the worst Sunday school class ever.

The first day of confirmation class was an uneasy truce. Ursula was there, and I sat beside her. Isabel was also there, and I had not sat in a room with her since I abandoned her at the beginning of ninth grade, a year ago already.

"Now, let's start with the story of the Good Samaritan," Pastor Brown began. "Who has heard the story of the Good Samaritan?"

No one answered. Pastor Brown examined us. "I know you all know it. Someone give us a brief summary."

Isabel sighed, twirling a length of hair around her index finger. She was dressed in iridescent green parachute pants and a stiff black jacket made out of some sort of polyurethane-coated leather.

"Who told the story of the Good Samaritan?" Pastor Brown asked.

"Jesus," I answered. I glanced at Isabel. She did not look back, but I thought I caught a flicker of a smile cross her eyes.

"And why were the actions of the Good Samaritan so noteworthy?"

"Because he was a nice guy?" a boy named Daniel suggested.

"Yes, but what else?"

"He cared for his neighbor," Stacy, who had supposedly slept with Jared Pinter, chimed in. "He was, like, really kind to people."

"That's right, Stacy. He cared for his neighbor. Who was he like?"

Pastor Brown waited. Isabel's plastic outfit creaked as she leaned back in her seat. Daniel picked his ear. Stacy draped her upper torso across the table. I stared out the narrow window, wondering why none of my classrooms ever had enough windows.

"Isabel? Stacy?" Pastor Brown was determined to get through the entire volume of *Catechetic for Lutheran Seekers—The Teen Edition*. "Who does this make him like, Isabel?"

Isabel said, "Jesus."

I grinned. From across the table, Isabel caught my eye. "Jesus!" I mouthed.

After that, things deteriorated. Stacy asked why Jared had stopped going to Forbearing Emmanuel, and Daniel said it was because I cut off his penis.

"I did *not* cut his penis off!" I protested.

"She just nicked it with a ball point pen." Isabel smirked. "He had it coming."

"You're such a lezzie," Stacy said with a pout.

"Am not!" I said, too forcefully. Everyone looked at me.

"I'm just kidding," Stacy said.

"Jared was a jerk," Isabel grumbled.

"Are you going to let Stacy use homophobic language, Pastor?" Ursula demanded. "Do you realize there are people in this church right now who are actively working to make homosexuality illegal?"

"They're not ..." Pastor Brown sighed.

"They are, and we're sitting here talking about the Good Samaritan, and we're not even talking about the things that are happening in our state right now! I'm not getting confirmed. I'm not going to stand in front of a bunch of people and declare that I believe God was 'begotten, not made' and that Jesus loves us when the church won't take a stand on any *issues*!"

"Like how old Stacy has to be to have sex with Jared?" Isabel said under her breath.

It took Pastor Brown three Sundays to quit our confirmation class. He said that the lessons of the catechism would be more powerful if they came from the laity. "All Christians must participate in the education of our youth," he said in church on Sunday, but his face said, "I'm not getting paid enough for this."

The next week we had a new teacher.

It was not Pastor Brown's wife, nor Jared, nor his Fun in the Son ilk. They were not brave enough for our tenth-grade class. There was only one person selfless enough, saintly enough, just one woman so humble she could take our barrage of missionary jokes.

My mother.

My mother was a no-guitars, high communion parishioner. She loved the liturgy—the same stately words repeated over and over like the tide washing against the shores of everyday life. She loved the slow drama of communion and the silence that descended over the sanctuary after the last offertory hymn.

She wanted to share this with us.

She wanted to share this with me.

She wanted something that was hers.

So there she was, reading from yet another Jesus-only Sunday school text. We sat placidly before her, chewing on our pencils. If the other students had once felt, as I had, a thrill of divinity beneath the sanctuary rafters, they did not say so. If they felt that, as children, we had been steeped in sacred waters and now, as we grew up—fifteen, how old we were!—some sacred spring dried up within us, they kept their secrets to themselves.

"Tom and Tina have been dating for two years," my mother read from *Catechetic for Lutheran Seekers—The Teen Edition*. "Before they leave for college, Tom asks Tina to sleep with him.

He says it will cement their relationship." My mother adjusted her glasses. She had a round face—an Estonian face, she said—that gave her a perpetually innocent expression.

Isabel was writing a letter to a friend in California. Ursula had dyed her hair orange and was pulling on one livid strand. Daniel and Stacy slouched in their chairs, occasionally flipping ahead in their readers to see if there were pictures of Tom and Tina doing it.

My mother held the staple-bound book in one hand, reading the passage in her gentle, modulated voice. "Tina really loves him, but she wants to wait until they are married in the eyes of God. What should she do?"

Isabel shrugged and said, not unkindly since she liked my mother, "She should ask Jesus to guide her."

"What do you mean by that?"

"Jesus will tell her what to do."

"Does the Bible say anything about Jesus having sex?"

I heard a fly bumping against the fluorescent light above our heads.

"Ursula, what do you think?"

Ursula pushed her bangs out of her eyes with an orange-stained finger. "I wouldn't do it," she said.

"You wouldn't pressure Tina to have sex?" Daniel added.

"I wouldn't have sex with Tom if I didn't want to. It has nothing to do with Jesus," Ursula said.

"She could become a nun," Isabel suggested.

Everyone laughed.

My mother leaned back in her chair, her hands in the pockets of her elastic-waist skirt. "Do you think Jesus cares if you have sex?"

"Yes," Stacy said.

"Why?"

"It's a sin."

"Jesus didn't have sex," Isabel added. "Ever."

"How do you know Jesus didn't have sex?" my mother asked, leaning primly but forcefully on the tabletop. Her voice had a "so there!" quality that I was not used to.

Ursula cocked her head and nodded.

"I don't know what you have been told," my mother began, "but I don't think Jesus is sitting in heaven on a cloud keeping track of who has sex and when."

I looked around the classroom, sensing with animal clarity that embarrassment was imminent. But yet not present.

"I think that God grieves for our suffering, and having sex when you're not ready can cause a lot of suffering, but that does not mean God is keeping a ledger of your sins. God the Father. The Son. The Holy Spirit. The Lamb. The Good Shepherd. Even Hell. These are just metaphors. And, for myself, I don't think that a metaphor that has the all-loving God doing nothing but counting our sins makes any sense."

"What do you think about the gays?" Daniel asked.

"Yeah," Ursula said. "Triinu and I went to a town hall meeting. There are people who say homosexuality is the same as bestiality."

My mother glanced at me. I had not told her about the town hall meeting. But all she said was, "There are people who think that, and that is their opinion."

"That's not fair," Ursula protested. "You can't just say, 'That's their opinion.' What if they wanted to kill babies? Would you say 'That's their opinion'?"

My mother shot a pointed look at Ursula's purse, which was decorated with its usual assortment of political buttons. "I might say it was their choice," my mother said. "But more than that, I would say that I can't read God's mind."

She continued and we listened. She said that God was more complex than the drawings in our textbook. He was more than the shadows in the sanctuary, more than the Lutherans and our hymnal, more than the Christians and our Bibles. He was ours, and he was not ours. He belonged to the Jews and the Muslims, and he did not belong to anyone. He was larger than the night sky filled with stars and smaller than a tweedy snail making its silver path along the garden hedge. She wanted us to see and be filled with wonder, and, for a moment, we were, although the following Sunday we behaved just as badly.

Lesbianism: The Right Choice for Girls

It was almost Christmas and almost time for the confirmation ceremony. Ursula called one Saturday and asked if I wanted to spend the night at her house. Delighted, I arrived at the house with my neatly rolled sleeping bag and my overnight bag. Everything at the Bensons' house was Christmas themed: big, happy, American Christmas decorations with Jesus and Mary and Joseph and Santa Claus.

On our mantle, my mother had arranged a set of tiny French *santons*. There was Jesus, Mary, and Joseph, of course; but there were also figures of an onion seller, a cobbler, two school boys, a cow, and a flock of geese. The Holy Family was almost superfluous, three figures among the myriad of farmers, laborers, animals, and children. It was all so subtle, like the quiet war my mother and I were waging over my confirmation dress. She wanted white; I told her kids got confirmed in all colors of dress, even jeans.

At the Bensons', everything was red and gold and green. Even Scotch, the maniacal black lab who barked spittle and rushed at me as I knocked on the door, wore a red and green kerchief. Mr. Benson grabbed him by the collar, holding the door open with the other hand. "Stop it, Scotch. Eat your baby." He pushed a fleece doll in the dog's mouth. "Come in, Triinu. Soup's on. Hope you're hungry."

Behind me, a holiday wreath jingled on the door. At the table, the dishes were printed with poinsettias, and even the salmon was sprinkled with tomatoes and green onions. Mr. Benson took a slow sip of water and rested his hands on either side of his plate. "So Triinu," he asked, "how have you been?" Mrs. Benson whipped his napkin off his plate and served him a portion of fish.

Ursula's little sister, Lindsey, rushed by with the cordless phone in her hand, her curly blonde hair lifting off her shoulders like a spray of baby's breath. "Hi, Triinu," she said as she hurried by. "Ma? Did Jessica call?"

"Are you having dinner with us?" Mrs. Benson asked her younger daughter.

Lindsey slid into place between her parents. "Yes. But, Ma, I have to go in ten minutes. Jessica's parents are taking us to the movies."

"Dinner at the Bensons'," Mrs. Benson said. She carried a piece of salmon across three place settings, depositing it on my plate. "Don't mind the reach."

I didn't.

After dinner, Ursula and I helped with the dishes, then retired to her room. On every wall, posters of The Cure and Siouxsie and the Banshees stared down at us balefully, their mouths outlined in red. On top of the posters, Ursula had pinned mementos: a dry corsage, a blue ribbon, an airline ticket stub, a photo of her best friend, Chloe Lombardi. I could have sat in her room forever, just examining the memorabilia, but as soon as Ursula heard her parents retire to their bedroom, she moved us into the family room. "We can talk here without anyone hearing us," she said.

She closed the door to the family room, turned out the light, and opened the woodstove. The light of the fire filled the room. "You know what Chloe said?" she asked as she stirred the embers with a sooty poker. "She said she was in love. Can you believe it? Chloe is so boy crazy. That's all she thinks about."

88

Ursula set down the poker and settled onto the floor in front of the sofa. "Anyway, I told Chloe I was looking into this Rotary Club study-abroad program for junior year. She said she would only go abroad if her boyfriend was going. She said she didn't want to miss out on spending time with him. Can you believe that? What's special about time in high school? It's not like she's going to marry him."

I didn't want Ursula to go abroad, but junior year was an eon away. "That's very closed-minded," I said, seriously. "Has she even heard of feminism?"

"She can't be a feminist because she's in *luuuv*." Ursula pronounced "love" with a mocking French accent. Then she added, "You know, for me, if attraction was, like, something you could break into percentages ... I'd be eighty percent attracted to guys. Most of that would be Derek Potter's cute little butt. And I'd be twenty percent attracted to girls. I don't think it's all or nothing, and I read that that's normal for girls anyway."

A log in the woodstove broke apart with a crack.

"Did you know Deidre Thom?" I asked.

"No," Ursula said.

"She was a senior last year. She's graduated now."

"Yeah?"

I paused. "She was pretty."

Ursula touched my ankle, tracing the ankle bone with one finger. I felt a shiver of sparks fly up my spine, and for a moment I could not speak.

"So?" she asked gently.

"When I was ten, I told my mom I'd never kiss boys."

"All little girls say that."

"That's what my mom said. She said I'd grow up, and I'd want to." The woodstove sparked, and I caught a whiff of smoky pine. The smell of home, of Oregon, of Christmas. "But

I don't. It's like I'm still that little girl. All the girls I played with thought it was gross to get boy germs. Isabel thought it was gross. Then they all changed. But I didn't."

I could not believe I had just spoken.

"Is that what you get if you don't use a condom?" Ursula teased. "Boy germs."

"I know it's dumb." I turned away, my face as hot as the woodstove.

"I didn't mean it like that." And suddenly Ursula's cool hand was on my face, turning it toward her. "I'm just playing."

The log in the fire sparked again. Ursula dropped her hand and leaned back on the sofa. She appraised me in the orange light. Then she picked up my hand and turned it over, like she was reading my fortune. I didn't move.

"It makes so much more sense," she said. "We're friends with girls. We talk to girls. Girls understand each other. Why shouldn't girls date? Especially at this age." Ursula sounded parental: *at this age.* "If girls dated girls it would cut down on teen pregnancy."

"I think they should make a health video on it." I was suddenly giddy. *"Lesbianism: The Right Choice for Girls!"*

"Lesbianism," Ursula repeated, dropping my hand. "Lezzzbian. Lezzzzzbian."

"I'm here to tell you about a healthy new lifestyle for girls," I said in a TV-announcer voice. "Thousands of American girls are in danger of becoming pregnant by dorky boyfriends. The epidemic has reached enormous proportions, as the number of dorky boys has increased by thirty-seven percent since 1975."

Ursula covered her mouth with her hand.

I continued, "But there is hope for the next generation! Girls, make the right choice for you!" I punctuated the last declaration with a sweep of my arm and knocked over the 7 Up I had been drinking.

Ursula laughed, wiping her eyes, and leaned over my out-stretched legs to blot at the spilled soda. "It's okay," Ursula said as I tried to help. "You're so funny."

I felt, as one sometimes does in dreams, that in just a moment I would remember how to fly.

"Hey, you want to go somewhere?" Ursula asked. "My brother used to sneak out to the park down the road. We could do it."

We crept out of the family room. A light above the stove lit our path, twinkling in the household darkness. In Ursula's bedroom, we slowly pulled up the Venetian blinds. They were broken in some places and the slats rattled.

"Shhh," she said. "If Scotch wakes up, he'll bark. I hate that dog."

She took the bar out of the window. We leapt to the ground, the ivy silencing our landing. Then we walked to the end of Ursula's street, where the houses of a half-built subdivision stood covered in blue tarps.

Ursula stepped out into the middle of the road. In the blue light of the moon, I could see strands of her hair escaping their bun and a faint rawness around her jaw and temples like a fading rash. In the darkness, her eyes were neither blue, nor brown, nor black.

"Look, it's not raining," she said, stepping on the center line like a tightrope walker.

"Get out of the road. You'll get hit."

"Who's going to come around at this time of night?"

She was right. In a few years, cars would start speeding up and down the road. The subdivisions would light up. Developers would till under half the park to make way for a Montessori school. In the distance, a Safeway would advertise all-night bargains. But not the night that Ursula and I went out, telling secrets. Two black-clad figures in the vast exodus of suburbia.

"You're a good friend," she said as we strolled down the center line of the empty highway. "You're my best friend."

My best friend! I walked, repeating the words in my mind: *You're my best friend. My best friend.*

I put my arm around Ursula. Before us the highway stretched into the distance, disappearing only when it met the dark feet of the foothills. The moon had set, and yet the whole scene seemed lit from within, as though, even in the absence of light, there was a great phosphorescence—the light of God, the flame of Pentecost, in everything and in me. And I thought, *I'm in love.*

I came home the next day, marched into the kitchen, and told my mother no.

"I'm not getting confirmed. I don't believe in it."

I was thinking about the homosexual issue. Now that I had started to look for it, it was everywhere. Gays were rallying. The group Ursula had told me about—the Oregon Citizens Alliance—was lobbying to get their candidates into offices across the state. I had even overheard Pastor Brown talking to one of the parishioners.

"I just don't see why they have to push this issue," the woman had said, her hands on the hips of her floral jumper. "They flaunt it in front of everyone when it's a sickness, a perversion."

"They're saying it's not a choice," Pastor Brown had said.

"Sin is not a choice?"

Pastor Brown had sighed. "No. Sin is always a choice."

"We can't have people like that in our church. You have to do something."

"I know."

"'If a man has sexual relations with a man as one does with a woman, both of them have done what is detestable.'" The woman had persisted. "'They are to be put to death; their blood will be on their own heads.'"

"I know." Pastor Brown had sighed again. "I know."

I told my mother that the church was just a bunch of old people worrying about death. It was one big, stupid potluck with Jesus's face plastered all over it. I didn't believe in God. I didn't believe in the Creed, and no one else did either. Daniel was only getting confirmed because his mother had promised him a camera. Isabel planned on skipping church that day. Ursula refused to be confirmed as a matter of principle. If my mother cared about the integrity of confirmation, she would not make me stand in front of the congregation and swear I believed a bunch of mumbo jumbo that even she had her doubts about.

My mother looked away, picking up a piece of cutlery from the sink. She washed it and let it slide back into the cloudy water. "After you are confirmed, you are an adult in the eyes of the Church," she said with the halting dignity of someone who is not crying.

"You're not treating me like an adult."

"It would mean so much to Vanaema Emi to see you confirmed before she dies."

Perhaps I was a coldhearted child; perhaps I really was the death's-head floating down the hall. In the rock-paper-scissors game of human relationships, self-righteous, adolescent integrity trumped dying grandmother for me. I did not care if Vanaema Emi saw me confirmed or died believing I was an unrepentant sinner.

I was not convinced Emi cared either. Emi never seemed

particularly happy or unhappy. My American grandparents did; they were as complicated as reset bones. Sometimes they would catch me with their watery eyes and say, "I love you so much," as though they were trying to stave off an inevitable parting. Vanaema Emi just smirked. She smirked and bounced checks and watched static on the television. She lost bills and saved junk mail. She answered sales calls and hung up on friends. When we asked why, she just clucked her tongue and said, "Ah, ze young people," as though we were all idiots.

I didn't care what Emi thought, but my heart just broke when my mother said, "I bought you a confirmation dress. You look so beautiful in white."

From the picture taken on the morning of confirmation, it was hard to tell if I looked beautiful or not.

Isabel stood in the back row, squeezed into a recycled bridesmaid's dress. Daniel frowned grimly; he had not gotten his camera. Ursula sported a jungle-patterned dress and purple pumps. "Don't ask," she sighed and looked over at her mom. I wouldn't have asked. I knew.

I stood in the front row in a cream-colored gown, white nylons, and white flats. At the moment the photographer snapped the picture, I was staring down and slightly to the left, my lips pursed, as though at that last moment, when gracious compliance would have cost me nothing, I chose insubordination. But that's not what it was.

It wasn't scorn that drew my eyes away from the photographer and the parents fluttering behind him. It was remorse. It was the weight of the white dress and my mother standing at the back of the sanctuary, caught in the light of a stained glass window. It was the smell of Christmas in the eaves of the church. It was the fact that Ursula had just brushed my hand with her fingertips. It was my body warming to her touch. It was Pastor Brown sighing and saying, "Sin is always a choice." It was the fear that I would not be welcomed back when the longing for Easter pulled at my heart like spring.

That night, I sat in my room, staring at an empty notebook. My hands were shaking. I had lied to God, and I was in love with a girl who felt like a goddess to me. I was alone.

My father knocked on the door.

"What now?"

"Would you like to come see the Christmas display at the Pepsi plant with us?"

"Why?"

"Please just come. It'd be something nice for your mother."

How little they knew about the exact moments of my life. Suddenly I thought how sad that must be. They loved me so much, wrapped as I was in my impenetrable privacy.

I bought you a white dress.

"Okay," I called out. "One minute."

The winter rains had made deep puddles outside of our house, and my mother and father and I splashed through them on our way to the car. We brought Vanaema Emi too, almost carrying her. Overhead, the trees dripped on our backs. Behind us, the house glittered with light, our enormous Christmas tree visible in the window.

My father drove us to town and through the Christmas display with its crude plywood cutouts of Disney characters, angels, and Santa Clauses. A simple motor carried the Three Little Pigs around on a tiny Ferris wheel while Santa's reindeer jiggled up and down to the sound of canned Christmas music.

We drove very slowly. The large Buick in front of us was full of children. I could see their heads bouncing as they tried to take it all in. I stared out the car window and thought, *I'm in love. I'm in love. I'm in love.*

Meanwhile, my mother said, "We're really going to have a nice Christmas. Roger, your mother outdid herself this year. Packages have been coming in every day."

"Forgive me if I've told you this before," my father said, to me as much as to my mother. "When my mother—your grandmother—was a little girl, she went to one of those Christmas exchanges. She was desperately poor at the time. And all the other girls got beautiful dolls, but she only got a tin box."

"A box?" I asked. "Why?"

"I don't know. I don't know if it was a deliberate slight or if someone thought she had so little she would appreciate anything. But I think that experience defined her. Somehow all this Christmas bounty, all those presents she sends us ... that box devastated her."

He spoke slowly but not tragically. He didn't tell us the story to make us feel sad or guilty. He simply said it as one might sing a snatch of a remembered tune, or as a passenger looking out the window of a car might see a hitchhiker and remark, "Gosh, some people have it tough." He just said it because it crossed his mind and because it was true. Because everyone was present that Christmas. Like the *santons* on the mantle, everyone was represented: the bounty of presents, the girl and her tin box, the familiar pleasure of the Pepsi bottling plant Christmas display, the sudden bewitchment of young love. All of us looking into the dome of God, guarding our secrets in our hearts.

The Blue Bird of Happiness

Lying in bed at night, I imagined myself speeding along a dark, empty road, driving a car as wide as the night sky, with Ursula by my side. "I love you, Ursula," I whispered, thinking of the sound of the receding highway. "I love you. Until I met you I was nothing." As I said it, I pictured myself leaning my whole weight on the accelerator. The car flew. We plunged over Earth's convex surface, falling into a horizon of stars. "I will love you forever." I had read Greek mythology. I transformed us into constellations. Triinu and Ursula, those two bright stars above the tree line.

I felt as though love called me to a sacred order. I felt like an acolyte, although to which church I no longer knew. As I lay half-asleep, my dreams were so absolutely real I could smell them in my hair. However, as I stumbled into another day of P.E. and driver's ed, my dreams seemed to soar away, as unreachable as the constellations. How could I step out of my life of Scantron bubbles and No. 2 pencils and say, "Until I met you I was nothing"? My dreams balanced between possibility and impossibility. One thing, I thought, could tip the scales in my favor. It wasn't gay rights. It wasn't magic.

I was fifteen. It was a car.

It was, specifically, a 1980 Chevrolet Cavalier station wagon. My parents had bought it because it was safe and had vinyl upholstery that could be wiped down with a rag. While a later Subaru kept its new-car smell until almost the end, the Blue Bird of Happiness, as my parents incongruously dubbed the Cavalier, grew old like a smoker. Neither love nor money could force it over fifty-five miles per hour, and after a few years of my mother's gentle driving, it had rust in the wheel wells, three missing hubcaps, bubbles in the paint, half a rubber guard strip hanging off the driver's side door, and a bad cough.

I thought it would change my life.

If I got my driver's license and if—I told myself not to hope, but hope pulled on me—my parents gave me the station wagon, all things would become possible. Behind the rubber steering wheel of the Blue Bird of Happiness I would have the courage to confess my love to Ursula. Then perhaps we would fly away, our suitcases plastered with stickers. At the very least, we would spend the short eternities of our evenings alone together, beyond the peripheral vision of our parents, beyond the ever-present possibility of running into our parents' friends, a possibility that turned the whole town into a Forbearing Emmanuel Lutheran coffee social. We would drive into the darkness, away from the one-way streets of the university campus, away from the downtown with its municipal petunia plantings, and find—hope pulled on me—a place where nothing could trample my love.

My father taught me how to drive, late in the summer of 1990.

"That's the gas pedal. That's the brake. And you never press them at the same time."

Once, during that first lesson, my father yelped, "Triinu! What are you doing?!" but never again. I was an attentive student, and he was a good teacher. He never screamed, "Slow down!"

I never whined, "Dad, you're making me nervous." He gave some instruction in a professorial tone and then leaned his seat back and stretched out his legs.

We took long drives in the bright evenings. After dinner, my father would toss me his keys in their worn leather case, and we would climb into the car, redolent with the smell of paper grocery bags and carrot tops. Down the gravel drive. Past the ranch homes that lined the frontage road. Into the grass seed fields. The Grass Seed Capital of the World looked sleepy in late summer, the occasional tractor moving slowly through the fields, just joyriding, like we were.

As we drove, my father told me stories. "Have I told you this before?" he would ask.

Sometimes he had. It didn't matter. I would no sooner say, "Yes, you've told me that story before," than I would say, "The story of Christmas? Oh yeah, I already heard that one."

"Please tell me," I begged.

Far away, a tractor lumbered across a field, tossing up a cloud of dust that the sun illuminated, like a sunset dispersing over the fields. Even when the tractor disappeared, the air glittered as though all the tractors of the valley had thrown a mist of gold into the still September air.

"My friend Harold and I used to go driving around my hometown," my father began. "And after I went to Penn State, I used to come back on the weekends. I was bored. Lonely. I guess we both were. So one evening Harold and I decided to go up to a dance they held in a mining town about twenty miles away. We decided to invent new names, new histories. We said we were air force pilots. And we met two pretty girls, which would have never happened back in Millersburg."

"No?" I pressed the brake gently as we rounded a curve in the road.

"Oh, I was awkward, shy, socially hopeless. And Harold ... Harold was lazy. He didn't have any ambitions. Everyone knew us in Millersburg. But with a car, and an evening to ourselves, in a town where nobody knew us ... that was exciting."

99

He cleared his throat almost imperceptibly. "Well, Harold fell in love with the girl he met, and she fell for him, too. They saw each other throughout the summer. But there was a catch: eventually Harold had to confess everything, first to the girl and then to her father. He was an old miner. I remember Harold told me he had pale eyes that seemed to cut right through him."

My father paused, glanced absently out the window. For a moment we could see the whole valley. To our left, the blue slope of the western foothills. To our right, a snow-streaked peak in the distance. Then I turned, and we glided down a ribbon of highway into the bowl of a grass seed field.

"I guess we all have that moment." My father tapped his fingers on the dashboard as though figuring out a quick calculation. "When we have to confess our sins."

"Because we're in love?" I asked. *Could he know? Could he possibly know?*

All he said was, "The old miner let her marry him anyway. What could he do?"

During another one of our drives, months later, the sky fading to milk-blue, the foothills darkening before us, my father told me about the car his parents gave him as a college graduation present: a reliable Chevy from the hometown dealership. He drove it across the country and traded it in for a white BMW with red upholstery.

My father sighed. He had hurt his parents. He had sold their present for less than it was worth, stepping outside the economy of Fords and Chevrolets. By that time he was gone from Millersburg. Night after night, he dreamed about the Susquehanna Valley, but he never went back for more than a fortnight, although his mother pined for him fiercely.

100

"And the BMW," he concluded, "broke down as I was driving it off the lot."

I thought, *Oh! If you give me the Blue Bird of Happiness I will love it forever.*

And they did.

Sitting around the dinner table one evening, my mother said, "Roger, should we tell her?"

My father spoke slowly. "We wouldn't want to be hasty. We wouldn't want to … rush into anything."

"Oh, Roger, tell her."

"Well, you know how profligate your mother is, Triinu? How she likes fancy jewelry, young men, fast cars?"

"Oh, Roger!" My mother reached across the table, scooping up my empty plate and my father's and stacking them on top of hers.

"Well, your mother has put her foot down and said that she's tired of driving a station wagon with mildew on the upholstery. I don't know why that bothers her. You remember when I had the VW; I grew mushrooms in the back seat."

"One mushroom, Roger. When we let the car sit for a month. Don't exaggerate."

They were both smiling.

"Your mother would like a new car."

"Oh!" I clasped my hands to my chest.

"We were wondering if you know anyone who might be able to use the old Blue Bird of Happiness?"

I squealed, leaping up and hugging my mother and then my father.

"Thank you, thank you!"

My mother said, "Triinu, we're proud of you."

On my sixteenth birthday, I took the driver's examination and passed with seventy-five points, the lowest score you could get and still pass. I was a good driver, and my father was a good teacher. However, neither of us had taken much pleasure in driving around town, practicing unprotected left turns and four-way stops. The clutter of traffic confused me, and for no good reason I listened to the advice of a girl in my English class who told me to stop briefly before proceeding through every green light. The driving examiner looked worried as he handed me my paperwork.

In the license photograph I smiled like a wedding.

Later, I called Ursula. She said she could go out for a few minutes even though she had a test in the morning.

"You kids grow up too fast," Mrs. Benson exclaimed cheerfully. "Don't kidnap our Ursula, mind you. We want her back in one piece, and you, too." She squeezed my shoulders.

Ursula appeared in the hall, her purse in one hand and a cardigan in the other.

"She let you out of the house without a lecture," Ursula commented as we settled into the car's cool plastic seats. "So, where do you want to go? The Beanery? God, you wouldn't believe what Chloe was wearing today. I think it was a lace teddy over a bra. I'm sorry … call me conservative … I couldn't believe her mother let her wear that to school. So, the Beanery or what?"

I was trembling, waiting to feel the car plunge over Earth's convex surface and fall into a horizon of stars. I was waiting to confess everything, waiting for the words to pour from me: "I will love you forever. Until I met you I was nothing." I was ready to elope, to cast off my pedestrian life, to launch my declaration of love into the sky like a guiding star.

Unfortunately, we were still parked in front of the Bensons' green mailbox. The Bensons' dog, Scotch, was still barking to the point of self-strangulation. And Ursula was still talking about Chloe's lingerie top.

"Let's just drive around a bit," I said.

"Okay," Ursula said cheerfully. "But you know what I'd really like first? A Slurpee."

A Slurpee? Oh, prosaic world! How was I to say, "You are the burning light of my heart," to a girl drinking a Slurpee? And what if I felt compelled to buy a Slurpee myself? Could I say, "Without you I am nothing," if in my hand I held a Slurpee, the spade-shaped straw making a little *wheek-wheek* sound as I pushed it in and out of the lid?

I didn't think so, but I said anyway, "A Slurpee it is."

As it turned out, we spent an hour looking for the perfect Slurpee.

"It has to be white cherry," Ursula said, sampling a grape flavor and then tossing her cup in the trash. "Nope. That's not it. Can we keep looking?"

"Anything for you."

This was not what I had planned, but, admittedly, there was something marvelous about circling the town in search of the perfect Slurpee. We could never have talked our busy parents into this. It was the kind of spectacular waste of time available only to girls with their own steel-blue Chevrolet Cavalier.

When we finally found the ideal Slurpee, Ursula put her arm around my waist, gave me a playful hug, and said we had to go to the Beanery next.

The Beanery was situated at the south end of town, near the waterfront. It was the last place to eat before downtown petered away to nothing. The tables were scuffed, the chairs mismatched, the tile floor cracked. The bussing trays overflowed; the punk baristas could not be bothered to empty them. Nor did they bother to charge the regulars for their coffee. The sole unisex bathroom smelled of urine, and the walls were covered in graffiti. "Gay rights are human rights," someone had scrawled across the toilet paper dispenser. Beneath it, someone else had drawn a crude picture of George Bush and written, "I am Ozymandias. Look on me and despair."

I had been to the Beanery before, but always as an interloper, lingering for a nervous half hour and then fleeing. I had never had the courage to ask for my thirty-five-cent refill. With Ursula, I was no longer a stranger.

She bought me a coffee. Then she led me to a bench seat by the window, and we spread the paper in front of us, giggling over the personal ads. A few of Ursula's friends stopped by our table, including Chloe Lombardi in her lingerie top. Chloe even asked for my phone number and gave me hers, after which Ursula scoffed, "Don't wait for a call. She never follows through on stuff."

I didn't care. Ursula was sitting so close to me I could feel her hip against mine. I could feel the wool of her sweater against my wrist. I could feel her breath on my hand, and the desire to lean over and kiss her temple was so deep it made my bones ache, but, of course, I didn't kiss her. I just smiled and stared out of the window, past the congregation of skateboarders jumping on and off the curb, a street light casting their orange shadows on the pavement.

An hour later, the Beanery closed. We deposited our cups in the bussing trays and lingered outside with the skaters for a few minutes. Chloe joined us and smoked one of her mother's menthol cigarettes. A boy named Aaron told an incomprehensible joke about sheep. The failure of the joke was offset by his handsome profile, and we laughed obligingly.

"That's a good one, isn't it?" he said, pushing a length of hair behind his ear.

Someone asked, "What's open? Where can we go?"

The answer was nowhere. Even with the Blue Bird of Happiness, the only places open were the twenty-four-hour grocery store and an old diner with bright lights. We had killed our appetites with caffeine. Besides, we weren't lingering in the darkness because we wanted a steak and gravy dinner. We were lingering in the possibility of the evening, each of us pondering it in our hearts.

Ursula was the first to say goodbye. "You guys can stand out here all night." She tugged her sweater over her hips. "I should get home."

I dropped her off at her house and watched her disappear inside, relieved that I had not declared my love, relieved that I had done nothing to spoil the possibility of having another evening exactly like this one, right down to the white cherry Slurpee.

Then I went home and wept.

I decorated my car shortly after I got it. For a dashboard ornament, I chose a small glow-in-the-dark nativity set that I had had since childhood. The figures were about the size of wedding cake figures, but they were formed out of lumpy, mushroom-green plastic. My American grandmother had bought them for me at a five-and-dime.

Ursula disapproved. "Someone might be offended by that," she pointed out as she settled into my car one evening.

I jerked the car into drive and took a fast left turn. "I didn't make them. I just put them in my car."

"Still, it's kind of irreverent. Don't you think? I mean, I think it's important to respect other people's religions."

"It *is* our religion," I countered.

"It's what we grew up with, but you can't really say it's yours. I mean, not if you like girls."

I glared at the road ahead of me, feeling wounded. I wanted her to laugh. I wanted her to slap the dashboard and say, "Ha! These are great. You're so funny and clever." I drove in silence.

"Are you okay?" Ursula finally asked. "You seem kind of quiet."

"I'm fine."

"It's just that you seem like you've got something on your mind lately."

"I was thinking about this homework I have to do."

Ursula plucked Joseph off the dashboard, reformed the clay around his feet, and replaced him carefully.

"I don't just mean today. You just seem ... I don't know ... distracted?"

I opened my mouth. A motorcycle sped by us. A search beam advertising a used RV dealer swept the sky. I heard myself say, "I'm just thinking about homework, really."

I wanted to slam on the brakes, screech to a crooked stop in the middle of the road, scattering the cars behind me, and say, "No! That's not what I meant. Listen to me. Let me give you my heart." But I kept driving.

Ursula stretched back in her seat and said, "Well that's good. I'm glad. Hey! Guess what I found out today. My Rotary Club host family has two kids: a girl and a boy. Eleven and fourteen. I'm really excited. I think it's important that they have kids. Chloe didn't see why it mattered, but I still think it's cool."

"That's great," I said, glaring at the road.

Later that night as I drove home, I pounded the steering wheel at every stop light.

"Why? Why? Why didn't you say anything?" I whispered each time I hit the wheel, but there was no answer. The

106

steering wheel took the beating silently, the horn having given out years before.

I carried on like that for months. I lived to see Ursula. Still, when she did call, I was distracted, easily miffed, at turns sullen or obsequious. Often I just stared at her, thinking, *I'm going to tell her in three ... two ... one.*

"What are you thinking?" Ursula would ask.

Three ... two ... one.

"Oh, nothing."

When I finally spoke, it was like the first time I jumped off the diving board at the municipal pool. I had been trying for weeks. My patient mother had watched me—a slight seven-year-old girl with stringy, wet hair—walk to the end of the diving board again and again. She'd watched me contemplate the water, watched me turn back.

The rough plank had bounced under the weight of my breath; the water had stared back at me. It had seemed impossible that I should jump. Yet it had seemed equally impossible that I should have come so close to the edge, seen the water beneath me, and turned back. Again.

Minutes had passed, and, as they did, some internal scale that had previously hung in the balance tipped toward courage. Before I had known that I would jump, my knees hit the water. Chlorine struck the soft tissue at the back of my nose. My hair fanned out above me. I'd surfaced, coughing, wondering how I had been so brave.

Ursula and I were driving along an empty stretch of highway, our Slurpee cups squished together in the well between our seats. Around us the grass seed fields stretched to the dark horizon. We had been quiet for a long time. I had been counting down from three for months. Then suddenly I heard myself say, almost conversationally, "I've been thinking … you know how you're going away on the Rotary exchange program? You're leaving pretty soon, and it seemed to me that since we both have been thinking about girls … that we like girls. Maybe … we should kiss. Before you go, I mean. Just to see."

I did not say, "Until I met you I was nothing." But I said something.

Over the noise of the road Ursula said, "I'd like that."

That was all. That was enough.

That night I took the long way home, past Isabel's driveway. I passed it once, then I doubled back and drove by again. It was not quite midnight. A light was on in her room. She was probably reading one of the old paperbacks that had belonged to her father, wearing the red, white, and blue lamé pajama set she had been so proud to find at Goodwill, even though it made her look like a cellophane balloon. I knew that if I tapped on the window, she would open it. She would be glad to see me. She would toss me a dog-eared Louis L'Amour, and I would sit on the floor with my back against the foot of her bed. And when I was ready to talk to her, she would listen. But I could not bear her forgiveness, and so I continued on down the road into the moonlight.

What I Knew About Love

I became Estonian in the summer of 1991, the summer I asked Ursula to kiss me and she said yes. Of course I had always been half Estonian, but I was the kind of half Estonian who spoke English, lived in America, listened to My Life With The Thrill Kill Kult, and drove a Chevy station wagon. I had eaten pickled herring, that Estonian delicacy, exactly never. But Ursula was scheduled to depart on her one-year exchange program in France. She had bought a dozen guidebooks. She planned on visiting Germany, Italy, and Spain. No foreigner or exchange student introduced around the table at the Beanery was safe from her interrogation. That summer, Ursula was enamored by all things foreign, so I had to become foreign, too.

I had the perfect accomplice: Vanaema Emi.

In truth, no one in the family was particularly fond of Emi. My mother hated tending to her aging mother, a woman with whom she had never been particularly close. My father found Emi exasperating. Although he must have known it was futile, she drove him to torrents of frustrated questioning. "Why, Emi? Why?!" he would protest, as though sense might wing its way into her head like a swallow into a barn.

But Vanaema Emi wouldn't say anything. She would just smile, and her smile seemed to say, "You're a silly boy, but I won't fuss." It irritated my father to no end, drove my mother to tears, and seemed proof that Vanaema Emi had no soul.

My mother said I was good with Emi. She said I was a good person, a *kullake*, a sweetheart. In my black dress and veiled hat, I must have looked like an Old World daughter helping

Vanaema Emi into the car. I brought tea and sandwiches to her room. When the mood struck me, I put pink curlers in her hair. If Vanaema Emi turned the television to static and sat in front of the blur, I switched to the next viable channel. I never asked, "Vanaema, do you see anything on the television? Vanaema, what *program* do you want to watch?" I just changed the channel and let her be.

Still, in some ways, there was more human connection in my father's exclamation of "Emi, what are you thinking?" I cared for Emi in the same way I cared for the rangy begonia in our living room, turning it toward the light. She didn't exasperate me because I didn't care that her brain was failing. It didn't bother me that sometimes she walked outside at night and picked camellia blossoms or that she believed JFK had been murdered in her bedroom. *She's a nut case,* I thought, and I put the camellias in water and walked away.

Behind her back, however, I extolled our noble Estonian heritage.

"Being Estonian, I don't always fit in here ... you know, in America," I told Ursula casually, squinting up at the blue sky.

Ursula and I had driven to the park by her house. We had walked over the lawn and into the unclaimed grassland that surrounded the park. In the tall, dry grass, on top of a slight hill, Ursula had tossed down a blanket. "Two more months and I'm out of here," Ursula sighed. She sat cross-legged on the blanket, wearing a straw hat cocked at a jaunty angle.

"Lie down." I patted the blanket next to me, but Ursula didn't seem to notice.

"My mom is driving me crazy over this France thing. She keeps badgering me to do stuff, to pack, to clean up my room. In two months I'll be gone. I'll be in Europe! I love her, but I'm going nuts." Ursula lowered her voice to a conspiratorial whisper. "Did you get the pot?"

I had procured ten dollars' worth of marijuana from Pru-Ann's friend Brent Macintosh, who was no longer straight edge.

"You don't even smoke cigarettes!" he had said. "Who are you gonna smoke it with?"

"A friend," I had said, but it felt monumental. She was so much more than a friend.

I handed my purse to Ursula, and she opened it like it was her own.

"Come here, Ursula. Lie down." Ursula leaned back on her elbows, not quite brushing my arm with hers. "I hope you get to Estonia when you're abroad," I said. "I really … miss it. Can I say that, even though I've never been?"

Ursula stared at the horizon. "What would you do if the cops came?" she asked meditatively.

I sat up quickly and scanned the sky for the shadow of a policeman stomping toward us. "You don't think they will, do you?" Between us and the horizon there was nothing but grass, and even up on my knees, my head barely cleared its tasseled ends. A grasshopper landed beside me, snapping its wings shut.

"Relax," Ursula said. "Nobody's coming." I lay back on the blanket, lit the pipe, and took a quick drag. "What would you do though?" Ursula asked again. "If the cops did come? I'd pretend we were having sex." She giggled.

I imagined the police officer like McGruff the Crime Dog. I saw Ursula stuff the pipe under her back while I leapt on top of her, the buckle of her jeans snagging my shirt. She would push her lips against mine in the same way she talked about politics, rough and accurate.

"I'm sorry, Officer," Ursula joked. "We're not smoking pot, we're just having sex."

"And practicing witchcraft." I laughed.

"And plotting against the government."

"*Elagu Eesti!*"

"*Vive la France!*"

I thought this might be the right time to lean over Ursula and kiss her. But I didn't. I didn't want either of us to look back on that kiss and say, "We must have been high," even though the sticky clot of marijuana had done nothing but make my mouth dry.

"You know, it might not be a good idea," Ursula said.

"What?"

Ursula sniffed the burnt remains of the pipe. "Saying that we were having sex. It might be safer just to say we were smoking pot."

"But pot is illegal."

"If the Oregon Citizens Alliance gets that measure on the ballot, it will be illegal to be gay."

"They can't do that."

I didn't want to talk about politics. I wanted Ursula to lie down beside me, take my hand and clasp it to her chest. In my daydreams she said, "Oh, Triinu, I can't bear to leave you. I'm staying in Oregon. Is that wrong?" In real life, she asked, "Have you heard of *Bowers v. Hardwick*?"

Of course I hadn't. I felt small. "No," I said sullenly.

"Michael Hardwick was this gay guy. He was going down on a guy in his *own bedroom*. The cops came in and arrested him because gay sex is illegal in Georgia."

"Still?"

"Yes, still! Right now. And the OCA wants to make it illegal in Oregon too."

"But I thought they just wanted to teach that it was wrong in sex ed and stuff. They didn't want schools 'promoting' homosexuality." I had read that in the paper. I comforted myself that no one listened in sex ed anyway.

Long spikes of grass poked through the blanket. I broke one off and held it up to the sky. Through the center of the straw I could see a tiny dot of blue sky.

"They want schools to teach that it's wrong." Ursula was using her teaching voice. "They don't want gay teachers. They don't want any gays working for the state. They don't want money going to any organization that helps gays, even if it's a food bank or a health clinic. Don't you see? This is just a start. They know they can get people to vote for *this*. The next step is to make it one hundred percent illegal. The next step is to come into people's houses and arrest them for being gay. The next step is rounding people up and sending them to prison."

"That's like the Holocaust. That's not going to happen here."

But even as I spoke, I thought of Vanaema Emi. The night she left Estonia, she left everything. Had she stayed, men would have come in the night and dragged her into the dark, taken her to a prison in Siberia. It happened in Estonia. What made me so sure it would not happen to me?

"Hardwick went to the Supreme Court," Ursula said. "And he lost. Everyone thought he was going to win, but he didn't. They said that rejecting homosexuality is, like, a fundamental American value."

"Maybe gay people will have to tell the cops they're just smoking pot." I meant it as a joke, but my voice sounded lonely and far away.

Ursula rose up on one elbow and looked at me. "There are places in this country where if I kissed you right now we could go to jail for twenty years."

Her eyes were an ambiguous blue-brown color. Although I knew she was not the prettiest girl I had ever met, I thought

113

she was so beautiful, so smart, so strong. I thought, *Kiss me. Twenty years would be worth it.*

Ursula flopped back on the blanket. "People smoke pot in Amsterdam," she added. "Europeans are cool about stuff. They're not uptight like Americans."

Behind our heads, the grasshopper started singing. Then it clicked its wings open, like the lid of a tiny jewel box, and flew away. Above our heads a coyote-shaped cloud stretched across the sky, its jaws opening slowly.

Ursula sighed. "I can't wait to get out of here. But I'll miss keeping up with Oregon politics. You have to promise you'll send me the paper if anything important happens."

"I'll miss you," I said, with too much verve.

Ursula broke a stalk of grass in half and twirled it between her fingers. "I'm glad I don't have a boyfriend." She paused. "Or a girlfriend. It's really hard to go abroad if you have someone. You know what I mean? I think I'm ready to date, but I wouldn't want to get into anything too serious. It would have to be for fun, not for real."

I closed my eyes against the sunlight. I must have been high; I didn't weep. "You don't think you could fall in love?" I asked.

"And marry someone from here? I'm too busy to fall in love. I've got too many things I want to do."

"Me too." I said. "I have *so many* things I need to do."

But when I went home, I sat in my room counting the hours until I would see Ursula again. The room was dim and hot. I didn't want to be there. I wanted to drive into the summer night with Ursula. I wanted to linger beneath the sky. I wanted to sleep under a wave of gossamer netting, her head on my shoulder. But Ursula was at a Rotary fundraiser, and I was stuck at home.

My father called from outside my door, "Triinu. Come here. Come on out."

I shuffled to the door. "What?"

"Quiet," he said.

I followed him, dragging my feet down the hall as though walking the length of the house was a great imposition. He eased the sliding glass door to the deck open and motioned for me to follow him. Standing at the deck railing, my mother looked down on the lawn. We joined her. Beyond the circle of house light, two raccoons perused the grass, gently fingering it with black hands. Behind them meandered a trio of tiny masked faces.

"Babies," my father whispered. "The raccoons have been busy."

"*Pesukaru*," my mother said. "The Estonians call them 'washing bears.'"

"I feel like those *pesukaru* sometimes," I told Ursula later in the week when she called on the phone. "They're in the garden, but they're not part of it. My mom and dad sit up and read poetry and watch the *pesukaru*. And, I mean, I like poetry and I like raccoons …" Ursula laughed. "… but they're just …" I didn't know what to say.

"I know what you mean," Ursula said gently. "I feel that way about my trip. My mom tells me to clean up my room and come home on time. I know she's just being Mom, but I want to tell her that in less than two months I'll be in France! I'll practically be an adult."

"Do you want to spend the night?" I asked, forcing my voice through the telephone lines. Ursula rarely visited my house, arguing that it was too far out of town. If we wanted to go to the Beanery, we'd have to turn around and drive twenty minutes back into town.

But she said, "Well, if you can show me some raccoons …

but you'll have to think of something else, too. What else can you show me?"

I stuttered. "I—I've got some old photographs."

"That's a start."

As it turned out, we did not see the raccoons, nor did we look at old pictures. We stayed in my room talking. Ursula stretched on my bed, while I sat on the floor beside her. Eventually, I heard my parents go up to their bedroom. Ursula and I crept downstairs without turning on any lights. All the while my heart pounded against the prison of my ribcage. I bumped my way to the television and turned it on. In its static glow, I fumbled to turn on the VCR. Ursula sat cross-legged on the sofa watching me. "What's your favorite movie?" she asked.

"This one, I guess," I said, holding up *Pump Up the Volume*. I put it in. The previews flashed to life, and I scooted back toward the couch, positioning myself on the floor beside Ursula's knees. "I like the way Christian Slater speaks his mind. I like the way he says what everyone else is thinking but is afraid to say. I like the way he says we should break out of our little suburban neighborhoods and really live life."

Ursula touched my hair with her fingertips as though smoothing a slight imperfection. "What are you thinking about right now?" she asked.

The Earth's convex surface falling into a horizon of stars. I love you, Ursula. Until I met you I was nothing.

"Nothing."

"Come here." I got up and sat at the other end of the sofa. "I said come here." But before I could move, Ursula moved toward me, reaching behind me to adjust a pillow. Then she pushed me gently back. "There." She turned around so that she could stretch out on the sofa and place her head against my chest. "That's better." She folded her arms around mine.

I looked down at her bare arms. And hope and certainty met. Until that moment, there had been only impossibilities.

Then Ursula smiled at me. "*Oui*," she whispered.

And my hair fell across her face, and I kissed her.

When I stopped, she kissed my palm, my wrist, my fingertips. "Again?" she asked.

Again. It was nothing like Ralph's tongue on my neck. The feeling that suffused my body was sweeter than any romance novel I had ever read, even though I felt the rough texture of her tongue and tasted the long day on her breath.

"This wouldn't look good if your parents came downstairs," she whispered.

"We could just pretend to be having sex or smoking pot."

"Let's go back to your bedroom."

We made our way upstairs again and slipped into my bed. A tooth of moonlight extended beneath the curtains. And we left Vanaema Emi alone in the basement, for she had never been more than a few feet away from us, behind the closed door of her bedroom, staggering in her unimaginable dreams.

The next day I wrote Ursula a letter detailing my love. It was a silly letter, full of abashed qualifications. "I didn't want to … I find I cannot … Please forgive me … I don't suppose …"

I carried the letter in my purse all the next night as I drove Ursula around town, stopping to say goodbye to her various friends. Finally, I drove her home. As she got out of the car, I pushed the letter at her.

"What's this?"

"It's a letter," I said. "It's for you. I wrote it." She didn't take it. "I'd like you to read it because it's something that I wrote. And it's for you." I pushed it at her, and finally she slipped it into her purse. "Call me," I said.

She hopped out of the car without looking back. I sat in the driveway for a long time, watching the place she had stood.

In the morning I called her as soon as I woke up. "Mom is totally freaking out," she announced. "She says I have to finish packing, but I *am* finished … almost. I just have to get it into my suitcase. Maybe you can help."

"I'd do anything for you."

"Can you fit six sweaters in one carry-on?"

In Ursula's bedroom that afternoon, I saw that no amount of devotion would fit her packing list into the modest suitcases her mother had purchased. I watched her fold and refold her clothes, trying increasingly ingenious techniques, as though one of them might bend the laws of physics and create, inside her suitcase, a space that was larger than its length and depth. I watched her with such intensity I could feel the texture of her T-shirt, the warp and weft, the spandex-cotton blend that clung to her body. I watched her hair fall between us like a veil. I watched her hands and the dot of blood beside her left thumbnail where she had bitten the cuticle. I was only sixteen, but I knew that if she loved me, she would look up. She would look at me, and, brushing the hair from her eyes, say nothing.

As it was, she stood up and pulled a baby-doll dress from the closet, and said, "Do you think I can wear this with jeans? I've seen Chloe do it, but I just don't know. It's one of those things that I thought was cheesy, but then I saw it, and I kind of liked it. How many socks do you think I need?"

I stared at the suitcases and pulled two socks out of a pile and put them together, rolling them into a ball and pulling the lip of one sock over the other, the way my father rolled his long black socks.

"Don't do it like that!" Ursula complained. She performed a modified sock roll and tossed it at me. "Better, right?"

The effort it took not to cry bruised my lungs.

"It doesn't help me if you don't do it right." Ursula added. "And I wanted to talk to you about the sweaters." She pulled a limp pile of sweaters out of the suitcase. "If you fold them like this," Ursula squared a sweater on her pillow, rolled it. "See?"

I imitated what she had done but came out with a lumpy knot.

"Don't tease," Ursula laughed.

But I wasn't teasing. I was desolate. "Ursula, did you read my letter?"

She spoke reluctantly, as though I had just pulled a dead snake out of my pocket and asked, "Do you see this?"

"Yeah."

"And?" My voice was raw. I already knew the answer. My father had read me "The Love Song of J. Alfred Prufrock." I knew she would not sing to me.

"I told you I wasn't looking for anything." Ursula dropped her voice as though afraid someone would overhear. "I don't want a relationship. And Triinu, I'm not gay. I think it's cool that you are. And I like girls, I mean … I like them some. But I'm going to Europe. I never said I would be your girlfriend. We're not going to prom, okay?"

Prom. I wasn't asking her to go to prom. I was offering to cut my heart out with a stone knife and lay it, bleeding, on the altar of my love. I was walking into the lion's den because the Lord God would defend me. I was standing in the garden at Gethsemane, crying, "Why have you forsaken me?"

"I don't want to go to prom," I whispered.

"Good," Ursula said. "'Cause we're great friends. You know that, right? You're my best friend."

When I got home, I threw myself on my bedroom floor, sobbing. I cried for the sweaters and the socks and the casual way

Ursula had said, "I'll probably see you again before I leave." I cried for the airplane that would sweep Ursula away. I cried for the letter that carried my message of love and the possibility that Ursula had buried it in the bottom of a trash can like a cigarette butt. I cried, convinced I had lost everything I could have possibly lost.

I cried until my father knocked on the door and opened it without waiting for a reply. Before I had time to pick myself up off the floor, he was at my side, his long arm around my shoulders. "What's wrong? Triinu?" A real edge of worry was in his professorial voice.

For a breathless moment, I thought I might tell him the truth, but I did not know one other gay person in the whole world, let alone someone who had looked their father in the eye and spoke the words, "I'm gay. I'm in love." As far as I had proof, it had never been done.

"Ursula's leaving," I sniffled.

"Was tonight the last time you'll see her?" he asked.

"I don't know … but she's still leaving, and I'll miss her so much."

"I'm sorry," he said.

I leaned my head on his shoulder. I could smell his deodorant and, beneath that, a faint smell of sweat and dry pine needles. He had been in the garden that day, raking bark dust and tying up lilacs.

"I'm fine," I whimpered.

"You will be."

A few minutes later, my mother woke from a nap. Sensing that melancholy had crept into her house while she slept, she came downstairs to battle it back. She appeared at my door with a rented video in one hand. "I don't want to impose on your sadness, but I am watching a video. Do you want to join

120

me?" she asked, her accent lending a formality to everything she said. It seemed to make no difference whether I watched a video or not, so I dragged downstairs behind her. We settled onto the couch in front of the television, side by side.

The room held no trace of the evening Ursula and I had spent there, nothing to suggest that this room was a secret cave submerged beneath my parents' ordinary life. If there was a striking feature, it was the painting of a rough-hewn cross. We had inherited the painting when my uncle died, driven to drink and then to death by the grief of leaving Estonia. Everything else was faux-wood paneling and beige carpet.

The movie my mother had rented from the foreign section at American Movie Rentals must have struck her as an unfortunate choice. It was a modern silent film that retold *Alice in Wonderland* with marionettes. The drama took place in a dilapidated dollhouse. The marionettes were made out of old dolls with rolling eyes and teeth, and the rabbit was a plush lump with nearly human eyes loosely affixed to either side of its head. For an hour and a half the characters chased each other through a nightmare of closets, Alice's teeth clacking as though hungering to bite the fingers off a small child.

Oddly enough, I felt a little bit better after it was over.

My mother smiled and said, "Well, I like foreign films, but that was very strange."

"It's okay," I said. "It wasn't boring."

"I love you, Triinu."

"I love you too, Mom."

Every night during the summer, my parents sat in a pair of moldy Adirondack chairs on the deck and sipped wine. That night, my mother pulled a dining room chair onto the deck for me. My father poured from a bottle of red wine, giving me a thimbleful at the bottom of a tall glass. We sat, drank our wine, and listened to the screech owls until the raccoons came back.

"Is one limping?" my mother asked.

"I think so." My father rose from his chair and leaned on the railing. Below, an ancient raccoon winced across the grass. "Looks like he's seen some hard times."

"Maybe we should put out some kibbles for him," my mother said.

My father went inside. I heard him pour dog food into a metal bowl. When he walked outside, the raccoons scattered to the trees. Their claws sounded like rain as they scrabbled on the bark. They stared down at my father with smart, reflective eyes.

When my father returned to the deck, he held a dog-eared, yellow book in one hand. "What have you got there?" my mother asked.

"Auden." My father leafed through the book while my mother took a deep sip of her wine.

"'Lay your sleeping head, my love, human on my faithless arm,'" he began conversationally, barely glancing at the page in front of him. "'Time and fevers burn away individual beauty from thoughtful children, and the grave proves the child ephemeral.'" He was a bass in the church choir, and his voice was rich and confident after years of lecturing. "'Every farthing of the cost ...'" Beneath us, I could hear the old raccoon crunching kibbles in a steel bowl. "'All the dreaded cards foretell, shall be paid but from this night ...'"

My mother finished from memory, "'... not a whisper, not a thought, not a kiss nor look be lost.'"

Did they know?

They read Auden all the time. Had they been preparing me for years? We were so close, my parents and I, even with my secrets balled up in my hands like tearstained tissues. We were so fond of each other. We, the young people.

When my father finished reading, we sat in silence for a while. Then eventually, my mother said she had to check on Vanaema Emi. Emi's health had deteriorated, and now she had to be diapered at night.

"Why check if she's sleeping?" I asked.

"If she's soiled herself," my mother sighed, "I'll need to change her before bed."

"But if you check on her now, and she soils herself in ten minutes, it'll be the same as if you don't check on her at all." I hated to see my mother go downstairs. I hated the long, uncomfortable silence as we listened for the sound of the shower that would indicate Vanaema Emi had to be washed. I resented my grandmother—when I bothered to think of her at all—for the trouble she caused my parents, their grief and revulsion at her gray body and its excrement. I cleaned Vanaema Emi, too. I walked her to the toilet, pulled her pants down, wiped her anus with a lemony towelette, but it didn't bother me; I didn't see her humanity. She was a litter box to be scooped, a dog pen to be hosed down, a bag of trash to be lugged out to the end of the driveway, just another household chore with its attendant smells.

In the end, Vanaema Emi was an eccentric immigrant who came to this country in middle age and never learned the workings of American society, eventually sickening and becoming a burden on her family. Emi Luhavalja, at the end, so passive and uncomprehending that she slept in her own shit, although she was strong enough to walk to the bathroom had the notion occurred to her. There she was at the end of life, her granddaughter's bragging right, a factoid with which to impress an adolescent love interest. *My grandmother the immigrant. Aren't I different? Aren't I cool?* That is one way to tell Vanaema Emi's story.

This is another:

Long ago, but still on the cusp of modern history, in that abandoned Estonia had been invaded before, and Vanaema Emi had been part of the resistance. She was a doctor, and she posed as a proponent of the occupations, forging medical documents and saving Estonians from the labor camps. My mother had also suggested that Vanaema Emi had been one of the Forest Brothers, a guerrilla fighter. By the time she told me this, it was too late to verify any of the facts; still, one marvelous photograph found in a manila folder made me quick to believe.

It was a graduation photograph from Vanaema Emi's medical school. The photograph showed two rows of solemn Estonian men. Seated in their midst were Vanaema Emi and one other woman, together the first two women to graduate from the school. Everyone wore white coats. Their hands were folded in uniform arrangement. They looked reverent and sorrowful, except for Vanaema Emi, who did what no Estonian ever did in photographs, even at weddings: she looked straight at the camera and smiled. Pretty and small, her hair curled in a pert bob, her lips closed in a natural smile, she looked enormously fetching. A desiccated corpse lay on the wooden table before her, a prop to mark the students' arrival in the medical community. Before Vanaema Emi, the sunken leather of the dead man's body sucked up light. In the contest between his death and her smile, I could see my grandma looking down the scope of a rifle.

Nonetheless, on the night of the Soviet invasion of Estonia—not even a sidebar in my history textbook—Vanaema Emi fled. Paulus and Feliks, only teenagers at the time, arrived

124

at the house with two cars, one hitched to the other. They whispered something terrible in the nervous light of the kitchen.

What they said. Where they had been. How they got the cars. Who hitched them together and with what choking urgency. No one would know. Grandpa Aivo, Paulus, and Feliks were all dead by the time I sat on the porch, pining for Ursula Benson. My mother, only a little child at the time, remembered this: before they left, Vanaema Emi placed an open Bible on the kitchen table beside a vase of flowers. When they left, they left the door unlocked.

The Luhavaljas left both cars on the edge of the Baltic Sea and boarded a greasy fishing boat with nets piled fore and aft. My mother remembered vomiting on a green and blue plaid blanket. She knew that her mother stood beside her on the deck and watched the Soviet airstrike sink every ship that followed, the boats filled with people Vanaema Emi knew.

After that, the family lived in German refugee camps, four to a room. In the camps, which were not like the death camps but rather Germany's best attempt at housing the lost and the unclaimed, the Estonians set up schools and churches, and Vanaema Emi ministered to them with her nostrums. She picked wild mushrooms, and Paulus picked wild strawberries, which he saved for my mother. He took photographs of the Estonians in high-collared jackets. And once a Nazi officer patted my mother on the head and gave her an orange, a fact that confused me as a child. I had read Anne Frank's diary, and I knew who the villains were.

Exactly why and how they arrived in Germany—a country that had itself occupied Estonia at one time—and why and how they were eventually ferried to San Francisco remained a vague background to the story. They came to America, bypassing Ellis Island, which was fine with them.

"We were not 'the wretched refuse of your teeming shore,'" my mother said once when I came home from a school lesson on the Statue of Liberty, brimming with fourth-grade patriotism. "We weren't 'huddled masses.'"

By the time the family arrived in America, a quarter of the Estonian population had been killed or sent to Siberian labor camps. In Estonia, there was one Soviet soldier for every twelve Estonians, and the KGB was everywhere. No one spoke. Nothing was safe. The Soviets outlawed Christmas trees. Even singing hymns was cause for imprisonment. A third of the slaves in the Siberian labor camps were children.

My family moved to America, the land of promise, carrying the sorrow of Estonia with them, and made do. My grandfather worked as a caretaker at a Lutheran Bible camp while the family learned English. He was never able to parlay his Estonian engineering license into an American profession, but Paulus became an engineer in his footsteps and my mother excelled in English literature. Vanaema Emi obtained a license to practice homeopathic medicine, and the family bought a house in the Oakland hills.

In a family photograph, Vanaema Emi, Grandpa Aivo, my mother, and Paulus stood in that living room. They were so dignified. No one smiled. No one gave two thumbs up. No one had been caught in a half sneeze before the flash. They could have been carved out of stone, they were so still. All photographs are motionless, but the Estonians' stillness sang of the Old World. Even my mother's hair, flowing long and natural over her shoulders, seemed restrained. They were so achingly handsome in their high collars.

My mother stood up, her Adirondack chair creaking. "I have to check on her."

"Aww, Mom," I protested one last time. "Just leave her. Emi'll be fine."

My mother stood up, turning from the evening darkness toward the house light and her duties. "No," she said simply, her shoulders sloped and her head bent.

"Why does she always have to do that?" I asked my father when she had disappeared.

"Your mother?" he asked, as though I might be asking about someone else. "She does what she has to do."

"It just doesn't make sense." I sighed and returned to dreaming about Ursula, thinking I knew everything there was to know about love, not realizing how deep the river is into which we dip our feet at sixteen.

Satan's Lab Partner

Those first days back at school after Ursula's departure my junior year were hard. I couldn't call her. An international call cost three dollars a minute, plus a connection fee of nine dollars and ninety-nine cents. Even if my parents had allowed the expense, there were no hours in the day when we were both awake and in the house, and the pressure of talking at that price would have killed the spontaneity of our conversation. And without Ursula, I did not have any friends. Pru-Ann was at a different wilderness camp, and I could not crawl back to Isabel.

At school, I wandered listlessly through the career center, where the librarian had installed a rack of local newspapers for our edification. A hand-stenciled sign read, "Keep Up with Current Events!" Ursula had asked me to keep her abreast of Oregon politics. I squared my shoulders and scanned the headlines.

"Gay Teen Suicide Rate Higher, Advocates Claim"

"Oregon Citizens Alliance Say Youth at Risk, Targeted by Pedophiles"

"Homosexual Gangs!"

The Oregon Citizens Alliance was already lobbying for the antigay ballot measure they planned for the following year, 1992—my senior year. They hadn't won yet, but it was just a matter of time; all the political commentators said so. "The gay issue is not going away," one editorial read. "The OCA's antigay initiative is certain to take the state next fall."

Later that week, the Democracy Club featured a debate on the homosexual issue. I wasn't sure I wanted to go, but I didn't have anywhere to eat lunch. The Democracy Club at least gave me a place to sit.

I took my hard plastic seat in the front row. The club had promised a debate, but I could only spot one presenter. The man looked vaguely familiar. I thought I might have recognized him as an itinerant member of Forbearing Emmanuel Lutheran, one of those church members who showed up every fifth or sixth Sunday.

Principal Pinn stood at the man's side, shaking his hand and slapping his back. "So good of you to come, Chuck." Shake. Shake. "I know you're going to be able to tell these kids some things that put this all into perspective." Backslap. "We need that with all these liberal parents at home."

"Well, Rick," the man guffawed. "I don't think I've really got a *perspective*, unless you count being a God-fearing Christian a perspective." The man had a thick, black mustache and a gut that he probably mistook for muscle.

"Kids, you're in for a real treat." Principal Pinn slapped his guest on the back one more time. "Now, let's hear a word from our student leader: Pip Weston, the president of Students for Family Values."

Pip leapt up from his seat and hurried to the front of the room. He pumped his fist. The boys behind me barked their approval. I heard a girl whisper, "I love him."

Pip took a piece of paper out of his pocket. "Today, I want to welcome two speakers. Chuck Garst of the Oregon Citizens Alliance." The boys barked again. "And Mary … Diz … gin … ik?"

As he butchered the name, a woman with a gray ponytail moved to the front of the room. I hadn't noticed her hovering by the door.

"She's from special rights something." Pip sneered.

"I'm Mary Deljenick with the Coalition for Equal Rights," the woman corrected, but her voice was lost in the laughter of the crowd. Principal Pinn grinned.

"A very good introduction," Chuck Garst said, his mustache twitching. Then he bellowed so loudly, I jumped in my seat. "We don't believe in special rights for ho-mo-sexuals. These people are degenerates, child molesters, sodomites, delinquents, predators, beast lovers, scat lovers, perverts, and vampires sucking the blood of our society. Do you want these people teaching your classes? Boys, do you? Do you want them in the locker room? To be your coaches? Your doctors?"

From the front row Pip yelled, "No way!"

Mr. Garst nodded and went on. "The Oregon Citizens Alliance and myself, we want to keep this country for God-fearing heterosexual Americans and not some perverts asking for special rights. Are you with me?"

The crowd stirred. A couple of girls clapped and squealed. Two of Pip's friends gave each other a high five, as though they were personally saving children from the homosexual agenda simply by being seventeen-year-old assholes.

"Excuse me." Ms. Deljenick skimmed through her notes, sipped her water, and whispered, "May I present the opposing side? We at the Coalition for Equal Rights believe in the democratic principles of freedom and equality for all citizens." She sipped her water again. "Historically ..." She shuffled her notes. "Historically ..."

Speak up! I pleaded silently. *Tell him he's a fucking asshole and he'll burn in hell.*

"Do you know how hot the fires of hell are?" Mr. Garst said, as though he had intercepted my psychic message to the gay-rights advocate. "I suppose we're not supposed to talk about church in school. But let's just say, I think there are places for people like this."

130

I glared at Mr. Garst, hoping he could feel my stare burning through his chest, through the hard mountain of fat, and into his entrails.

He grinned. "Think about it, people! Homosexuals can't breed, but there are more and more of them every year. Do you know why? They recruit. They're outside middle-school playgrounds. They trap vulnerable children in their sick lifestyle, and it spreads like a cancer. But if we get our measure on the ballot next year, we're going to stop that."

The crowd cheered.

"We're going to make sure that every school in Oregon teaches kids about the homosexual threat, and we'll make sure not *one* Oregon tax dollar gets spent on the homosexual agenda."

Ms. Deljenick coughed. "Excuse me."

Mr. Garst kept talking.

"Excuse me," she tried again. "Are you saying the Oregon Citizens Alliance would ban homosexuals from public employment?"

He smiled as though she had just handed him a piece of pie. "We sure would like that. Yes, ma'am. We'd like to ban homosexuals from working with children, from coaching, from teaching of any kind, from positions of authority where they can spread their lies. We'd like to ban them from government, universities, schools. Naturally, we wouldn't want any tax dollars paying *gay* salaries."

I thought of my father in his office at the university. It had never occurred to me that I might want to be a professor. Suddenly I felt the office door close. I looked around. Everyone was smiling.

"But there's more," Mr. Garst said. "Let's get serious about this." He brought the microphone close to his lips, so his whisper roared through the room. "They don't become predators at eighteen when they graduate high school. They start young." He shook his head. "My hope is that one day soon, we won't have homosexuals in our schools at all. One strike. I say, as soon as a student is suspected of homosexual behavior, they're out."

Finally Ms. Deljenick raised her voice over a whisper. "What are you going to do with these children you have labeled as homosexual? Two little girls kiss on the playground. What are you going to do to them?"

"Oh, we've got a very successful facility in eastern Oregon. We employ all the latest science and technology. Drug therapy. Talk therapy. Shock treatment under very, very controlled settings …"

"To do what?" she interrupted.

"To cure them."

Suddenly I had to pee. My hands felt cold. I thought I might throw up. I rose, stumbling into the girl next to me.

"Whoa!" Pip called out. "There's your first one, Mr. Garst."

I pushed past the girls in my row and ran from the room. They were going to come get me. The ballot measure would pass. The Oregon Citizens Alliance would win. Then one day, I'd disappear, just like Pru-Ann, only it wouldn't be my parents who sent me away. It would be Principal Pinn. My parents would stand on the sidewalk in front of the bus lane, crying and waving. My mother would mouth the words, "I love you." I would watch her for as long as I could, until she became a tiny dot and then disappeared. Then Chuck Garst would take me to the desert and torture me because I loved Ursula Benson.

That night, I lay in bed and cried. I thought about telling my mother. I remembered being six and curling up in her arms, her kisses in my hair. "If ever somebody is mean to you," she whispered. "Anybody. Even if you think you're not supposed to tell, you can tell me."

But how could I tell her that the whole state had reared up its head and said, "She's not ours"? How could I lay that weight on my mother, in whose face I saw that old Estonian sadness? She had enough to do caring for Emi, who was bedridden now. I could almost see her dreams slipping away as she diapered her own mother and poured Ensure into a plastic cup.

What was I going to say?

Do you remember the last boats to leave Estonia? Do you remember the torpedoes that sunk them all? It's happening again.

This time it's happening to me.

The cruel thing about adolescence is the way it heaps insult upon insult. Not only was I a flounder with one enormous labia whom the Oregon Citizens Alliance hated because I wanted to kiss Ursula Benson, I was now a junior. That meant biology. That meant dissections, because apparently seeing cancerous lungs in jars was not sufficient for our edification. It was time to open the jar up and take out our scalpels.

At the beginning of class, Mr. Litel, the biology teacher, assigned lab partners. "Ben Sprig and Julie Cotswold," he announced.

A few tables away, Ben, a stocky, pear-shaped football player, came to life. He threw his upper body across the black laboratory table in front of him. "I don't want to work with Julie *Fatswold!*"

Mr. Litel went down the list, unmoved. "Pip Weston and Triinu Hoffman ..." Some of the girls in the class actually sighed when our partnership was announced. Pip had, I hated to admit, grown handsome over the summer. Even I could see it. He had finally had his growth spurt. Now he was six long feet of elegant, lanky boyhood. Still, I knew the devil in all his guises.

"Aw! No way, man!" Pip protested. "I can't work with her. I'm president of Students for Family Values."

"Well, maybe you can share some of your values with her." Mr. Litel said it like he really thought that might happen. "A strapping young fellow like you, I think any girl would be happy to be your partner."

"She's a frickin' lezzie Satanist." Pip's voice soared to a melodramatic high. Ben chuckled.

The late September sunlight teased through a narrow window at the back of the biology lab, catching in a row of formaldehyde jars placed above a high cupboard. I felt, as one does in dreams, that there had been a terrible mistake, that instead of my fall schedule printed on dot-matrix printer paper, I should be able to produce a passport I could show Mr. Litel. "See? I'm not supposed to be here. I got the wrong class, the wrong life. Sorry for the trouble. I'll see myself out."

Mr. Litel continued down his list of names. I stared intently at my textbook, ignoring Pip with all the gothic decorum I could muster. I didn't have the heart to fight back, not without Ursula, not when the whole state had turned against me.

Pip moseyed past my table. "I just wanted to know, do you dress that way 'cause you're, like, a Satanist?" I opened my textbook and pretended to read.

He smacked his hand down in the center of my book. "I'm talking to you, perv!"

I had fallen back on the old public school adage: "Ignore a bully and he will go away." I knew it was a lie, but I didn't know what else to do.

Mr. Litel sauntered up. I knew too much to hope for salvation. He put a big, manly coach hand on Pip's shoulder. "Maybe you can turn her head," he said smiling at us both. "You know … before she goes too far down the wrong path."

That evening after dinner, my father and I took a long walk in the woods. "How was school?"

I could not tell him the truth: that I was being picked on, teased, bullied, like a shy kid on the back of the bus. Somehow he seemed to know.

"Forgive me if I've told you this before," he began. "I used to hate the start of school. I got picked on something terrible when I was about eight or ten." He broke off a stalk of grass and tucked it in the corner of his mouth. "Kids were just mean. One kid in particular. He would pound my head into the playground every chance he got."

My father pulled the grass out of his mouth and tickled my ear with the fringed end. I swatted it away. "What did you do?" I asked.

The answer was simple. He grew up. He grew tall. He grew into a lean bear of a man with great paws and a chest like a drum.

"Sometime in the fifth grade I realized I was bigger than the rest of the kids were." Around us the forest crackled with the sound of life. "So I sat on their heads," my father said, without unnecessary satisfaction. "And I beat the snot out of them. They never bothered me again."

I appreciated the story, but it didn't seem like a workable solution for me.

The next day in biology, I sat in a foursome with Ben, Pip, and Ben's lab partner, Julie. In this close proximity, Ben and Pip kept up a constant patter of insults. "Weston, I think you'd better clear this up if you two are going to work together," Ben said. "Is she a dyke Satanist or isn't she?"

"Like you have to ask. Look at her! Why don't you ask Julie how she got so fat? I mean, seriously, how does that happen?"

Julie *was* fat. Her buttocks hung over the seat of her lab stool. She wore white cotton turtlenecks that accentuated her rolling stomach. On her binder, she had taped Bible verses, Oregon Citizen Alliance slogans—"Love the sinner, hate the sin"—and photographs of little boys, probably her nephews. They had crew cuts and open mouths and little doll teeth. They looked like boys who would grow up to ask girls, "Do you pose for fatty magazines? Are you, like, a fatty porn star?"

Ben chuckled. "Hey, Julie, I was wondering ..."

But Julie was an amazing person. She must have been working on a modified version of "Ignore a bully and he will go away." She was better at it than I was. She turned to Pip and Ben and smiled a bright, loving smile. It was unnerving. Everything about Julie was fat, clean, wholesome, and sexless. Still, watching her smile as Ben said, "I heard Jenny Craig is hiring," was like watching Pru-Ann press a safety pin through the skin between her thumb and forefinger.

"You crazy boys, you better watch it," she said, her voice cheerful. It was surreal.

Pip turned to me. "So? Would you like to sacrifice Fatty here to the fuckin' Lord of the Underworld?"

"Is swearing part of your family values?" Mr. Litel chided Pip, without any real ire in his voice.

"No, sir," Pip said, straightening and folding his hands in front of him. Out of the corner of his mouth he hissed, "Dyke."

"Okay, kids. Time to get your frogs out of the cooler," Mr. Litel said.

Principal Pinn often began the morning announcements by telling us that these were the best days of our lives. But when in adulthood would I be forced to dissect frogs with a man who thought I was a Satanist? I waited for Pip to retrieve our frog from the cooler. He slapped the tray down, splattering form- aldehyde on the tabletop. He picked the unhappy creature up and held its stiff body toward me.

Behind us, Tori Schmidt squealed, "Oh, Pip! Don't touch it!"

"Triinu wants to eat it." Pip waved the frog in the air.

"Put it down!" Tori shrieked.

Pip put the frog down and wiped his hand on his jeans. He leaned toward me. "Come on, tell me. You worship Satan, don't you? You get up late at night and have sacrifices and fuck virgin girls and shit." He raised his crossed index fingers in my direction. "I think you're sick," he growled. "You're a pervert."

I tried to ignore him and focus on the lesson, but there was no lesson. Our books were closed, and Mr. Litel was on the other side of the room arguing with a young animal rights activist. We were just waiting: twenty-some teenagers with carcasses, waiting for Mr. Litel to hand us each a scalpel, to pierce the skins, to prick open the intestines, the stomach, the heart.

I liked frogs. I had raised them when I was young. In the early springs of my childhood, I would check the cold mud puddles in the gully beyond our house every day. Waiting. Then one day, as though God had breathed life into the water, the pools would swarm with tadpoles. One day each year, I would clamber up the side of the gully, blackberry brambles grabbing my socks, yelling, "Mom! I need a bucket!"

A few weeks later, the puddles would dry up. The tadpoles that I had not transferred to my aquarium would die. They were easy to catch right before the puddles disappeared, their black, fishy bodies pressed together in the last inch of water. I felt responsible for them.

Mr. Litel handed Pip his scalpel. Pip held it over the carcass like a fork.

"You know, this is what someone should have done to you." He waved the scalpel. "When you were in the womb."

137

"I thought you were pro-life," I said, finally meeting his eye. "You should stick to the same bullshit story, or no one's going to believe you."

"Yeah, well, it doesn't count for Satan worshipers."

I had had enough.

"I don't just worship Satan," I said. "I *am* Satan." I held up my index finger and pinky the way I had seen rockers do in heavy metal videos. "Fucking six, six, six."

At the adjacent table, Ben tipped his stool back casually. "Man, she just told you she's Satan." He glanced back at Tori and tossed her a smile. "And you know what, Weston?" Ben brought all four legs of his stool down with a clang. "She can make your balls fall off."

"I can," I said.

There was a time when Pip would have mocked me in a squeaky, nasal voice: "'I'm Satan. I can make your balls fall off.'" But he didn't. Something had shifted. Pip crossed his legs and watched me.

From then on, Pip still picked on me, but being Satan gave me something to say when Ben prodded him with, "Ask her if she sacrifices virgins."

I said yes. All the time. I couldn't remember how many virgins I had sacrificed. I'd sacrifice his sister if he had one.

At the front of the classroom one morning, Mr. Litel introduced our next project. We would be growing water cultures, he explained. Starting with a bucket of pond water, we would create an optimal growth environment by adding light and vegetation. Under a microscope we would see the diverse life forms that live in a single drop of water.

Around the room, students scratched pictures of the tiny monsters they found in their water cultures. Everyone said,

"Wow, that's amazing!" or "Ew, gross! I'm never going swimming again." Except for Pip. Every day he put his eye to the microscope and saw nothing.

"I killed them," I told him.

"You poisoned my water culture?"

I shook my head. "I didn't poison them. I cursed them."

"It's a fertility thing," Ben told Pip. "You just don't have that generative power."

"What?" Pip looked up.

"Generative power." Ben grabbed the crotch of his baggy jeans and shook it. He lowered his voice. "It means that your balls are falling off." He nodded toward me. "She put a spell on you. First your bugs die. Then your balls."

Pip stared at me. Then he returned to his project for a moment. And then he examined me again, intently.

"You really freak those guys out," Julie whispered, peeking over her microscope. "It's too funny."

I furrowed my brow. Julie and I did not talk a lot. "Being Satan has that effect on people."

"Pshaw," Julie snorted. "You're not Satan. Pip is looking at your legs."

I was surprised that Julie knew about legs. I assumed that she sat in class thinking about Baptist Jesus and how much she loved her nephews.

"I mean, he cannot stop looking," she said. "You totally freak him out."

"No way."

"Yes way. He can't stop staring at those suspender things you got on."

I was wearing a black trapeze dress, cut on the bias. Around my neck I wore a bundle of dagger-shaped charms, and, for Pip's benefit, a pentagram. I was also wearing a proud new addition to my wardrobe: a pair of thigh-high stockings held up by a real garter belt.

"You can't …" I said. But you could. Sitting perched on a lab stool, my skirt rode up, exposing the garter and an inch of bare thigh. I glanced down. "I guess you can."

"Yeah, you can." Julie sounded vaguely disapproving, but, more than that, she sounded conspiratorial. "Pip can." She bit off the last word like it was a chocolate bar.

In Hollywood films, popular boys see the untapped potential in shy, unpopular girls. The soundtrack soars as the boy looks on, startled at his own recognition. She is beautiful. In a series of close-ups, the girl is coiffed and put in a diaphanous pink dress. The boy then ushers this girl, newly made, into the life she always deserved. The whole school marvels as she glides into the prom.

This does not happen in real life.

This did not happen to Julie.

This did not happen to me.

Still, a satisfied silence fell between us. Julie and I could never be friends. She was a Baptist. I was goth. She wore white turtlenecks, and I wore velvet cloaks. She loved her nephews "to pieces." I had read "A Modest Proposal," and I didn't think it *had* to be a satire. And then, of course, there was the whole business of kissing girls. We couldn't be friends, Julie and I. Yet I imagined she was thinking the same thing I was thinking. For at least a moment, I was, for Pip Weston, an unmentionable desire, and to be an unmentionable desire for someone you despised, well … that was as sweet as any chiffon prom dress.

At the next table Tori tittered, "What sign are you, Pip? I'm a Scorpio. Do you think I act like a Scorpio?"

Pip didn't answer. I could feel his gaze on me. I let one foot slip off the lowest rung of my stool so that my leg dangled to the floor, exposing another inch of thigh. I felt the garter strain. I brushed my dress, as though absently chasing a piece of lint. Pip was thinking about sex. I could almost smell it. I let my leg sway. Then I turned to the front of the room and studied the overhead projection of mitochondria that Mr. Litel had left on the screen.

Pip whispered, "Hey, Satan, I have a question."

But I was paying close attention to the lesson, so I ignored him.

After class, Pip hurried out of the room without the parting insult he usually hurled at me. I noticed that he had left his microscope and his defeated science project on the table. I went to put it away. Before unplugging Pip's microscope, I put my eye to the lens to look at the devastation I was accused of having wrought on his water culture. I winced. The light coming through the microscope was blinding. I could see nothing but white. I reached under the slide tray and found the small silver knob that controlled the light.

I turned it, and as I dimmed the light, a world of multifarious creatures came into focus.

The bacteria and the protozoa, the algae and the rotifers. I admired them for a moment. Then I turned the microscope off, leaving the light at the correct setting so that the following day when Pip took out his experiment, all his bugs would be magnificently, inexplicably restored to life.

The next morning, I found a note taped to my locker door, the words *"Die you motherfucking dyke bitch"* typed in neat lettering along with a computer-generated picture of a gun, beneath which two stick figures engaged in sodomy. I was holding it in my hand, staring at it as though it might suddenly come to life, the stick figures pumping away, the imaginary gun firing a rain of bullets, when a shadow fell over the paper. I jumped and spun around, but it was Isabel, leaning over my shoulder.

"That's fucked up." It was the first time she had talked to me all year. "What lesbian is going to fuck some dude up the ass? But, hey, forget those assholes. I got something for you."

She looked down at her shoes and then held out a piece of paper. For a second, I thought it was going to be one of Pip's "Homosexuality Is a Sin" fliers. It was the same size, the same orange paper, probably stolen from the school's AV room. I imagined the insincere pleasantry that would follow: "I just wanted to share the love of Jesus Christ with you ... before you fry in hell!" It was hard to square that message with Isabel's black polyurethane jacket and shiny red stretch pants, but what else could it be? The whole state had turned against me, why not Isabel? She had more reason to hate me than Pip. I took the paper reluctantly.

"Pretty cool, isn't it?" Isabel said shyly.

I stared at the paper. It was a xeroxed copy of a hand-drawn picture of a giant squid eating a man. The man wore trousers and loafers and held a briefcase, but his head and upper body were already inside the belly of the beast. "Molotov Squid" was written, ransom-note style, using letters cut out of magazines. The fonts were strangely feminine, as though the artist only had access to *Seventeen* and *Woman's Day*. Yet across the entire piece, someone had stamped the anarchy sign in green paint.

"Wow," I said. I was fairly sure it was not antigay propaganda.

"I know." Isabel was blushing. "It's crazy, but you know ... carpe fucking diem, right?"

"Right?" It came out like a question.

Isabel pointed to tiny lettering running the perimeter of the flier. The Xerox had cut off the last millimeter, but I thought I could make out the words "bass" and "guitar" and "vocals by Isabel."

"You're in a band?" I asked.

"I started working at this sandwich shop downtown. One of the guys, Greg, is the lead singer in this band, and we were hanging out, and their other singer didn't show up to practice, so ..."

"It looks great." It looked like something.

"So ..." Isabel fidgeted with the strap of her backpack. "I was wondering if you'd come. It's next Saturday at the Armory. You could stop by with your other friends if you wanted. Just for a minute. But you're probably busy. Anyway, I've got to go." The words came out in a rush, and then she was gone.

I held the two pieces of paper in my hands. My mother always said that people should do good in the world, because sometimes good and evil hung in such a perfect balance that the smallest deed tipped the scale in one direction or another. "If you pick a snail off of the sidewalk," she had said once, "and it doesn't get crushed because you put it in the bushes, you might have saved the world."

"I'll come."

I wasn't sure if Isabel heard me, but I thought I saw her side ponytail bounce a little bit higher.

I yelled down the hall. "Isabel, I'll come!"

She spun around and grinned, strumming an imaginary guitar, then spun back around and kept walking.

I stared at the other flier. "Die you motherfucking dyke bitch." I thought about Ursula. What would she do? I had not received any letters from her. I assumed they had not reached me yet. I imagined her thinking about me, watching me. If I was going to love her, I had to deserve her. I tiptoed into the administrative office.

"Is there someone I could talk to?" I asked the secretary.

"About what, hon?"

I held out the flier.

"Oh, well, I guess Principal Pinn will want to take a look at that."

I shook my head. "I don't think he does … I mean … is there anyone else? Like a guidance counselor or teacher?"

The secretary cocked her head. "The principal is the one we talk to about things like this. He's a very nice man. Do you know him?"

I moved toward the door. "Yes. No."

The secretary rose from her seat. "Now, you can't just leave, Triinu. It's not passing time. If you're not here to see the principal, I'll have to cite you for skipping class." Like Mr. Litel, she said it with a smile. One big joke.

I was going to say, "Fine, cite me," but I thought of my parents. What would I tell them? Why had the flier ended up on my locker? Why couldn't I tell Principal Pinn? If Ursula was there she would walk right into his office and argue with him, just like she had argued with Jared Pinter.

"Okay," I said. "I'll talk to the principal."

Principal Pinn greeted me with narrowed eyes and a wide grin. I gave him the flier. "I found it on my locker," I said.

He studied it, shaking his head. "You've heard about the OCA. I've seen you at our Democracy Club meetings."

I nodded. Very quietly I said, "You always say in your morning announcements that if we want to make the school a better place, we should report things."

"And you should. Drugs and bullying. Fights. But I think what we've got here is just some people having a little trouble

144

finding the appropriate way to express their political convictions. That's a lot of bad words, isn't it? But they typed it." He chuckled. "It's always better to type your papers. Right?"

"I don't know." My voice had fallen to a whisper. The surge of courage I had felt earlier had drained out of me. If good and evil hung in the balance, it was just as likely that evil would win. I could pick up the snail, but Principal Pinn could send me to eastern Oregon, where they would shock love out of me.

"You can't hold it against them," Principal Pinn said. "I mean, we do hear that kind of language in the hall sometimes."

I didn't mind the swear words. I minded the death threat. "No," I said, staring at my hands folded in the lap of my black gown.

"We've got a group of concerned citizens out there right now." I knew he wasn't talking about the gay rights activists.

"You know this isn't about equality," Principal Pinn continued. "The homosexuals aren't asking for equality. They want special rights. They want laws to protect their deviant behavior, their sex fests, their pedophilia. We are going to win next year." He pointed a finger at the surface of his desk. "This time next year, me and your parents and every student who's over eighteen is going to have a chance to vote for the American family. Do you know what I'm talking about?"

"No," I said. But I understood.

"I'm talking about perverts and criminals asking for special rights." He emphasized the words "special rights." "You can see why people are getting eager. Every day that passes, the homosexual agenda is in our schools, in our parks, in our government, asking for things you and I don't get. The right to break the law, that's what the gays want."

"They're not breaking the law," I said so quietly I was surprised that Principal Pinn heard.

"You like to play devil's advocate. That's good. Keeps us thinking. But I'm afraid you're wrong there. After next year's election, it *will* be breaking the law. We're going to criminalize sin. Makes sense, doesn't it? Criminalize sin." He chuckled to himself. "Criminalize homosexuality and say no to special rights. Like the sound of that, don't you?" Principal Pinn was skinny, with a long neck and too many teeth. He looked like a cartoon character. I kept waiting for his head to telescope off his neck and come bobbing into my personal space.

"They said they were going to kill me." I pointed to the flier. "That's a sin."

"They didn't mean you. That could have been any locker. There's no reason to take this too seriously. Right, Triinu?" He picked up a photograph of his wife and sons and turned it so that they grinned at me with big, widely spaced teeth. "Right, Triinu?" It wasn't a question; it was a threat. He was thinking about the facility in eastern Oregon. "I'd be pretty disappointed if I had a reason to think this was personal."

"But ..."

I wanted to say, "It's not fair! I didn't do anything wrong." But the words got lost somewhere between my mind and Principal Pinn's toothy smile, reminiscent of his sons' smiles in the photo on his desk, but without the gaps; his teeth had closed ranks.

"We'd have something to worry about if you were ... you know. But we don't, right? Just kids messing around, right?" He held out the flier. "Do you want to keep this?" I shook my head. He took one more look at it. "The things kids do with computers these days."

Then he crumpled the paper into a loose ball and handed it to me. I did not know what he wanted until he lifted up his trash can. "Make a basket!" I tossed it, overhand, into the can.

"Game point!" Principal Pinn said in a sports-announcer voice. "And our new all-star basketball player is Triinu Hoffman!" He retrieved the crumpled paper and handed it back to me. "Can she do it again from the free throw line?" I could tell by the look on his face that he was going to go home to his wife and tell her how he mentored me and how much fun we had playing basketball in his office.

I missed the next shot on purpose. Principal Pinn sighed.

When I exited the administrative offices, Pip Weston was leaning against the wall by the door. At first, I thought it was coincidence. I put my head down and tried to hurry past him. He lunged at me, grabbing at my crotch. "Your fly's undone, Satan."

I was wearing a dress. I smacked his hand away with my book bag.

"Maybe you just need a real man," he taunted, jumping back and then feinting another grab. "Isn't that it? You're just too fucking ugly to get one."

"It was you!"

"Me, what?" He opened his eyes wide and pouted his lips. "I didn't do anything."

"You put that sign on my locker."

"It's a free country."

I turned to flee, but Pip was too fast. He pushed me up against the lockers. "You gonna go cry to Mr. Pinn? He doesn't give a shit. He thinks I'm right. This whole fucking country would be better without you." Pip's voice had lost its nasal whine. He sounded like a man. I felt my animal heart squeeze into a bloody fist. *He wants me dead.*

Pip leaned forward, his voice deep. "You'd better be careful," he said very slowly. "Because one night you're gonna go out to that shitbox of a car, and I'm gonna be there, and you're gonna get it, and nobody in this whole fucking state is gonna care."

That weekend I drove to the Armory. I looked around twice before getting out of my car, sensing Pip in every shadow. If a girl was to get killed by her lab partner, the Armory seemed like the place it would happen. The building was just a concrete bunker with a single door. In front of that, a flame flickered on a pedestal. It looked like a tomb.

No one took my payment as I entered, although the flier said I owed five dollars. Inside, the performance space was a cement floor, like a gymnasium but without the basketball hoops. The stage was a black-painted box. A few young teenagers sat against the walls. I didn't recognize anyone, nor did I see any sign of Isabel. I asked a boy in a black trench coat when Molotov Squid was going to play.

"I'm here for Poison Death Ray Garbage Man," he said.

Three girls in tie-dye told me they were waiting for Reeferatica.

Finally, I spotted Brent Macintosh. To my surprise, he hugged me. "My friend is in this band, Nosferatu Pigeon," he said. "But I don't know when they're going on."

"My friend is in Molotov Squid," I told him.

It felt good to call her "my friend."

We waited for almost an hour before the first band, Reeferatica, came on. It was just two girls with an acoustic guitar, and they kept giggling and starting their songs over from the beginning. No one even bothered to dim the lights until the second band came on. They introduced themselves as Spire of Madness, and they sounded like a semitruck driving into a giant trash compactor. Brent and I kept glancing at each other and exchanging melodramatic winces.

When the set ended, he apologized and said he had a midnight curfew. He would have to miss Nosferatu Pigeon. The lights grew dimmer. Some of the kids on the floor stood up. The room wasn't crowded, but there were probably fifty or sixty people.

The next two bands failed to introduce themselves, which didn't matter since they sounded exactly like their predecessors. Then the girls with the guitar came back on and giggled some more. There was a short intermission. I checked my watch. It was almost three. If my parents woke up, I would be in trouble. I thought the show would have ended hours earlier. Someone yelled, "Molotov!"

The lights went out entirely. There was one second of black silence, and then a guitar screamed. A black light illuminated the stage: the band had appeared out of nowhere. Their faces were outlined in DayGlo paint, and it burned ferociously under the black light.

"Rage, rage, rage!" a man yelled into a microphone. The squeal of feedback was phenomenal, but none of the band seemed to notice.

"Rage!" the crowd screamed back.

I recognized Isabel behind Greg, the lead singer. She clasped her guitar to her hips. She was wearing shiny red stretch pants, a black plastic jacket, and the "Pow! Bang! Shazam!" T-shirt—basically the same outfit she'd been wearing since seventh grade. But it worked.

"Rage!" Greg howled.

Isabel struck her guitar. The bass player nodded his head without moving any other part of his body. The drummer looked like a man having a seizure. The crowd cheered.

A little mosh pit formed in front of the stage, and the girls in tie-dye jostled me into it. I resisted for a moment, then let myself get carried into the bob and sway of the pit, back and forth, my shoulders bouncing off strangers, shoved and caught simultaneously.

"Rage!" the song went on.

Isabel's voice joined Greg's. "Fight, fight!"

Someone grabbed my arm and swung me around. Through the whirl of lights, I could see that the whole crowd was suddenly swinging and stomping, like a mad square dance careening its way to the edge of some unseen cliff, children playing Red Rover at the end of days. Everyone was screaming, "Rage, rage, rage!" their voices joyous. And it didn't matter that I didn't know anyone. It didn't matter that our dance looked like a barroom brawl. It didn't matter that the stage was a plywood box. It didn't matter that the feedback was as loud as the bass. It just mattered that Isabel was there, and that this time I had waited for her, as I always should have.

At the end of their set, Greg yelled, "We're Molotov Squid, and before we go tonight, a special song by Isabel 'The Angel' Avila!"

The crowd cheered.

Isabel walked to the front of the stage. One of the girls in tie-dye ran up and took her electric guitar, handing her an acoustic. Isabel plugged it into the amp.

"Can we get the house lights up a little?" Isabel said to the darkness above our heads.

She sounded like a real performer. *Can we get the house lights up?* Where had she learned that?

Someone produced a stool, and she sat down, her plastic outfit glinting in the low light. "We sing a lot about rage," she said, strumming the guitar once. "But music isn't all about anger, so this one goes out to my dad." Isabel's voice trembled and fell a little flat on the high notes, but the refrain was sweet. "You went off into the distance, the distance. You went off into the distance to die."

It was an odd picture, her outfit a combination of RoboCop and Michael Jackson, the melody half-cribbed from a Guatemalan folk song. It struck me that she had started wearing all that vinyl the year her father died. He had died and she had wrapped herself in plastic. Impermeable. Indestructible. It made me miss our old childhood, but I knew why she did it. She looked good in the glow of the house lights. Even when her voice cracked and she said, "I'm sorry. I can't finish," she looked like a rock star.

Behind me, I heard a guy say, "Molotov Squid is like, really *real*."

A girl whispered back, "It's like she really shares something with the audience, you know?"

The lights dimmed again. I saw Greg wrap Isabel in his arms and kiss the top of her head. Afterward, I waited for her to rejoin the crowd, but she didn't. As I was leaving, I recognized Mrs. Avila's bumper-stickered van in the parking lot. Glancing around quickly in case Pip was waiting for me, I dug around in my car for a pen and paper and wrote Isabel a note:

> Isabel,
>   You were amazing! Your father would have
> loved that song.
>
> Triinu
PS Call me.

Dance, Then, Wherever You May Be

"I think you all know why you're here," Mrs. Pendergrass, the school guidance counselor, said.

I was sitting on a hard chair at the Singing Oaks Conference Center, surrounded by about sixty other students, half from my high school and half from Ursula's school. Someone had tried to arrange the chairs in a circle, but there were too many students and not enough space in the long, narrow room, so we looked like two armies facing off across a gulf. In the gulf stood matching guidance counselors, Mrs. Pendergrass and Mrs. Fincks.

"I hope you're all as glad to be here as I am," Mrs. Fincks added, her blonde ringlets bobbing in time with her voice.

I *was* happy. Three days at the Face It! Youth Leadership and Self-Esteem Conference meant I would miss the better part of the fetal pig dissection in biology. The conference seemed a little corny, and I wasn't sure if I was there because I was a student leader or because I had come home at four in the morning from the Molotov Squid concert and my guidance counselor told my parents that meant I was "troubled." Either way, it was better than prying the eye out of a dead pig alongside a boy who thought I was a Satanist.

"While we are here, we're going to set up some ground rules of trust," Mrs. Pendergrass said. She wore heavy beige foundation, and there was a clear delineation where the makeup ended and her neck began. I wondered if she thought it made her look tan. As a girl who mixed blue eye shadow into my white face makeup for added pallor, this puzzled me—both the desire and the execution. Didn't she know about her neck?

"Who has an idea for our Trust Board?" Mrs. Pendergrass hovered a blue marker over a sheet of butcher paper on an easel, her foundation cracking around her smile.

The other students looked as perplexed as I felt. "Don't be mean?" one girl ventured.

"What a great statement," Mrs. Fincks said, her hair dancing. "Don't you think so, Carolyn?" Mrs. Fincks addressed Mrs. Pendergrass by her first name, something we never heard in school. "Here in the trust circle, we won't judge anyone. We will listen *compassionately*."

"How about 'everything said in this room stays in this room'?" Mrs. Pendergrass suggested. She wrote the words on her butcher paper without waiting for a response.

"And how about 'no assumptions'?" Mrs. Fincks suggested. "Because you know what assumptions do?"

Like a vaudeville act, Mrs. Fincks and Mrs. Pendergrass leaned their heads together and fanned their fingers out as they chanted together. "When I assume, I make an ass out of you and me!" Perhaps they thought we'd be shocked because they said "ass." We would think they were wild and "on our level."

I took out my notebook and tried to write a poem about the conference, something that would convey the humor and the inanity of it, a kind of free verse *No Exit*. I had gotten as far as writing, "A rift in the butcher paper. Blank! Blank like your soul!" when the door to the conference room flew open. A girl with a shock of bleach-blonde hair and no shirt burst through. To her credit, she was wearing jeans, a blazer, and a fairly modest purple bra, but definitely no shirt.

"I am so sorry!" She was flustered, tripping over the leg of a chair in her haste to take a seat. "I was supposed to get a ride to school with Lillibeth, but my brother told her I had left, so my mom let me take the car, but 84 and I-5 look the same when you're coming over that big bridge and I got turned around."

I was waiting for her to notice the absence of her shirt. I had dreams like this. I would walk into biology class and Pip would say, "Look! Triinu forgot her pants." In my dream I'd tell him to fuck off, but when I took my seat and looked down, it was middle school all over again. Only this time, my fly wasn't undone: it was gone. I was naked from the waist down, clothed from the waist up, which somehow made it worse. Full nudity was a statement; half nudity was a nightmare.

The girl just plopped her bag down and pulled up a chair next to me. "Whew! What a trip," she whispered.

She looked vaguely familiar, but I could not look directly at her in just a bra. I was waiting for the guidance counselors to tell her to go back to her room and put on a shirt, but perhaps she had not brought a shirt. If she had, it would probably be back in her car. But if this was her naked nightmare, she probably would have lost her car. If she ran to retrieve it, she would find that zombies were chasing her, but she couldn't move her legs. Then she would realize she had never graduated from middle school, and she'd have to do it all over again. Nude.

All Mrs. Fincks said was, "Let's welcome Chloe to our circle of trust."

Chloe! That was where I knew her from. This was Chloe Lombardi, Ursula's former best friend, the one I had bested. She was the boy-crazy girl who would turn down a chance to travel because she didn't want to leave her boyfriend.

"Thanks, Mrs. Fincks," Chloe mumbled.

Mrs. Fincks turned her attention to the group. Chloe dug in her bag as though hunting for a secret key that would get her out of the room. I wanted to say, "It's no use. There's nothing you can do."

With a satisfied "Ah ha!" Chloe pulled out a lipstick and applied it liberally, and I saw that I was wrong. The lipstick perfectly matched the purple of her bra. She had worn it on purpose. She had deliberately eschewed the shirt. She hadn't just walked knowingly into the nightmare; she had accessorized it.

"Wet n Wild," she said, turning the lipstick over to show me the bottom of the tube. "Passionate Plum."

It was awe inspiring.

"Who'd like to start the sharing?" Mrs. Fincks continued. "How about you, Bessie?"

My heart went out to the plain-faced girl Mrs. Fincks nodded to, but Bessie didn't seem to mind. "I feel really alone?" She ended every sentence with a question mark. "And my boyfriend, he's really popular? So other girls talk to him, and he says it doesn't matter, but sometimes I get jealous?" She went on.

I felt Chloe lean toward me. "Don't worry," she whispered. "I went to one of these last year. You don't have to talk, just tell them you want to share a moment of silence with the trust circle."

Bessie had started to tear up, and Mrs. Fincks had given her a tissue. "Thanks, Bessie. That was really brave." She put her arm around Bessie's shoulder, and Mrs. Pendergrass hugged Bessie from the other side. Then both the counselors started tearing up.

"I just feel so close to everyone in this room," Mrs. Pendergrass said.

The students must have been specially chosen for this trip, because no one snickered.

"I think we all do," Mrs. Fincks concurred. "This is a safe space for everyone."

Next we heard from a boy who had failed to make it on the basketball team three years in a row. "Now I'm a senior, and I know I'll never be on the basketball team." He sniffed. "And everyone on the team says I'm a fag, but I'm not a fag. Just because I can't make a layup doesn't mean I'm a fag."

"I don't think you're a fag," said the girl sitting next to him. She touched his hand. A couple of other girls giggled, and one of Bobby's friends elbowed him.

I thought about a story I had read in the paper. A boy in eastern Oregon had come out to his family. His two cousins had dragged him to the edge of their property, locked him in a shed, and set it on fire. His mother had called the police, but not until the roof was blazing. Local police had said the cousins would only get manslaughter because the boy had provoked them.

"You're a handsome, smart, athletic young man," Mrs. Fincks said. "I don't think there's anything gay about you."

I glanced at Chloe. She rolled her eyes. "I hope they don't have crap for lunch," she whispered.

At lunch, Chloe beckoned for me to join her at a small table in the corner of the conference hall. "Chloe," she said, extending her hand. "Lombardi."

"I know." I shook her hand. "You were Ursula's friend."

"Were," she said dryly. She poked at her lunch, something that purported to be soufflé but looked gray on top. "No kidding. I haven't heard from her since she left."

I had received one short missive on a postcard. It read,

> L'Europa is better than anything I could have
> imagined. *Le meilleure!* I don't know how I'll live
> back home. Perhaps I'll join the foreign legion

and be *un soldiere de fortune*. Still, there is one thing I miss back in *l'Etas Unis*. That's you.

♡ Ursula

I had treasured that heart, but it was a cold comfort.

"You know," Chloe said, her mouth half full of soufflé. She had pushed the gray part off and dug into the yellow middle. "I was wondering … 'cause I knew you were going to be here … would you like to be my friend? I know it sounds massively dorky, but I was thinking that you were probably missing Ursula, and I was missing Ursula, especially now that we're back in school and, you know, she's not. So I was wondering if you'd like to hang out sometime. You know: be my friend?"

I remembered that night in the warm darkness of the Bensons' woodstove when Ursula had sighed and said, "Chloe said she'd only go abroad if her boyfriend was going. She said she didn't want to miss out on spending time with him. Can you believe that?"

I had shaken my head, enthusiastically shocked.

Another time, Ursula had told me that Chloe had dated a twenty-one-year-old when she was just thirteen. "And her mother approved," Ursula had said, as though that was also Chloe's fault. "I hope that my mother would never let me go out with a twenty-one-year-old, at least until I was … say … *eighteen* and *legal*! Chloe is so boy crazy. I hate to say it, but she's kind of a slut."

I had trilled, "That's awful," and my heart had opened like a gilded cage. Ursula liked me better! But now Ursula was in France; it had been forty-two mail days since her postcard.

"Yeah. I'd like to be your friend." I heard the question mark at the end of my sentence, but Chloe didn't.

"Great! Awesome!" Chloe waved at a boy on the other side of

the room. "That's my boyfriend, Aaron. I told him to give us some time so I could talk to you. Come on over, Aaron. She said yes."

I had to laugh. "Did you think I'd say no?"

"Ursula said you and I had nothing in common. She said you were an *intellectual*. Are you?"

"I don't know."

"Well, whatever. I thought if Ursula liked you so much, I'd probably like you too."

I was still puzzling over the bra.

"Ursula thinks I'm slutty," Chloe said, as though reading my mind. "Am I slutty?" she asked the lanky, dark-haired boy who had just appeared at her elbow. "This is Aaron."

Aaron seemed perfectly balanced between fish-eyed adolescence and beautiful adulthood. One moment I thought his Adam's apple was about to pop out of his neck, he was so skinny and gangly, but then he'd turn to look at Chloe and his concentration was handsome beyond measure.

"I don't think that," he said thoughtfully. "I think what a woman does with her body is her own business."

I stared at them. Aaron wore a dress shirt, tie, and sweater vest. Chloe had matched her lipstick to her bra.

"So what do you like to do?" Aaron asked, taking a seat next to Chloe.

"Nothing. Write." I shrugged.

"Cool," Aaron said. "You going to eat that?" He pointed to the gelatinous lump of egg on my plate.

"I'm trying to quit," I said.

He laughed. "Mind if I do?"

I shook my head.

"If you like to write, you might like this," Chloe said. From her bag, she withdrew a handful of small handmade books, each with a staple-bound spine and a hand-lettered cover.

"What are they?" I asked.

"Friendship books. See? You write your name and address and what bands you like, then you send them to one of your pen pals. I have ninety-eight pen pals. When you get a friendship book, you can write to anyone in it. If they like you, they write back."

I flipped through one of the books. The first entry read:

Tanya "Ya Ya" Carbesso
Columbus, Ohio
I love: Ministry, Pet Shop Boys, Morrissey
I Hate: Janet Jackson and Richard Marx.
A/A I mean it!

"What's A/A?" I asked.

"Answers all. She'll write to anyone who writes her."

Forty-two days since Ursula had written me, but Ya Ya Carbesso in Columbus, Ohio, would write to anyone. I could just post a card in the mail and say, "Dear Ya Ya, I'm a lesbian, but I can't tell anyone. I love Morrissey, and I don't have a lot of friends. Sometimes I'm really lonely, but I think it's dumb to say that at a youth leadership conference. I hate Janet Jackson too. Please write back." And she would.

"Have you heard from Ursula?" Chloe leaned her head on Aaron's shoulder.

I wanted to say yes. I wanted to say, "Of course I have. I mean, she is my best friend. She writes all the time. She says Europe's great, but she really misses me."

"She sent me one dumb postcard," I said out loud. "The picture was a statue of a kid peeing. I mean it was a *real* fountain, and the water was his pee."

We all laughed as though somehow that explained everything.

That night we were housed dormitory-style in cabins set throughout the wooded conference grounds. I cringed at the thought of lying in my bunk bed listening to Bessie sniffling beside me.

Worse yet, I hoped I would not cry. I felt the tears pressing at my eyes. It was nice to meet Chloe and Aaron, but lunch had been followed by another round of trust circle. The confessions shared in the afternoon had seemed genuine and unforced. One girl was pregnant. One boy had just learned that his parents were divorcing. A pair of sweethearts had broken up; they knew they were wrong for each other, they fought all the time, but they were still in love.

"Why is this so hard?" the girl had pleaded, looking across the room at her ex-boyfriend, who sat with his head in his hands. "My mother said it's just puppy love."

Mrs. Pendergrass had put her hand on the girl's shoulder. "If your mom meant that that makes it easy ... well, she was just wrong."

All the while I had stared at them thinking, *What about me?* The Oregon Citizens Alliance had blanketed the state with advertisements. On our bus ride to Portland, I had seen a billboard commanding, "Choose Not the Sin." Another sign read, "Homosexuality is an Abomination. Leviticus 20:13." At home, we had received a flier in the mail addressed to "Caring Resident," titled "Gay Rights: Fact or Fiction." It read, "93% of homosexuals engage in rimming, 53% engage in fisting, 46% in golden showers, and 17% routinely smear their sexual partners with feces. They are 90% more likely to be pedophiles, and 28% have engaged in sodomy with over 1,000 different partners."

I wanted to grab the counselors by the neck—Mrs. Well-Meaning and Mrs. I-Could-Be-Spending-the-Weekend-with-My-Husband-and-Kids-but-I-Chose-to-Mentor-You-Instead—

160

and tell them that this was all a big, corny lie. If this was a leadership conference, they should teach us to be leaders, not sniveling brats who broke into tears because—surprise—life was hard. If this was meant to be a self-esteem builder, then they shouldn't elicit secrets that would go public the minute we returned to school. As soon as we were back home, everyone would run straight to their twelve closest friends and relay every detail of the conference, down to the imperceptible bulge in the pregnant girl's belly. If they couldn't see that coming, they shouldn't be high school counselors at all. I wanted to scream, "I'm gay! Open your trust circle up for that!" But they could not open the circle wide enough to include me, and I turned my face to the wall and pretended to sleep while the other girls chatted about nothing. I had chosen between self-esteem and fetal pig, and I had to live with my choice.

Finally, the girls in my room retired to bed. I heard Bessie climb the ladder behind my head, then felt her weight rocking the bunk bed as she settled in to sleep, and a moment later I heard her snoring. She wasn't crying. She had played her part in Mrs. Fincks's trust circle, and now she slept peacefully, probably dreaming of happy hours spent gathering cans for the student government fund drive. It was me who lay awake with tears seeping out of the corner of my eyes. *Sniveling brat*, I thought, and it just made me cry harder.

I had been feeling sorry for myself for about an hour when I heard the door open. I saw a crack of darkness slightly lighter than the darkness around me, and I thought maybe I had drifted off unknowingly. In that time, one of the girls had left the room and was now coming back from the bathroom. Then I felt a shadow move over me. A hand reached under my blanket and touched my shoulder. I opened my mouth to protest, but somebody's hand covered my mouth. I smelled cologne. In the moonlight, I saw a forest of dark hairs on a man's wrist, the tail of a black pea coat, and a belt buckle. I couldn't see his face.

"Shhh," the figure cautioned in a deep voice. "Get up."

"No!" I pulled away, knocking my head against the wall.

The figure dropped down to my level. "Do you want to wake everyone up?"

It was Aaron lurking in the darkness, and he looked nothing like a fish-eyed teenager. He looked handsome in a way I knew I should have liked as a goth girl—lean, dark, his brow furrowed, his sweater vest exchanged for a billowing white shirt, open over a tank top. I could see his ribs.

He pressed a finger to his own lips. "Come with me."

"No."

He glared at me, his gritted teeth saying, "I can't talk to you here."

"What?" I spat when we were in the hall.

He held up his hands in protest. "Nothing!"

He was standing too close to me, conspiratorial and eager, his hand resting on my lower back.

"Good, because I like Chloe," I said, stepping away.

"Yeah, me too."

He was playing dumb. I was sick of it. First Jared, then Ralph, then Pip. I was tired of them eyeing me. As though it somehow wasn't enough that I was gay or that Ursula had left me. It wasn't enough that the whole state was against me. I had to sit stoically while I listened to a bunch of breeders talk about how misunderstood they were. I had to take a moment of silence when my turn came. Now I had to fend off Chloe Lombardi's boyfriend because some great force of nature thought I should open up my legs to every boy who came along smelling of Jōvan Musk, because that was apparently better than the starlight yearning I carried for Ursula.

"Leave me alone!" I hissed. We weren't supposed to be up. There weren't supposed to be boys in this cabin. "I'm not interested. Can't you get that?"

Aaron's face melted into puzzled embarrassment. "You aren't? Chloe was sure you'd want to go."

"I don't … go where?"

"Wait. You didn't think I was …" Realization dawned on his face. "Oh, God, no. That's not what I meant. I thought Chloe told you. Chloe and I … there's this underage dance club. We heard about it from her brother. Some people say it's run by a pedophile, but they play *Bauhaus!*" He stopped, obviously waiting for something. "We're going right now. Chloe's got her car. We're practically in Portland. You've got to come."

The conference center was located in a network of faux-woodland trails. It was nothing like the real forest that surrounded my house. Those woods were rough and strangled by blackberry vines. If a girl looked closely, she could find owl pellets, little balls of gray fur in which the ghostly skulls of the owl's prey peeped out. An eye socket. A jawbone lined with tiny teeth. There were no bones at the Singing Oaks Conference Center, but the manicured woods presented their own dangers.

"This way," Aaron said, touching my elbow gently. "We've got to meet Chloe outside the conference building."

I stepped into my shoes, which I had left by the cabin door. I was still wearing a long velvet nightgown.

As soon as we exited the cabin, we saw Mrs. Pendergrass and Mrs. Fincks coming toward us on one of the winding sidewalks that laced the grounds. It had started to rain, and their heads were bowed against the cold drizzle.

We ducked back into the cabin. Aaron looked at me. They were heading toward us. He wasn't even supposed to be in our cabin. I, at least, could leap back into bed, but what would he do? Roll under my bunk? "Bathroom?" he mouthed.

I thought it through quickly. We could hide in the bathroom. He could squat on the toilet seat so his legs did not show, and I could pretend to be sitting in front of him. It would account for my absence from bed. But one could only pretend to pee for so long.

I heard footsteps on the cabin stairs behind us. Mrs. Pendergrass said, "It's raining cats and dogs." Her voice was muffled by the door.

"Come on," I said. "We can do this."

My blood raced through my veins. I was not sure if I was afraid of getting in trouble or afraid of running into the night with a boy I'd known for about five hours. I felt as I had after I'd stabbed Jared Pinter and run into the woods with Isabel. I felt as though there was another world in which none of this happened. I was still the little girl who pressed her face into her mother's shirt, who rode on her father's shoulders as if on the back of a gentle bear. I was still there, standing in my childhood, waving as the world carried my other self away.

I lunged for the cabin's back door. Aaron followed me, but we stopped short as the door opened. Ahead of us was another cluster of adults. I recognized the physics teacher from my school.

We were surrounded, but my childhood in the woods had prepared me for this. I grabbed Aaron's sleeve because there was no time to speak. I yanked it, looked him in the eye, and then I ran. I raced through the woodscape, leaping over the artfully planted ferns, darting through a stand of pines, careening through a snowberry bush, twigs snapping as I flew. I was vaguely aware of the teachers greeting each other behind us.

"… that sound …"

"A nice facility …"

"Must have been deer."

"Here in Gresham?"

And then we were out of earshot.

I had a good sense of direction, and in a few moments we pulled up short at the edge of a cluster of rhododendrons. The conference center rested in a pool of orange light in front of us.

"Over here." Chloe waved from behind a tree.

The rain had increased to a downpour by the time we reached her car, and we were drenched. I was shaking, but I did not know if it was from the cold or the excitement.

The club was in a section of town that appeared to be nothing but warehouses.

"I don't think this is right." Chloe's knuckles had been white on the wheel ever since we pulled out of the Singing Oaks parking lot. "I hate getting lost."

I was not sure if we were lost or if we had simply arrived at the end of the world, but when we turned the next corner, I saw a group of people huddling around a card table on the unlit sidewalk.

"Is that the club?" I asked.

"No," Aaron said. "I think those are the protestors." He scoffed. "Supposedly the club is run by this guy who wants to give street kids a place to go at night, but some people say he's a pervert."

"They're all rumors," Chloe added. "People say there's drugs, you know, prostitution. Shit like that."

"But the music is good," Aaron offered. "I heard they play Joy Division."

We were sixteen. Pedophiles and prostitution be damned, we loved Joy Division.

As we drove closer, one of the protestors lifted a hand-lettered sign reading, "Love the Sinner, Hate the Sin."

"Is that for the pedophile?" I asked.

"No ..." Aaron drew the word out as if pondering whether to say more.

He didn't, and we parked and got out about half a block from the door we guessed to be the entrance, although it looked like a warehouse loading dock. "Are you sure this is it?" Chloe asked.

Some of the protestors beckoned to us. I heard a murmured prayer, or maybe it was just conversation. I caught the word "repent." Behind their murmurs I heard something else. A heart-beat. Boom. Boom. Boom.

"Let's do this," Aaron said, and he took both our arms.

As we neared the loading dock, the protestors detached from the wall and started coming toward us. "Hey," one man called. He was a little older than us. He looked like the college students who flooded our town every fall, only harder. His thin lips were set in a mean smile. "Can I talk to you for a second? I just want to talk."

An older woman in a white rain slicker asked if we wanted some hot chocolate, but there was nothing gentle in her voice. Behind her a man yelled, "Faggots!"

"What the fuck?" Chloe said. She pulled closer to Aaron. I also drew in closer, keeping the protestors in my peripheral vision as we hurried up the concrete stairs that supposedly led to the club.

"Perverts!" someone yelled. "Burn in hell."

"The wages of sin is death."

"Do you want a hot chocolate?"

"It's probably poisoned," Chloe whispered.

We mounted a short flight of stairs on the outside of a

loading bay. When we got up close, I could see "The City Nightclub" stenciled in gray paint on a black door. I pulled on the door, but it was locked.

The young protestor was at our side now. "I just want to talk to you. Can't you even talk to me? Come on. You're hurting my feelings."

You're hurting my feelings. He was Pip Weston all grown up. *I'm sorry. Your fly is undone. I just wanted you to know you're a lezzie Satanist, and you're going to burn in hell forever.*

Aaron pounded his fist on the door.

"Open up," Chloe called.

"It's not too late to accept the Lord Jesus Christ into your life." The protestor hovered a few feet from the door, as though he was afraid he might get sucked in.

"I have!" I shot back.

Aaron hit the door again. "Help," he called.

To my surprise, the door opened. We were hit with a wave of noise and a blast of warm air. Then a man with a bald head and a T-shirt that read, "I had sex in the bathroom at the City Nightclub" filled the doorway. He looked us up and down. I was not sure what he was looking for. In what world would we pass muster? Aaron looked like a pirate, Chloe was wearing her bra, and I was still draped in the long burgundy velvet gown that passed for my nightgown. But the bouncer beckoned us in and shut the door in the protestor's face. We stood in a kind of antechamber lined with black sofas and neon lights.

"Five dollars," the man roared over the music.

I had not brought my wallet, and I had a vision of sitting outside on the loading bay waiting for Aaron and Chloe. But Chloe grabbed my arm. "I got you," she yelled over Soft Cell's "Sex Dwarf," which blared through the speakers at a heart-stopping volume.

With the bouncer appeased, we moved through the antechamber and into the next room. A dance floor filled most of the room. I could see it clearly because it was composed of illuminated squares, their lights changing to the music. Surrounding the dance floor were huge speakers, the source of the awe-inspiring sound. On the speakers, lean boys gyrated their hips. A girl in a gown not unlike my own strode across the dance floor like a runway model and then twirled, her dress flaring out at her knees.

"Sex Dwarf" morphed into a Eurythmics song and the dancers changed their tempo.

"It's cool," I yelled to Chloe.

"I knew you'd like it."

Then, as I watched, the whole scene disappeared as the room filled with a heavy white fog. A strobe light flashed through the mist. I caught a glimpse of a leg, the hem of a dress, a girl's face in white makeup. The fog smelled of vanilla, cologne, and something vaguely chemical.

It was glorious, and it was more than just the dancing. As the fog cleared and my eyes adjusted to the dark, I saw two of the boys lean over and kiss each other, their kiss keeping tempo with the music. On the other side of the dance floor, a tall woman all in black pushed her tattooed companion against the wall and pumped her hips. I saw that the person she had pinned was a girl. It was a girl who wrapped her hands through the woman's dark hair. It was a girl whose eyes closed as the other woman pulled her close and planted a long kiss in the curve of her neck.

"It's a gay club," Aaron yelled in my ear. "I hope that doesn't freak you out. You know, whatever people want to do, right? It's their business."

"It's not hurting us," Chloe added. "You don't mind, do you?"

"Live and let live," Aaron said.

"It's cool," I said. "No biggie."

On the colorful dance floor downstairs, we danced to Madonna, Erasure, and the Pet Shop Boys. Eventually we found our way to a narrow staircase that led upstairs, where Sisters of Mercy, Skinny Puppy, and Nine Inch Nails boomed from speakers set in the walls. Every surface was mirrored or painted black, and the dancers had lost their cocky strut. The girls danced by swaying backwards, seeming to drop and then swoop upward. The boys thrashed.

"I'm going back downstairs," Chloe said. Aaron followed her.

I stayed, lost in the music and the infinite loneliness of those songs that were written not for us, but for the lean boys on the dance floor and the girls with no suburban homes to return to. Of course there was another song about suffering, a song for those skinny boys, those hard-faced girls, those street kids for whom this club was a bed and a home. The song blared, "They buried my body, and they thought I'd gone, but I am the dance, and the dance goes on." I could almost see Him, moving between them, another figure, gaunt and grieving, nothing like the blond-haired buddy who rose from the pages of Jared Pinter's Bible.

I stood, swaying, when a new girl stepped onto the dance floor. She was petite, with a china-white face and lips painted in a bee sting. With her vintage dress and curly black bob, she looked like a little doll come suddenly to life in the strange forest of light created by the strobe. She started to dance, but she was far more graceful than I, so I backed away to give her space and to watch her. For it dawned on me slowly that I *could* watch. I was free to watch. She was lovely, and here in the darkness I was allowed to know that.

I was happy just to look, but a moment later the girl moved toward me. I stepped back again. She followed me, moving in that strange dance that all the girls had perfected, gracefully swaying backwards, falling and flying. With each movement she came closer to me until I could see the fine fabric of her dress, thin as new skin and trimmed with lace. I could see the swell of her breasts. I noticed the edge of her bra. Without thinking, I touched her waist with the tip of my finger. To see if she was real. To know if I was real.

Her black eyes flew upward and caught mine. Her face remained expressionless. She took my hand in hers, and we danced to those hard, angry songs. We barely touched. Only the outline of our movements intersected. She leaned back, and I leaned forward. She drew an arc in the air, and I followed her motion with my hand. She whirled to my right, and I circled to her left, interlacing the circles of our movement. We were like fire dancers, tracing the air around each other's bodies. I felt so finely tuned to the world, I thought I could feel the heat her hands left in the air. I knew if she actually caressed me, I would die.

In the back of my mind, I thought of the couples I had seen groping in the halls of my high school, their knees wedged between each other's legs, their lips so fully enmeshed I was sure they could fondle each other's epiglottises with their ordinary pink tongues. And I knew what I had always known: I would not trade my loneliness for the halogen glow of their certainty, their dissecting light, their public lust, so bright it scared God away as surely as the conference center lights scattered the deer that wanted to live in the ferns.

Eventually I saw Chloe enter the room. She waved with surprised recognition, and I thought she was waving at me until I saw the china doll wave back, her face suddenly animated and girlish. "Chloe!" I thought she had a British accent, but I wasn't sure.

"I didn't know you'd be here, Ava," Chloe yelled over the blare of music. "This is my friend Triinu."

"Hi." The girl waved at me as though we had not just been dancing.

"Hi," I yelled back.

"Ava goes to school in Eugene. She's one of my pen pals."

"Cool," I said.

"Anyway, Aaron says we need to go. The club's closing in half an hour, and we have to get back before everyone wakes up."

It was disappointing to leave the dance floor, more disappointing still to leave the beautiful girl, Ava. "What about the protestors?" I asked when we reached the door.

Chloe shrugged. "We can't stay."

The reality of it all rushed back to me. There, in the dark and the rain, was an angry mob, and we had left Chloe's car parked a few feet from their picket line. What would we do if they attacked? What if they had slashed her tires? I imagined the worst. The throng would have doubled. The hordes would have surrounded the car. I had seen footage of protests in Salem, the Oregon Citizens Alliance pressing forward, fists raised, placards waving, people yelling, "Burn in hell, Sodomites!" The police had barely contained them. And there would be no police in this abandoned district, anyway. Who even knew about this club besides the kids who whispered about it behind cupped hands?

"Hurry," Aaron said. "We've got to get back to the cabins."

"I don't want to go out there," I said.

"We've got to," Chloe said.

Then Aaron pushed the door open. Chloe grabbed my hand. And outside it was daylight. The rain had stopped. The sky was a pale white. The street was empty. Chloe's little car stood like the last car on earth.

I was still pondering these miraculous events when I returned to school on Monday. I arrived early and took my usual spot in the front hall by the counselor's office. It was the only place, aside from the cafeteria, where I could see out a window. I was alternating between staring out the window and writing in my journal when a shadow crossed the open page. I looked up. Isabel was looking down at me. She tapped the bottom of my shoe with the toe of her silver go-go boot. "Guess what?"

"What?"

"Guess who's in the hospital?"

For a moment, I thought it was one of her family members, but there was a gleam in her eye. "Who?"

"Pip Weston."

I struggled to my feet. She reached out a hand to pull me up. "What happened?"

"Asshole was riding his bike at night, drunk, all in black because he'd just egged Tori Schmidt's house with Ben Sprig. A monster pickup truck hit him. Supposedly he's in a coma. The principal's going to make an announcement. They think he's going to die."

I opened my mouth and closed it without saying a word. I wanted to race from the school. I wanted to run howling into the forest, gorged on the justice of life. I had danced with a girl, and Pip Weston was dying.

I looked at Isabel. She grinned.

Later that week, Kirkpatrick "Pip" Marcus Weston, born March 23, 1975, suffered severe bleeding in the brain. His

172

parents took him off life support. He died on the evening of February 19, 1991.

Principal Pinn found me in the hallway, where I was reading *Heart of Darkness*. "It's a shame," he said glaring down at me, "that we lose the best and the brightest, isn't it?"

I thought that even if, by some convoluted logic, he believed Pip was the *best* student, there was no way he could argue Pip was the *brightest*. I might give that to Isabel Avila. I might even take that for myself. It was definitely not Pip's honor to bear, even in death.

I shrugged.

"You think it's funny? Decent people die, and pedophiles and perverts think they deserve *rights*!" He was actually tearing up. "It makes you wonder if this is really America."

I thought of Deidre Thom, how she had exhaled cigarette smoke into Principal Pinn's face and flicked her ID at him. Untouchable. I stood up. I wished I had some document I could flash to win this argument that was no argument at all because I was not allowed to say what I believed: that my school, my life, and everything I loved was better because Pip Weston was dead, and that the same thing would be true of Principal Pinn, because he was nothing more than Pip all grown up and bullying the same sour hallways.

"I won't miss him," I said.

"How can you say that?" Principal Pinn hissed.

"Because it's true."

That night, Pastor Brown called me. I had not spoken to him since confirmation class. "I didn't know him," Pastor Brown said. "And I'm giving the eulogy at the school. Is there anything you can tell me, a story, a recollection?"

"He was a bastard," I said. I stood in the kitchen with the

phone pressed to my ear. At the counter, my mother was crumbling a piece of boiled cod, hoping to coax Emi into eating some solid food. Even the cod smelled wonderful because Pip was dead.

"I wouldn't have actually killed him myself," I said. "Because I don't want to go to jail. And I know I'm supposed to say it was a tragedy. Everyone is going to talk about how great he was, but it's all bullshit."

My mother glanced up. "Triinu!" she mouthed.

I waited for Pastor Brown to admonish me for being heartless and for swearing in front of a man of the cloth. I was, after all, a graduate of the worst catechism class in history.

He just said, "These things are complicated."

Later, we gathered on bleachers set up in the gymnasium. A few barred windows set near the roof let in unexpected winter sunlight. A sparrow, trapped in the building, darted from beam to beam in the exposed rafters. Pastor Brown stood on the stage. He tapped the microphone. Around me girls whimpered into tissues. Tori Schmidt wept openly, her sobs echoing against the high ceiling. Ben Sprig sat rigidly upright, his face a mask.

Pastor Brown began. "Kirkpatrick Marcus Weston was a precious member of our community."

I glanced at Isabel sitting beside me. Our eyes met. "He was an asshole," she mouthed.

Pastor Brown went on with recollections from Pip's classmates. The time in fifth grade when Pip dressed up as a farmer for Halloween and brought a live chicken to school. The time in seventh grade when he covered the math teacher's car in shaving cream. The time last year when he caught a twelve-inch trout with only a piece of chewing gum for bait.

Pastor Brown paused. "Pip had a path to travel and lessons

to learn, as we all do. We grieve for the steps he did not get to take, the dreams he never fulfilled, the apologies he never made. He died young, and his death was not divine punishment or karma or fate. It was random, and it was tragic. It is hard to make sense of a death like this, but I know this much is true: death took from him all that was culpable, and God has lifted the vast remainder into heaven. Blessed be the Lord who is our peace and our comfort. He ushers us into this world, and he carries us to his bosom in the end, knowing, as he is God our Savior, that this life is but a shadow of a shadow of a dream in which we glimpse the feast God has prepared for us, saying take and eat, this is my body, given for you."

I had arranged my face into a bored sneer, but now I felt the pressure of real tears behind my eyes. I did not know if they were for Pip or just for the language I loved so much. *The feast God has prepared for us.*

"The Lord bless you and keep you. The Lord make his face to shine upon you and give you peace. Go in peace. Praise the Lord."

"So much for the fucking separation of church and state," Isabel said, as the crowd rose in a wave of sniffles and sobs. Then she took a sharp breath and looked away, perhaps thinking of her father. We did not speak until we were outside the gymnasium and far from the crowd. Then she turned to me and did something she had not done since we were children: she hugged me. It was a hard, fast grip. She went to shake my hand, then made a fist around my hand and pulled me to her. Shoulder to shoulder. Fist to fist. We didn't embrace like Tori and her friends in their fuzzy cardigans and "RIP Pip Weston" T-shirts, draped all over each other and sobbing, "He was such a good guy." We hugged like soldiers, giddy and grieving, with nowhere to put our rage.

Our Beauty Was a War

In between my parents' bedroom and their shower was a carpeted antechamber with two sinks and a mirror that they called the vanity. Every time my mother mentioned the vanity offhandedly—to ask for the paper towels kept in it, for instance—my father would intone, "'Vanity, vanity, all is vanity.'" Every time.

If I called to my father from across the garden, "Father! Telephone!" he would come up through the garden reciting, "'Oh father, my father, the fearful trip is done, the ship has weathered every rack, the prize we sought is won.'" Looking up at me where I stood on the porch, he would rush through to the last lines. He did not particularly like the poem—he had been made to memorize it when he was in school—and he always recited the last line with humorous speed: "'Oh heart, heart, heart, oh the bleeding drops of red, for on the deck my captain lies, fallencoldanddead.'"

If, late at night, taking a final sip of beer in the kitchen, my mother sighed and said, "Is it midnight already?" my father would reply, "'It is midnight on the emperor's pavement.'" If, as he made this proclamation, the cat leapt onto his knee, he would pet it and declare, "'Tyger, tyger, burning bright, in the forest of the night.'"

My mother was not as prolific a quoter, but she knew all the quotations by heart and my father let her speak the best lines. Regarding the cat who looked up at him lovingly, he would say, "'When the stars threw down their spears and water'd heaven with their tears …'" Then he would pause and nod to his wife of twenty-six years, as one might gesture someone through an open door.

She would finish, "'Did he smile his work to see? Did he who made the Lamb make thee?'" Proof of their well-suitedness for each other: before they met they had purchased all the same poetry. Auden, Eliot, Shakespeare, Yeats, Blake, Gunn. They had marked the same poems with similar bookmarks, neither of them turning down the page corners because there was something slovenly—or perhaps blasphemous—about the practice.

My mother never got rid of books. Occasionally, she would prepare a bag of books to sell at the used bookstore, but the thought of those books cast out into the world, unreachable in the hands of another customer who would probably turn down the corners, would trouble her. One by one, sometimes at night, she would retrieve the books and return them to her shelves.

The house was full of bookshelves. My mother's books were not simply those books she had read or would read, no more than a librarian would read her entire collection. It was a cultural trust. It was her comfort, her world.

In the 1960s, rioters at U C Berkeley had threatened to dump out the card catalogues at the library. My mother had thrown her body against the catalogues to protect them from vandalism. "What good," my mother asked in her lilting accent, "is an illiterate revolution?"

I took Ms. Lanham's Junior Poetry class the way the good Lutheran kids took Bible study. It irked me that many of my classmates took poetry because they wanted to write about the evils of drinking after what happened to Pip, or because they thought poetry was easy because poems were short. I could have smacked them. I only restrained myself because I adored Ms. Lanham.

Ms. Lanham lacked the accessorized cheer of the other female teachers. She didn't wear holiday-scene sweaters or carry glittery tote bags or dot her i's with hearts. All of this made her seem less maternal and more vulnerable. She looked pained and whispery—as I thought a poet should—as she implored Ben Sprig to share his thoughts on cummings's "Buffalo Bill."

Ben tipped his chair back against the wall. "Dude. Buffalo Bill's been tokin', man!" He laughed too loudly. Then it seemed for a moment like he might cry, and he added, "It's all shit anyway."

It was not a promising start for the term, but Brent Macintosh was in the class, and at least he was not pining for Pip. There was also a foreign exchange student named Etti Clossen with whom I ate lunch occasionally. There were also about ten other girls who wrote poems with titles like "To Pip after the Big Game" and "Do You Know How You Hurt Me, Joe?"

One girl read her poem out loud. "If you want a drink, don't drive. You don't want to take a dive. You could lose your legs or die, or hurt someone you love and be a real dick." Brent and I rolled our eyes at each other.

Another girl read, "Joe, you make me feel so low. Don't go, I need you so. All I said was that I wanted to take it slow. Am I more to you than just a ho?"

Etti Clossen whispered, "In English how say you?"

"That sucks?" I offered.

By comparison, I felt like the next Mary Oliver.

At lunch, I sat by my locker and wrote, "Unsung, lonely, and alone. Who has walked through these mists, but me?"

The answer, had I been honest, was Mom, Dad, Chloe, Aaron, a good-sized group of their friends, Isabel, and even Brent. If someone had asked me, I would have told them that I was alone in the world. Despite this, Friday and Saturday afternoons elicited a dozen phone calls as an ever-shifting combination of girls and boys arranged to pile into someone's car. Going nowhere, going everywhere, laughing too loudly at our jokes, all the while the car stereo singing The Smiths' mournful ballads about loneliness, isolation, and a light that never goes out.

So it was that I found myself bustling out of the house one Saturday, a toothbrush tucked in my purse because I wasn't sure where the day would take me. My parents sat at the kitchen table. They were talking about Emi. Was it time to put her in a nursing home? The night before she had crawled out of bed, soaked in her own pee, and wandered into the garden. When they had found her, she'd said she was looking for the Forest Brothers. "The convoy is coming," she'd kept saying. "I have to warn them."

My parents had talked about a nursing home before, but the conversation had always been fraught, my father's calm proclamations fueling my mother's tears. Today they seemed peaceful. My father stirred a bowl of ramen contemplatively. My mother held a coffee cup loosely in her hands. The sun streamed through the kitchen window. "Is it time?" my mother asked.

"'To every time there is a season.'"

My mother sighed. "'He hath made everything beautiful in his time.'"

I did not want to interrupt their peace, so I spoke quickly. "Aaron, Chloe, and I are going to visit Chloe's friend Ava in Eugene."

I said it casually, but my heart had been racing ever since Chloe had said, "You remember that girl I introduced you to at the City? She wants to go to the coast or something with some friends. You want to come?"

"Who is this Ava person?" my father asked.

"She's Chloe's pen pal, and Ava's friend Christina and Chloe's boyfriend, Aaron, both want to go to the same college, so Ava's going to introduce them." The words tumbled out. "I'll pick up Aaron and then Chloe, and we'll drive down to Eugene to pick up Ava, then we'll go out to the coast to meet Christina. Then we might spend the night at Christina's house, and I'll call you if we decide not to. Can I go? Do you mind?"

"I wish a beautiful young woman would have picked me up when I was seventeen," my father said wistfully, spooning a boiled egg into his noodle soup. "Driven me around to meet friends and have adventures. That would have been nice."

My parents were not blasé about my safety, but they had started to comment, "In a year and a half, you'll be in college. You won't have us looking over your shoulder."

A time to keep, and a time to cast away.

"We weren't allowed to pick men up back then," my mother said.

"Pity that. Anyway, there were no girls who wanted to pick me up. Well … maybe one. I was adored once."

"I adore you, husband," my mother said, standing up and putting her plate in the sink. "You used to pick me up in a white BMW."

"With red upholstery," my father added.

"So do you mind if I go?" I asked again.

"Drive safely, sweetie."

I lingered in the kitchen doorway after this quick benediction, suddenly loath to leave them. *In a year and a half, you won't have us looking over your shoulder.* Then I put on my lipstick, grabbed a sweater, and left.

Aaron greeted me at his front door, still toweling off his hair. A few minutes later we leapt into the Blue Bird of Happiness. We picked up Chloe next and then drove the winding hour to Eugene, joking about the junk-strewn yards we passed. "Ooh, chicken-fried steak and livers, $3.99. Why aren't we stopping?"

"That's not just chicken-fried steak and livers, that's chicken-fried steak and livers in Junction City."

"Junction City, RV capital of the world. Can we stop?"

"I don't know if we're cool enough, but let's tell our friends we did."

In a large field, someone had planted a sign reading, "Three Gay Rights: Hell—Romans 1:27, AIDS—Jude 1:7, Salvation—1 Corinthians 6:11."

Aaron turned up My Life With The Thrill Kill Kult on the stereo. "If they're going to heaven, I think I'll take hell," he said over the music.

We picked up Ava in Eugene. I lingered behind Chloe and Aaron as they walked to her front door. I did not know what to say. I did not even know what to think. The night we had spent at the City Nightclub was as far from my everyday life as my dreams were. Like the one I had once had of eloping with Ursula in my blue Chevy Cavalier station wagon. I held my breath. Ava came to the door and hugged Chloe and Aaron and smiled at me.

"Do you remember Triinu?" Aaron said. "From the City?"

Ava cocked her head. There was something about her thin lips and her dark hair, bobbed like a 1920s starlet's, that made her seem much older than me.

"Of course I do." I had not imagined her British accent. Every word she spoke sung of white horses and red livery. "Hello, Triinu."

She opened her arms and, for a moment, I did not know what she expected. Then she hugged me gently, her clothes releasing a breath of linen and rosewater. She spoke into my hair, so quietly I was sure Aaron and Chloe did not hear. "I'm glad you came."

On the drive to the coast, Aaron, Chloe, and Ava chatted about colleges. Aaron and Chloe were seniors. Ava was in the last year of something called the sixth form, which I gathered was like senior year in England. I drove and sang along to the stereo, a mere junior with an eternity of high school still ahead of me. I sang softly so they would not catch the strain of sadness in my voice. Aaron was leaving. Chloe was leaving. And Ava was like a Pegasus descended from another heaven.

I thought, *Stay, stay, stay*.

"I'm thinking about Swarthmore," Aaron said.

"I'm with you, if I get in," Chloe said. To Ava she added, "Aaron's got better grades, and he took AP Physics. What about you?"

"Both my parents went to Oxford," Ava said. "I was going to go there, but now they're getting a divorce. I'm only in the States because my parents wanted me out of the house while they fought. Like I'm not going to notice that they're separating if I'm living with my aunt in America."

"How long are you here for?" Aaron asked.

"I don't know. Until my parents sort it out, I guess."

"Do you miss London?"

"I miss my mates. We've been in school together since we were kids."

"That sucks," Chloe said.

I watched Ava in the rearview mirror. "Yeah," she sighed, "but I'm glad I'm not living in the flat with my parents. I think their solicitors told them whoever moves out first loses the flat. Now it's war." Ava caught my eye in the mirror. "I always wanted to visit America, though, and I've met some great people."

We entered the coastal foothills, and traffic slowed to a stop. For as far as we could see, log trucks idled and weekend tourists leaned their heads out of car windows. Aaron rolled down his window and peered out. "There must have been an accident," he said.

"Want to have a smoke, Aaron?" Chloe asked.

They got out. Ava and I watched them saunter down the line of stopped cars, toward a hairpin turn in the road. On our left, the oncoming lane was empty. Beyond that, a thin guard-rail separated the road from a forested canyon. "I wonder if anyone died," Ava said in the silence of the emptied car.

The scene—the eerie stillness of the road, the mist collecting in the pines—combined almost everything I wanted in a poem: loneliness, fog, and the open-eyed contemplation of mortality. I imagined the accident, the car flipped over like a coin, for one weightless moment the driver staring at the milk-gray sky beneath her feet.

"It's the perfect place to die," I said.

Ava leaned forward so that her chin rested on the back of my seat, her lips near my ear. "Oh, Triinu! Don't say that! There's no good place to die."

I was going to say, "Of course there are good places to die. Our society just doesn't encourage us to think about the in-evitable." It was my typical goth poet stance: love, loneliness, fog, and death, but Ava's eyes pleaded with me in the rearview mirror.

I said, "I guess not."

We reached the coast. Along with Ava's friend Christina, we walked on the beach in a rain so absolute I could not tell where the ocean ended and the sky began. Aaron and Chloe kicked the waves with black boots. Christina stomped at the surf beside them. Ava slipped her arm through mine. "Kids," she said with mock seriousness.

She led me along the beach as though we were strolling on a sunny shore. Neither of us bowed our heads although the rain hit our faces like a wet sail. "I'm glad you're Chloe's friend," Ava said.

The sound of the ocean hid our words.

"Why?"

She looked up at me, her lips pursed. She wore six delicate rhinestone earrings in shades of garnet and black amethyst. Although the daylight had almost expired, I could see them glittering in her damp hair.

"If you weren't Chloe's friend, I might never have seen you again."

That night, we stayed at Christina's house, following directions that included, "Go until you are absolutely positive you're lost." At the end of that road stood a house like a grand lodge, a porch running its circumference. Lamplight and the smell of coffee spilled out of the front door.

"Don't worry," Christina said as she led us inside. "My parents are out of town." She pulled us into the kitchen. "Do you want coffee?"

Christina selected mugs from a rack above the stove. In the living room, Chloe and Aaron argued amicably. "What are you two on about?" Ava asked.

"Aaron says we're getting an apartment together at Swarthmore, and he's going to cover the whole thing with Metallica posters," Chloe protested.

Aaron pulled Chloe off the sofa in an avalanche of throw pillows. "How about Metallica and Bell Biv DeVoe?" he asked.

"Aaron!"

Christina plopped down in an armchair. "You two are cute," she said.

Aaron and Chloe looked up simultaneously, their hands around each other's wrists. "We're very fucking serious," Aaron said. Everyone laughed.

Ava settled into a loveseat upholstered in a pattern of cowboys and steers. She patted the seat next to her. "Come here, Triinu."

"Careful, Triinu, she bites," Christina said.

"I wouldn't," Ava protested with a smile.

There was a flurry of pillows as Aaron and Chloe wrestled. Christina tossed a pillow into the mix, and Chloe said, "Get her!"

"Aaron, help me!" Christina yelped.

"Stop it."

"Let go!"

"You're gonna spill my coffee."

They were all laughing. In the intimacy of their distraction, Ava took my hand. She lifted my fingers to her lips, and bit down gently on the tip of my index finger, the dry edge of her teeth just grazing the skin. "You see? I don't bite."

Ava let her arm rest on my shoulders all evening, sometimes pulling me close to her and whispering into my hair, sometimes lacing her fingers through mine and examining the pattern they made.

A few hours before the black sky faded to blue, Christina said, "I'm going to bed. Chloe, Aaron, you can sleep in my parents' bed. Ava, there's the couch. Triinu, you can have the recliner. It's not bad. There's also a futon on the porch. My mom thinks it's *liberating* to sleep outside. It stays pretty dry."

I was about to say that the recliner was fine, but Ava took my hand. "Triinu and I will sleep outside," she said. "With the mountain lions!" She pronounced 'mountain lions' carefully, as though this was a vocabulary word she had recently learned. "Cougars," she added, taking my hand and pulling me toward the porch. "That's right, isn't it? A cougar is a mountain lion?" I followed her outside. I did not look at the others. I was glad the porch was dark and Ava could not see my thoughts.

The futon was heaped with heavy quilts and sheltered under an overhang. The top blanket was damp. Ava touched it, then pulled back several layers of bedding. She pressed the mattress with her palm. "It's not wet." The rain had stopped, but the forest around the house was dripping. Through a break in the clouds, I could see the moon. "Come on. Get in," Ava said as she slid in.

She held the covers up for me. I climbed in, and the blankets settled over me like a gentle mountain, holding me down as I stared up at the roof above the porch. It was cool, and the air was damp, and the blankets were cold, but I felt only the possibility of Ava's body beside me.

"Do you think there really are mountain lions?" she asked.

"I don't know. You're the one who promised mountain lions," I teased.

"But you're from America."

I smiled without looking at her. "Yes."

"Have you seen one?"

"Once."

Ava rolled over on her side. I could feel her watching me. "When?"

I had only been five, and it was a dreamlike memory. I hadn't

186

thought about it for years. I traced it in my mind, speaking slowly. "I was little. I was walking with my father in the woods behind our house. It was late, and it was getting dark, but we know those paths so well, and then … there it was up ahead of us. It was the color of sand."

Ava touched my hand under the blanket. "He put me on his shoulders," I went on. "And he said, 'Katariina.' He never calls me that. That's my mom's name. I'm just Triinu. He said, 'Katariina, put your arms out like you're flying, and hold your coat open big.' Then he said, 'I'm going to turn around, but you have to look behind us and tell me if you see it coming.' Then he walked back the way we came, really slowly, and I watched it the whole time, and it watched me." I hesitated. Ava's hand was warm on mine. I wanted to say, "This is the one thing you should remember about America."

"What do you think he would have done if it came at you?" she asked.

"I don't know. He would have fought it, I guess. I know he would have died for me."

I stared past the roof, up at the stars, into the dome of God. I thought maybe I could tell my father. *A time to keep silence, and a time to speak.* I could tell him about Ursula and Ava and Deidre. He would understand how beautiful a girl could be.

"You weren't scared?" Ava asked.

I thought back. "No. I was just proud that my father trusted me. I felt like we had gone back to this ancient time when children could be brave. You know? There's no place to be brave anymore. You just show up and fill in the Scantron and wait for tomorrow."

"I think you're brave," Ava said. She rose up on one elbow and put her other arm across my chest.

And then she kissed me, moonlit, beneath that cedar sky.

My entire consciousness focused on the place where her lips touched mine, and I felt like we were the only people in the world. There was only the circle of our kiss, her fingertips on my cheek. We might have been the first two human beings formed of clay.

"Are you scared?" Ava whispered against my lips.

"No."

"You're shaking."

I couldn't speak.

"Are you ... you know ... gay?" Ava asked.

I nodded.

"Me too. Were you always?"

I thought of Deidre Thom gliding down the hall in her black dress, and then I looked at Ava and said, "Always."

"Come here." Ava pulled me closer.

A tear ran down my cheek and then another. Then a sob escaped my lips before I realized I was going to cry. "I'm sorry," I said.

Ava ran her fingers through my hair, pressing my face to her shoulder.

"I'm not sad," I whispered.

Then my lips were on hers. Her tongue was in my mouth. We found each other effortlessly. My tears in her mouth, the click of our teeth, our noses bumping, the smell of strong coffee on our breath: all of it perfect.

The heavy bedding held us down and held us together. I kissed her, and she ran her hands beneath my shirt. We kissed for a very long time. The first hint of gray dawn was rising from the forest floor when Ava finally pulled away. I touched her face, trying to read her eyes. She looked past my shoulder, up at the sky, and let out a laugh that was half sigh. "You're lovely," she said, but her voice was strained.

"What is it?"

She closed her eyes. She seemed irritated. Then she pulled me on top of her. I cradled her beneath me, afraid to let my weight settle.

"Please," she said, and she hugged me until our bodies were pressed tightly together, moaning as I settled on top of her. The sound sent a shiver of light through my body as though I had swallowed the whole sky, and all the blinking, white stars that filled the dome of God filled me.

"Um." She bit her lip. "I …" Her eyes opened and scanned the sky, now turning from black to navy, and the house windows, still dark. She looked anxious. She put her hands on my hips and pulled them closer, sliding one leg between mine, my jeans pressing into the soft rayon of her pants. I felt a sting of pleasure deeper than before. I pressed back and the worry on her face smoothed into a smile. She nodded. "Yes," she breathed.

I pushed against her again, making a slow circle with my hips. In the very back of my mind, I thought, *I'm going to make her come*. Nothing in the *Seventeen* magazine advice column had prepared me for this—not even for the thought—but her body knew and rose to meet me. A few moments later, I felt a little spasm run through her. Her head tilted back. Her hips bucked. She gasped once, then fell back on the pillow. I felt as though the entire world could end, melting away into individual atoms bound for outer space, and I would be happy and feel that nothing was lost.

Ms. Lanham, in her infinite compassion, did not chortle as I filled her inbox with melodramatic poems. Perhaps what I meant was, "Oh, Joe don't go. I need you so."

There was never a moment when I thought Ava would last. The week after we kissed, she wrote me a letter on scented paper. Her parents had reconciled. They wanted her home in London. They wanted to be a family. It was her last year of sixth form, and the friends she had had since childhood were celebrating without her.

She wrote to me, "You are so beautiful. Why did you come into my life now and here, when I'd been looking for you in London for so many years?" She didn't say that she was staying, but the following Friday, she met me at her front door and led me to her bedroom. Her room was clean and adult—no Cure posters, no blue ribbons tacked to the wall. The only decorations were a collection of roses, dried black and hung from the ceiling.

That night in Ava's bedroom, we listened to This Mortal Coil, and our clothes fell to a velvet pile on the floor. In the occasional flash of headlights, filtered through the rhododendron outside, I was aware of how exquisite we were. I wasn't proud. There were millions of girls as beautiful as we were. I simply saw it, as so few of my friends seemed to: our unblemished youth.

In some ways, our beauty did not matter. Ursula was not as beautiful. Her breasts hung down, a little lopsided. Her skin was rough. She bit her nails. But I loved her more than Ava. I loved her Lutheran face and her bright, bad lipstick, and Ava's beauty could not compete with that.

Still, Ava was lovely in all the ways an eighteen-year-old girl could be—not a pin-up girl, not a ripe peach, not an innocent, not a child. We weren't grown, but nor were we simple. Nor did we change the world, although she slid her soft arm around my shoulder and touched every bone of my ribcage, and I thought our beauty was a war we were winning.

Against the protestors outside the City Nightclub.

Against Principal Pinn and Chuck Garst and all the OCA bellowing, "Hate the sin!"

Against Pip Weston, whom I loathed even in death.

Fie on my detractors! What argument could they mount against our gorgeous, naked youth?

Even when she left, I felt victorious. On the day of Ava's departure, I drove to the airport in Portland and hugged her beneath her aunt's appraising gaze. "It's nice of you to drive all the way up to Portland just to say goodbye," her aunt said, a crease forming beneath her tightly permed hair. "Her other friends just said goodbye at school."

"I'm sorry," I said.

Ava squeezed my hand.

"Probably best that you girls don't see so much of each other," the aunt said.

Outside, the airport seemed to go on forever. The runways stretched toward the horizon, and at their outer ends stood rows of bunkers, warehouses, and hangars, all painted gray. A few hotel signs spiked the sky with their light-up hospitality, but even they seemed muted. It was late afternoon and the roads were unusually empty. The shadows cast by lampposts stretched across the asphalt. It seemed there was nothing beautiful in that landscape except for the memory of Ava's rhinestone earrings, the curl of her dark hair, her pale face, and the trace, however faint, of my fingertips on her skin. A cell, a particle, a slight altering of scent in the sterile terminal air, such that even as I drove home, some part of me lingered there, watching the airport ebb and flow like tides of dust on the moon.

I was sitting in the cafeteria alone, trying to capture it all in a poem, when Isabel came up and shoved a piece of paper in front of me. "Get this," she said. "The school's starting a literary magazine. We can write the worst poems ever, and then submit them under fake names like Ima Dick. Here's one." She took out a piece of paper and read, "There was a boy who was a jerk. In the halls he used to lurk, until one day a guy called Dirk came and squashed him like a turd. It's a slant rhyme," she added proudly.

Poetry was my sacred trust. I glared at Isabel.

"Or better yet," she said. "We can write them for other people, like love letters from Ben Sprig to Miss Charm." She sat down and pulled a glitter-coated pencil from behind her ear. She chewed on it for a moment. "Oh, Miss Charm." She wrote the words on the surface of the table. "I love it when you tell me about the harm of putting my dick where it doesn't ..." She looked at me, scrunching up her nose as she tried to think of a rhyme.

"Belarng," I offered.

Isabel let out a loud guffaw. A couple of freshman turned to watch us. "You do a stanza," Isabel said.

"Okay," I said, putting aside my reservations. "I hope I don't get anal polyps, because then you'll surely think I'm a trollop, but I really want to frolic in your ..."

"Lady bits," Isabel concluded.

"Oh yeah," I said. "Write that one down!"

We Were Everywhere

Aaron and Chloe left for college the summer after my junior year. Around the same time, the news reported that the OCA had gathered enough signatures to get their antigay ballot, Measure 9, in the 1992 election. But none of it mattered. Ursula was coming back! I counted the days.

Then one dry, hot August evening, Ursula came home—or at least someone came home wearing Ursula's face. She let me visit her the night she arrived. I sat on her bed marveling at her room and her things. It was as if nothing had changed: the curling posters, the dry corsage pinned to the wall, the jumble of books and socks, all so much more precious because they were hers. Time had rippled, and I had stepped from one year to the next. Her suitcases were still on the floor. Her bed was still strewn with clothes. There was still, unexplainably, an unopened can of mandarin oranges on her bedside table.

Ursula glanced up from the pile she was sorting, her gaze as sharp as a scalpel. "What are you looking at?" she asked.

I love you. Until I met you I was nothing.

"Nothing." I looked down at my lap. "I'm glad you're home."

"I'm not. I don't know how I'll survive here for another year. God! This place!" She dumped a small duffle bag onto the pile of possessions already on her floor. She examined the contents. "Why did I even bring this stuff home?"

She began tossing clothes, cassettes, and lipsticks into piles on the floor. I glimpsed the orange cover of Mary Barnard's Sappho translation that I had sent Ursula, inscribed, "To Ursula, with fondest love."

The book was a little heavier than a greeting card. The poetry was so simple and so lovely; from that mythical past the poet spoke, a voice calling across time. Then the book disappeared under a cascade of cassette tapes.

"Do you really think we'll all be listening to CDs soon?" Ursula asked, picking up a cassette and winding a few inches of tape back into its plastic housing. "I hope we don't get rid of records. Can you imagine?"

I turned away.

"What?" Ursula said.

"Nothing."

"You're talkative," she snapped.

I had waited so intently for our reunion.

"Come on," Ursula said, sighing. "Let's get out of here. I want to see people. I'm never going to get through all this stuff."

Shortly afterward, we sat outside the Beanery. The evening was warm, and I had dreamed about this night for a whole year, but it was all wrong. Ursula turned her back to me and struck up a conversation with a guy named Jason Price, one of her brother's friends, now two years out of high school. She carried a stack of European photos in her purse, and she pulled them out: a thousand tiled rooftops as unexceptionally perfect as the pages of a calendar.

"I miss France!" Ursula crooned the foreign names, elegantly enunciating them as she shuffled through the photos, "This is Looxembooorg. This is la Loirrre. Here's Longueville."

The baristas had set wrought iron tables on the sidewalk outside the Beanery. Ursula sat with her photographs, examining them in the fading daylight. Two boys played hacky sack in the street, calling, "Whoa, good save, man." A streetlight flickered on and off, uncertain about the twilight. Beyond that stood a row of ugly municipal buildings, and beyond those buildings the river and the fall peepers sang their late love song.

I wanted to grab Ursula by the collar of her jean jacket and shake her.

This is Luxembourg.

This is the Loire.

This is Longueville.

But that night outside the Beanery, that was ours.

Ursula leaned in toward Jason, drawing closer to him and to the memory, pointing to a photograph I could not see. Then I heard her say, *"That's Jessica in the middle, my best friend."*

Perhaps she meant only, "My best friend in Europe," or "One of my better friends." Perhaps she could only speak about Europe in superlatives. She had traveled for months with her friends Jessica and Halee. Europe opened itself to them, a continent of marvels unfolding as the train rattled from border to border, the girls eating baguettes by the window. Could I blame her for rhapsodizing?

Nonetheless, I had held onto our best friendship like a talisman. Ursula did not love me; I knew that. She had read my letter—"I cannot bear to see you leave without telling you that I am most deeply in love with you"—and said nothing more than, "Can you help me pack?" But our best friendship was a marriage I could settle for.

That's Jessica in the middle—my best friend.

"I've got to get back," I said, suddenly homesick for my bedroom, my books, and the quilt my mother had won for me in a church auction. "Ursula, if you want a ride home, let's go now."

"Can't you wait two seconds?"

"No."

Ursula glanced at her photographs, at Jason, and then at me, and said, "Okay, okay. I'm coming. What's the rush?"

Outside Ursula's house, I idled in the road while she yanked open the screen door and fumbled with her keys. I wished her dead at that moment, but I still waited to make sure she got inside safely. Just as she disappeared through the door, she put her palm to her lips and held it up in my direction, a single motionless wave. Or perhaps she was blowing me a kiss.

I drove away, grumbling, "Looxembooorg … la Loirrre … Longuevilllle …"

I remembered that kiss goodbye later and felt a flutter of remorse.

Senior Swap Day was a highlight of the social calendar for high school seniors in our sleepy town. Seniors worldly enough to have a friend at the rival high school signed up in pairs. Each pair spent one day at Middleton High and one day on the crowded stairways of South High. Ursula and I had been planning the swap since we were fifteen and senior year was a foreign continent. Then she said, "That's Jessica in the middle. My best friend." So instead I called a girl named Wren, a friend of Chloe's whom I barely knew.

I took my seat in Miss Lopez's anatomy class. Wren sat next to me. "Did you know," Miss Lopez said after the class had settled in, "that every few years all of the cells in your body are replaced? Think about that! How do *you* stay *you* when all the cells in your body have changed? Last year you were an entirely different person, but …" She raised one finger, her aqua tracksuit swishing. "Where do you think all those old skin cells go?"

We shrugged. We didn't really care, but Miss Lopez was so full of energy it was impossible not to follow her movements as she rushed back and forth in front of the classroom.

196

"Maybe the body recycles them?" one of the boys suggested.

"No," Miss Lopez said.

"Maybe they just drop off?" someone else suggested.

"And where do they go?"

No one knew.

"Dust bunnies!" Miss Lopez said triumphantly. "When you sweep up those clumps of gray dust under your bed, what you're sweeping is ninety-nine percent human skin."

The class groaned.

"Your skin cells are in the air and in the carpet." Miss Lopez brushed one finger along the edge of the overhead projector. "They're everywhere."

A popular girl covered her mouth and squealed.

In the back row a boy said, "That's how faggots get AIDS."

"That's how *you're* gonna get AIDS," the girl whispered with a flirtatious giggle.

Wren leaned over my shoulder. "Why are there so many idiots?"

I shrugged. "They recruit."

Miss Lopez broke us into pairs so we could draw the layers of the human skin.

"You hear from Chloe?" Wren asked as we colored our papers.

Chloe had written me several times, telling me about her life at Swarthmore. "Everything is better here," she had written. "All the assholes, all the guys spitting in the hall, and all the girls whose biggest dreams were to get pregnant at prom ... they don't make it into college. It's like natural selection. Plus they serve grilled cheese and tomato soup *every* Friday. It's awesome!"

I thought of Ursula's scant letters. They must have had grilled cheese sandwiches in Europe, but she couldn't be bothered to tell me. Chloe's letters came in regularly on Friday or Saturday, each written on blue stationery with her initials embossed in the corner and a little side note scrawled by Aaron in his almost indecipherable hand. "Hi Triinu. Hang in there. Aaron."

"She's doing good," I said, but I was thinking about Ursula.

After school that day, Isabel caught me in the parking lot. "Whatcha doing, Triinu?"

The parking lot was almost empty. I had stayed late giving Wren a tour of the school. I lingered after she left because I had promised my mother I would visit Emi at Pine Rest Care Center. I had been putting it off for weeks. I nudged the Blue Bird's tire with one foot.

"Gonna see Emi."

"At your place?" Isabel asked. She was wearing her ridiculous plastic jacket and a length of sparkly purple fabric draped around her neck like a scarf.

"No, my folks put her in a home."

"About time," Isabel said amiably. "She was crazy."

"Yeah. It's gross, though. That place smells. I mean, it's clean, but you can still smell it." I hated that sick-sterile smell. Death up close was nothing like my love-loss-death-fog poems. When I walked into the nursing home, I held my breath for as long as I could.

"I'll go with you," Isabel offered.

I looked up, surprised.

"Molotov Squid is supposed to practice this evening, and I don't want to go home before that because my mother is having some sort of hippie "No on 9" love-in-fundraiser-cook-a-thon. I'm not even sure what it is, but there are, like, twenty women with mustaches in my kitchen right now."

I laughed. "Crazy grandmother beats crazy love-in?"

"Yep!"

We slid into the Blue Bird of Happiness. Winter had come early. The night outside the Beanery with Ursula had been the last warm night. Now the damp cold got in everywhere except the Blue Bird. Something about the dark vinyl upholstery held in the heat.

"I love this car," Isabel said, her shiny black jacket squeaking against the seat.

I thought about saying, "I love you," but the love I felt did not feel anything like the love I had for Ursula, so I just turned on the radio and we sang along to "The Summer of '69," each of us trying to be more raucous and off-key than the other.

At Pine Rest Care Center, we found Emi in the common room, a pagoda-shaped space with windows on all sides and an array of armchairs, like a waiting room in an airport: designed to be attractive and to make one happy to linger, but stark. Where were the piles of books? Where was the stray coffee cup? Where was the sweater draped over an armchair? Most of the residents sat in wheelchairs beside the furniture, each one clutching a lapful of blankets and tissues, little islands of humanity among the dusty, rose-colored furniture.

Emi sat with her chin resting on her chest. I hoped this meant we could leave quickly. My parents said she had been agitated. She was back in the war. She was talking to people long dead. She only recognized my mother occasionally. I could tell them I visited, but she was sleeping. There was no point in waking her up and upsetting her.

She opened her eyes and looked up at both of us simultaneously. "Triinu?"

"Yes," I said. "It's me."

Emi looked at Isabel. "Triinu?"

Isabel shook her head.

"It's me, Emi," I said.

"Ze Forest Brothers," Emi said. "Ve have to varn zem. Vere's Paulus?" Her accent had gotten thicker. "Vhat happened to Paulus?"

"We're here to visit you, Emi. How are you?" I asked.

Her milky eyes scanned the distance behind my head, behind my life. "Zey are coming!"

A woman with a walker and a bouffant of orange hair sidled up to Isabel and touched her jacket. "Oh, honey, this is so cute!" she said cheerfully.

Emi stared at her with fear in her eyes.

"You are just a dollbaby," the woman persisted. "I wonder where I could get one of these."

Isabel smiled. "I got it at Goodwill."

"Well, aren't you just the thrifty little thing. And I bet it's waterproof, too."

I was pretty certain "Waterproof thrifty little thing" was not the look Isabel was going for, but she smiled warmly. "It sure is." The woman effused about the jacket for another minute and then wandered off.

Emi looked up at Isabel. "Triinu? Vere is Paulus? Vhere are ze Brothers? Zey have to know. Ve have to varn them."

"I'm Triinu," I said, tapping her hand. "Over here. You're in Oregon."

Emi tried to stand, but she was too weak. She struggled in her chair. "Vhere is he? Vhat happened to Paulus?"

"It's okay. Just relax. You're not in Estonia," I said.

Her eyes grew wilder. "Vhere am I? Vhat has happened to Paulus?"

"You're at Pine Rest." I did not say, "Paulus is dead. Paulus has been dead for years."

200

Emi tried to stand again. Her foot slipped off the footrest. I caught her as she stumbled forward and sat her back in her chair. Her body felt warm and fleshy and thin and dead all at the same time. I could smell her diaper. I looked around for an attendant, but no one was nearby. Emi struggled, and I held her back easily. She was like one of the birds that flew against the windows of our A-frame house. Stunned, they fluttered on the deck. I had picked them up, so light, so small. They beat against my cupped hands like a heartbeat, and then they died, and there was nothing left of them but feathers and a streak of pink blood on my hand.

"Should we go?" I mouthed to Isabel.

Isabel bit her lip and stared in the distance, as though searching for clues in Emi's field of vision. Then she knelt down in front of Emi's wheelchair. "Paulus already warned them," she said. "He got there on time and told them. Everything is going to be okay. Estonia won."

Emi clasped Isabel's hand. "Ve von? My vittle Katariina! Ve von?"

"And Paulus has gone to get a …" Isabel glanced at me. I shrugged. "A ham," she went on, "for the party. There's going to be a big ham and a band, and I'm going to sing. I am going to write a song just for you and for Estonia, and we're going to sing it."

Isabel talked until Emi drifted back asleep.

Walking out of Pine Rest, Isabel said, "That was weird. I'm sure she knows who you are."

I could still smell the nursing home on my clothing. "It's fine," I said, dropping into the driver's seat of the Blue Bird of Happiness. "She might have thought you were my mom. I don't really care." I pushed the car into drive and we headed down the street without discussing a destination. "You know my mom said Estonia really is going to win its independence? She says it'll happen. We'll see it in our lifetime," I said.

"That's cool."

I was thinking about Ursula.

We passed a house covered in "Yes on 9" signs, the words "No Special Rights" screaming from every side of the lawn. As though that was not enough, the owner had hand-painted another sign. "Kill Perverts! No Fags in our Town!"

"But it's too late," I said. I could hear the bitterness in my voice, and I did not try to conceal it. "Emi's worried that something happened to Paulus, and it did. He got out of Estonia. He escaped. But it's too late. And you know how he died? He was an alcoholic. My mom says everyone knew that, but no one talked about it. Then one day, he drives down to some rocky beach near San Francisco with a copy of this Estonian book, *Kalevipoeg*, in his pocket, and he just walks into the water and drowns. It was winter and it was cold, but he just lay down and died in three feet of water. Everyone thought it was because he was drunk, but when the police did an autopsy, he wasn't. It was probably the only time in ten years that there hadn't been any alcohol in his system."

"You didn't know him," Isabel pointed out.

I knew what she meant. She knew her father. Paulus was just a story.

"He's my family," I shot back. "I never got to know him." We turned down Eighth Street, with its majestic row of old oak trees. "Estonia might be winning its independence, but Emi is stuck in a nursing home," I went on. A spatter of rain hit the windshield. "Maybe we never get what we want. Maybe, even if we get what we want, who we want, it's all wrong, and it's too late. You know? Estonia gets free and then something

202

terrible happens someplace else. Someone walks into Emi's room and tells her everything is okay, but it's not. The good news that Paulus survived is so late that it's bad news because now he's dead. Maybe that's all we get. You don't get to be happy unless you're so out of it, you don't know shit about what's going on."

We turned. The "No on 9" signs and the "Yes on 9" signs warred with each other the whole length of Washington Street. Purple for the gays. Red, white, and blue for family values.

If you pick a snail up off of the sidewalk, and it doesn't get crushed because you put it in the bushes, you might have saved the world.

"Hey Triinu," Isabel said, "I'm sorry. You want to get a piece of pizza? My treat."

Ursula avoided me for several weeks after Senior Swap Day. When I finally saw her, she told me I had hurt her feelings. "I can't believe you did Senior Swap with Wren." We sat in the Blue Bird, parked in a strip mall lot. Ursula talked and talked. "It's been really hard for me to be back. I had all this freedom. I traveled, and I met great people. It was wonderful, but then I had to come back, and the one thing I counted on was you."

In front of us, a Meals on Wheels van stopped in the fire lane. A man got out and disappeared through a service door between the pharmacy and the craft store. A moment later he reappeared, rolling a rack of TV dinners covered with white lids.

"I never felt like I fit in here, but then I went to France, and I found my place. People liked me." Ursula gave a rueful cough. "Maybe they just liked me because they couldn't understand what I was saying. But no … I think I really connected."

The Meals on Wheels driver disappeared into the building again.

"I really miss Jessica, and I miss France, and I need you to understand that. I was so happy, and now that's gone. Even if I go back to Europe, it's not going to be the same."

I wanted to get out. I wanted to slam the car door and hurl expletives. I wanted to bite through the tendons on her wrist like a dog and shake her against the ground and scream, "You left me!"

Instead, I said, "My mom used to do Meals on Wheels."

I remembered. Before I was old enough to attend preschool, my mother had taken me on her Meals on Wheels route, delivering dinners to the infirm and the elderly. Slowly the old women would inch toward their tables. Resting her hand on their bowed backs, my mother would say, "It's good to see you, Pearl. How are you, Mary?" My young mother was gorgeous, like a Bergman starlet with her broad, mysterious Baltic face and her tender smile. Now I saw the same look in her face as she sat beside Emi's bed in the nursing home. I could not say what I wanted to say to Ursula: "You bitch! You faithless whore!"

A thin ray of sun pierced through the window. The car felt stuffy.

"I'm sorry." I didn't mean it. I wasn't sorry at all, but everything I wanted to say was too horrible for the girl whose mother had driven a Meals on Wheels route.

Ursula straightened up. "It's okay," she said. "I just wanted you to know. I forgive you."

I squinted into the sun for what must have been a long time. Ursula put her hand on my wrist. "Hey, it's really okay. I just needed to get that off my chest." I opened my mouth to speak, but as I inhaled, Ursula continued. "My mom's got leftover pies from the church supper. Let's go home and get a piece."

The next thing I knew, I was sitting down to a large slice of lemon meringue pie at the Bensons' kitchen table. Ursula cut a corner off her boysenberry pie and slid it onto my plate. Her mouth full, she said, "This is really good. You gotta try it."

"So how is your grandmother?" Mrs. Benson asked. "Did your parents put her in a retirement community?"

"It's a nursing home," I said. "She's okay. She doesn't notice much, but I still visit her. Sometimes my friend Isabel will come, too."

"You're a good kid," Mrs. Benson said as she patted my shoulder. "I know Ursula is glad to see you again." She turned to her daughter. "Oh, Mrs. Garst called. She wants you to house-sit for her. Chuck's doing some political work in California, and she wants to visit him."

"No way!" Ursula said. She glanced at me. "I won't house-sit so that she can go help Chuck Garst with his antigay agenda."

"I know, I know," Ursula's mother said.

"Can you imagine being married to Chuck Garst? Mr. OCA, Mr. 'Let's make homosexuality illegal'?"

"She *is* married to him," Mrs. Benson said.

"How could she do it?" Ursula shook her head.

"I told you before," her mother said. "She was forty-five. She was lonely. I think she convinced herself that his politics didn't have anything to do with their marriage."

"She used to be liberal."

Mrs. Benson shrugged. "Don't look at me."

"But you're still friends with her," Ursula persisted. "Doesn't it bother you?"

"We don't talk about politics, and we only visit when Chuck is out of town. It's too bad. She knows no one likes her husband."

"Because he's a homophobic asshole."

Mrs. Benson gave Ursula a disapproving look, but she

nodded at the same time. "When you've known people for this long, you just don't write them out of your life." She tucked a dishcloth over the faucet. "You girls eat up as much of this as you can. Lindsey's boyfriend is coming over this evening, and there won't be anything left after that."

Ursula sifted through the newspaper spread out on the kitchen table. "Antigay Ballot Measure 9 Gains Favor," the headline read.

"I don't know if I'll house-sit for her," she said after her mother had left the kitchen. "It feels wrong."

"Go ahead and do it," I said, full of pie and suddenly feeling charitable. "Maybe my parents will give us a couple of beers and we can watch dirty movies."

"Where are we going to get dirty movies from?"

"Aw," I growled. "That filth is everywhere. Young people today have no morals."

Ursula laughed a sweet, high laugh.

A month later, Ursula was inserting bits of seared steak into the head of Mrs. Garst's jawless cat. "That is too weird," I said. "I love my pets, but there comes a time when you just put them down."

Ursula stroked Smokey's back. "He's doing pretty well for not having a lower jaw. I guess the cancer didn't spread."

"What's she going to take off next? His legs? His tail?"

"Don't listen to her, Smokey." Ursula held up another bit of steak so that the cat could tongue it into the back of his throat and swallow. "She should keep Smokey and put Chuck down."

I stroked Smokey as he ambled back and forth across the kitchen table. Ursula pulled a piece of plastic wrap over his steak and returned it to the refrigerator. A chime on the refrigerator door tinkled a few notes as it swung shut.

"This is definitely a woman's house," she said. Everywhere

we looked there was some bit of homespun cuteness: a sun catcher lighthouse, a stencil of ivy around the ceiling. On top of the cupboards rested a blue, fish-shaped soup tureen.

"It's a lonely house," I said, glancing around.

Ursula cocked her head. "How so?"

"This," I picked up a rabbit doll sewn out of a hard, nubby fabric, dressed in an apron. "This is sad."

"I thought it was cute."

"It's all cute, but it's empty. It's like she sits around making these instead of having a real life."

"I know. My mom said she married Chuck because she was lonely. Now he's working on an antigay campaign in California, and none of her friends will see her because they hate him. I don't even know if they care about gay rights." Ursula poured herself a soda and hopped up onto the counter. She sniffed disdainfully, although the room smelled of fabric softener. "He's just such a pompous asshole."

I looked around. On top of a pile of mail lay a videocassette. I picked it up and read the blurb from the back of the box. "The Homosexual Agenda is a nationwide campaign, fueled by Pedophiles and Infidels, to corrupt the American Family, sodomize our children, and Spite the tenets of the Christian Faith. Do not be Fooled by leftist propaganda. The Homosexual Agenda is Everywhere."

I passed the video to Ursula. "Check out the capitalization. Maybe that's the problem with the homosexual agenda. They don't randomly capitalize common nouns." I paused. "I wish we were everywhere. I'd like to spit in Chuck's food, and then crank call him and say 'You ate gay spit.'"

"That's what I've always liked about you, Triinu. You're so mature," Ursula said, but she was watching me with a curious smile. "So you're really gay?"

"Yep."

I wanted her to say, "Me too," but I knew she wouldn't.

She took a sip of her drink, then put it down. "You know, it would be a shame to let this opportunity go by."

"What opportunity?" I asked, but I looked up at her and I knew, and I knew that I would say yes, and I knew, in my deeper heart, that this was not what I had waited for.

"Well ... I don't think we should spit in Chuck's food," Ursula said slowly, "but we should probably kiss while we're here. Just to say we did it."

When we had first kissed it had been through a tangle of hair, the obligatory ponytails of tenth grade loosening with our kiss. Now our hair was short and kissing was an efficient business. I went straight into her mouth. She pushed back, her tongue exploring the connective tissue along my gums. Not wanting to be outdone, I opened my mouth until I could feel the edge of her teeth against the back of my tongue. She might have gagged, except neither of us were breathing.

Ursula pulled away for a second. "You've gotten bold," she said, then grabbed a fistful of my hair and squeezed.

I reached under her sweater and yanked up her bra. The underwire caught on her nipples. I pinched the soft skin underneath. She squeezed her legs around me until I could feel the rubbery heels of her Doc Martens. My pubic bone ground into the edge of the counter.

"Come here," I said. I put my arms around her and slid her off the counter, then pushed her up against the wall beneath a shadow box full of papier-mâché vegetables. She wedged her leg between mine, stretching my skirt and throwing me off balance. I clung to her.

"What are you going to do to me?" She giggled.

I didn't know. I wanted to hold her. I wanted to return to the tender certainty of our first kiss. She had undone me, unwound me, and our kiss had been as sweet as the sunlight that filtered through my bedroom window. Now she was like an animal that I had caught by the scruff and could neither hold nor release.

Ursula bit her lower lip and pressed her leg between my thighs. I grabbed her wrists and pinned them against the wall. "I'm going to induct you into the homosexual conspiracy," I whispered.

"We can't do this here," she said, suddenly pushing me away.

I stepped back, covering my mouth. "I'm sorry. Ursula, I'm sorry."

"No, silly, I mean we have to do it in Chuck Garst's bed." She took my hand and led me onto the high, lonely bed. "If he only knew," Ursula said, flopping down with her arms above her head. "Well, come on!"

I eyed the thin strips of gray sky still visible through the half-closed blinds. I kicked my shoes off and laid next to her. We were fully clothed, but when I smoothed the front of her rumpled sweater I could tell that her bra had unclasped. I leaned on one elbow and traced her nipple through the soft knit of her sweater. Ursula gave a little snort, and wriggled out of her bra and sweater, casting them to the other side of the bed. I lifted one tentative hand to touch her face, but she pushed my hand to the waistband of her pants.

"That's better," Ursula said, but a moment later she half-guided, half-hoisted me on top of her, tugging at my shirttail until I lifted it over my head.

I straddled her, feeling the stiff weft of the bedspread imprinting my knees. I could feel tiny parts of myself falling away. Ursula raked her nails across my back, and I imagined the microscopic cells of my epidermis separating. Some were ground into the sheets; some were brushed off the bed. Caught in the current of hot air, those shattered cells drifted into the hall and into the kitchen. They landed in the blind eyes of the nubby bunny, while others sank into the cat's water bowl. The video was right.

I looked down at Ursula, her eyes an ambiguous blue-brown in the fading afternoon light. "We're everywhere!" I said.

We fooled around for an hour, shedding our clothes. Ursula's breath quickened and turned impatient, but she wasn't moaning for me—just for the collection of cells that would, by the next year, be entirely replaced by my new body.

Eventually the light outside faded, and she rolled over with a little sigh and switched on the bedside lamp. "I think I'll go down to the Beanery," she said. "You know what Jason Price said?"

I smiled, trying to catch her gaze in the lamplight. "I don't really care what Jason Price said."

I gave her breast a little nipping kiss.

"Well, I do. Pass me my sweater. I'm cold. He said there's a meteor shower tonight, and he'd watch it with me if the sky was clear enough."

I snatched Ursula's sweater off the floor and tossed it at her, then yanked my own skirt off the floor and stomped into it. "How all-American."

"Do you want to come?"

I didn't want to go. I didn't like the way Jason and Ursula talked politics. They prefaced everything with a genial, "You can't realistically argue that," and finished every statement with a hearty guffaw, although they agreed on absolutely nothing. It seemed to me they ought to just spit in their hands, shake, and give up, but they talked and talked, spinning endless circles of logic and eventualities until I wanted to scream.

210

I said, "I love meteors."

"Fine. Come."

We left my car in the gravel parking lot behind the Beanery.

"I know where we can go," Jason said, slipping into his leather jacket. "There are some grass seed fields out by the airport. They're state owned, so they're public."

"How do you know that?" Ursula asked.

Jason unlocked his truck. Ursula gestured for me to slide in first. "I was out with some of my buddies at the park and the cops stopped us. So we asked where we could go, and they told us about these fields. They're reasonable guys, cops."

"You've got to admit, your interactions with the police are influenced by the fact that you're a white, middle-class man," Ursula said.

Naked in Chuck Garst's bed it had seemed impossible to leave Ursula, to gather my shoes and wave goodbye, but squeezed into the cramped cab listening to Ursula and Jason argue racial profiling, I wanted to go home.

My parents would be sitting down to a bottle of wine, or eating crackers in the kitchen, or taking bowls of ice cream into the living room, where the last embers of a fire were glowing in the fireplace. The dog drooling at their feet. The cat dozing on the sofa.

Soon my mother would say, "I should get to bed. It's almost midnight."

My father would reply, "'At midnight on the Emperor's pavement ...'"

Then one or the other of them would finish: "Marbles of the dancing floor break bitter furies of complexity, those images that yet fresh images beget, that dolphin-torn, that gong-tormented sea."

211

Someone would say, "Full marks."

"Good night, Roger."

"Good night, Katariina."

It occurred to me that by the following October I would have only a dorm room to return to in the evening when I needed to bind up my heart.

"This looks like a good spot," Jason said, pulling into a gravel turnaround on the side of the dark road.

I did not take off my seatbelt. I presumed we would watch the meteors from the truck. We could roll down the windows, then drive back to the Beanery and go home. I would have a piece of buttered toast in my own kitchen before curling up under the church-auction quilt and dreaming the luscious, longing dreams of seventeen. The next time I wanted to be included in something, I vowed, I would have the good sense to say no.

Jason parked on the side of the road and turned the engine off definitively. "Let's go."

"Where?" I asked.

"Out there." He pointed to the field.

I liked the view of the landscape from inside the vehicle, the fields looping beneath a navy sky, but I did not want to walk out into the fields with nothing but Ursula and Jason's impenetrable conversation to take my mind off the rapists and murderers that were probably lurking in the dark.

Upon closer inspection, the fields were not a uniform sea of grass, but actually full of dips, rises, and dark patches that stirred in the still air. I watched sideways, remembering lively Miss Lopez lecturing in her aqua tracksuit about rods and cones.

Miss Lopez had asked us, "Why is our peripheral vision sensitive to dark shadows?"

Jerry, an ex-gang member who had been sent north to

reform, raised his hand. "It's so you can see shit coming at you at night."

"That's right," Miss Lopez had pointed at him. "It's so you can see stuff—stuff, Jerry, not shit—coming at you at night."

I saw stuff coming at me at night! Every time I turned my head I saw movement in the field. The line of trees on the horizon was alive with shadows. "This looks like a good place to watch," I said, staring longingly at the truck.

"Nah," Jason said. "Let's get into the middle of it." His cigarette glowed in the darkness.

"I don't know how you can say gun rights aren't in the Constitution," he continued. He and Ursula had been prattling back and forth since they got out of the truck, but I had lost the train of their conversation.

I heard something creeping through the grass behind me, crackling. "You acknowledge the Second Amendment, right?" Jason asked. Finally we sat down; the crackling in the grass drew closer, catching up.

"Yes, but the Second Amendment provides us with the right to form militias. I don't think that means every Tom, Dick, and Harry should be allowed to buy an Uzi."

I brushed at the back of my neck.

"Why are you so antsy?" Ursula asked.

"I heard something."

"It's just the grass settling." Jason hit the grass behind him with the back of his hand. "You hear it now?" The blades rustled and cracked and reshaped themselves. "Anyway, the rights of the Constitution have to be protected whether or not the Left thinks a few people misuse them."

"Are you calling me the Left?" Ursula scoffed.

I could hear the grass settling, but the sound behind me was more deliberate, a series of sharp, spiny legs clawing through the grass, reaching for me. "Teen Found Dead of Spider Bite," the headlines would read; "Girl's Body Sucked Dry."

This is my fault, I thought. *What a stupid, stupid girl I am.* I was a pushover. I could never say what I meant. I couldn't even say no to being eaten alive by giant spiders.

Jason went on, "You have to admit, you hold the positions associated with the Left."

"I think you assume that because I disapprove of gun ownership I'm left on everything, but I'm surprisingly conservative on some issues." We were about to be bitten by giant spiders, if not raped and murdered by the monsters stalking through my peripheral vision, and Ursula wanted to prove how complex she was.

"And I'm not conservative on all issues either," Jason said. "I mean, I don't think gays should have special rights, but the whole gay thing doesn't freak me out."

Ursula sparkled. "I think it's really brave of you to say that."

I wasn't listening. I had forgotten about the spiders, the rapists, and the murderers, because I now knew how we were going to die. All around us at the edge of the field, moving closer, I heard the cackling deliberation of madmen: a congregation of crazed, overgrown children conversing in their own twin-intimate language.

"Kla kla kla khoo."

"What the fuck was that?" I whispered.

Jason remained stretched on his back, the grass bending away from his head like a rough halo. "Coyotes. Fields are full of them."

"Shouldn't we go?"

I liked coyotes in principle. My mother gave money to the Sierra Club, and in Outdoor School I had chosen Coyote as my "nature name," but it occurred to me that I knew very little about them. Isabel's brother said they ate people.

Jason took a hand-rolled cigarette out of his tobacco pouch. "They won't come near if they smell smoke. It's a shame we haven't seen any shooting stars. Maybe it's the wrong time of year."

I thought of new headlines: "Stargazing Teens Eaten Alive: Meteor Season Over." "'She Died for Nothing,' Bereaved Mother Said."

"I've been housesitting for my mom's friend," Ursula said. "Her husband is in the OCA, and it really bothers me."

"What does your mom think?" Jason asked.

"Oh, she feels sorry for Mrs. Garst. I know it probably isn't such a big deal, but I care about this." Ursula spoke to Jason, not to me.

Jason tapped her on the arm. "Hold that thought. I've got to take a leak. I'll be right back."

He stood up. For a moment I thought he was going to unzip his fly and pee right behind us, but he waded into the knee-high grass and set off toward the dark line of trees at the edge of the field, his cigarette glowing like a firefly.

I could see the papers now. "'Many People Think Coyotes Are Afraid of Cigarette Smoke,' Urban Legend Expert Notes After Tragic Mauling of Local Boy." I took a slow, deep breath as Miss Lopez suggested we do before tests and sporting events.

Ursula looked at me from her place in the grass. "It's because of you, Triinu. When I think Mrs. Garst married someone who wants to hurt you, well … I could kill him. I really could. You know? I love you. You're like my family."

We sat together in silence, watching Jason's figure grow distant and indistinct. Above us, the sky was absolutely still. There were no meteors, but deep in the sky, beyond the brightest constellations, I saw a dim band of stars so huge it filled the circumference of my vision. "Look, Ursula." I said, my breath visible in the starlight. "It's the Milky Way."

"It's kind of romantic," Ursula said. "All those stars."

I was going to tell her about the dome of God, the child-hood vision of God as an enormous planetarium. I could almost see Him now behind all the pinpricks of light and in the velvety darkness between them, but then Jason sauntered back into our little circle, bringing the smell of cigarettes back into our midst. When he sat, he sat right next to Ursula. He put his arm around her. "You cold?" he asked her.

"Yes." She giggled and snuggled closer. "I miss France." She sighed. "It was cold there too sometimes."

"Tell me about it," Jason said.

Don't tell us about it. Fucking France!

"Well ..." Ursula shot me an excited look. I could read every thought in her face: "Jason put his arm around me, and he wants to hear about France!" She opened her eyes wider, as if waiting for my smile, as if I too should be thrilled by this unexpected turn of events.

She went on for a long time. Apparently it never rained in France. The butter didn't make you fat. The corner store was a historical landmark that made America look like a crumpled up McDonald's wrapper. And everyone in France was more interesting than anyone here, even when she didn't speak the language and had no idea what they were saying.

"And the cathedrals! Oh, they're so beautiful."

"I know something else that's pretty," Jason said.

I liked the metaphor—your body is my church; I kneel before your beauty—but I groaned inwardly at "I know something else that's pretty." Was I back in Ms. Lanham's poetry class? "You're so pretty. I'm so giddy. I want to pinch your titty." Lame! And yet, even in the starlight, I could see Ursula's face flush with pleasure.

Then, as though I was not there at all, Jason leaned over

and kissed her. I was shocked that he would kiss her in front of me. I assumed they would stop immediately. It was one of those fleeting gestures, almost involuntary. I was waiting for Ursula to pull away, laugh, wipe her lips, and say, "We'd better be getting back home."

She kept kissing him. Her hands grabbed his staunch middle as his hands wrapped around her thick-sweatered body. She seemed to devour him, as though at any moment she might unhinge her jaw and consume his head. A moment later I heard her issue a little moan. I looked away, and when I glanced back, Jason's hand was under her shirt.

I stood up, coyotes be damned. I would rather the whole pack tear me limb from limb than stay and watch Ursula tongue the back of Jason's throat. My headline could read, "Teen Lesbian Writes 'Fucking Breeders' in Own Blood before Dying of Coyote Bite."

I was several paces away when Ursula finally acknowledged my departure. "Where are you going, Triinu?"

I kept walking. I was waiting for her to run after me, to throw her arms around me, to cling to me, pleading, "Triinu, I was wrong!" Maybe this was the moment in which she would see everything clearly. I was already telling a story of our future selves, Ursula looking back on that night later, saying, "Do you remember when you were so angry and we saw the Milky Way, and I finally knew I loved you?" I was already forgiving her in my mind. The stars were so high and bright, God so clearly visible. I was ready.

Ursula just called out, "Wait for me at the truck, then."

I reached the truck, but I didn't stop. I wasn't going to shiver on the tailgate and wait for them to finish kissing—or worse. My heart was breaking. I was going home.

I had passed two mile markers on the rural highway when I finally admitted my mistake. I should have sat on the tailgate and waited. I should have said, "Goddamn you motherfuckers, if you're going to make out in the field, take me home first!" The road stretched ahead of me into infinity. Maybe it was the wrong road. Maybe I was walking toward the empty east, not the populated north. Maybe I was headed for the foothills. There were bears out there, and mountain lions, too. I missed the coyotes now; they felt like old friends with their amicable chatter, but I could not hear them. What lay ahead was dark and silent.

A car passed me. I waved. It had to be Ursula. I did not care if I had to sit sandwiched in between Ursula and Jason. I did not care if they kissed right over my squished-in knees. My jaw was stiff. My hands were numb. I had left my jacket in the truck. My teeth had begun to chatter uncontrollably, but the car sped away.

After what seemed like a very long time, I heard another engine. I turned and saw a set of headlights in the distance behind me. "Please, please, please," I whispered. "Don't leave me."

The vehicle approached, slowing ominously. As it passed, I saw that it was not Jason's truck, nor did it pick up speed after passing me. In fact, it was slowing to a stop. I tried to walk very tall. Miss Lopez had told us that rapists and murderers picked their victims based on body language. I squared my shoulders and held my head high. I saw the road in the car's brake lights; it looked like a crime scene.

The driver hit the horn. The noise startled me like a shot. I turned and started walking back the way I had come. The driver put the car in reverse. It was careening back toward me and swerving in the road.

I started to run, but there was no way to outrun it. I looked to both sides. On either side of the road was a deep channel full of water. Beyond it, I saw wire and the telltale lightning bolt placards announcing an electric fence.

The car reached me. The window rolled down. "Hey," a rough voice yelled.

I plunged into the gutter. I had never touched an electric fence. I hoped it would be like putting out a candle with your fingers. You just had to move quickly through the flame to the wick. Crush it. Then run.

The car's lights threw a pool of red on the road and the gutter. I scrambled down the side of the muddy bank. The creek was deeper and slipperier than I had expected. I grabbed one of the fence posts to pull it down, but it was as solid as the road behind me. Up close, the electric wire was as thick as the antenna of my car. A few sparks zinged across its surface.

"Hey, Triinu!" a voice behind me yelled.

I froze. It wasn't Ursula. It was a trick.

This is why when I was a child, my mother never bought me T-shirts with my name on them. Careless mothers did, and then kidnappers called their children by name, and the children skipped happily away with their abductor saying, "Mommy didn't tell me her friend was going to pick me up from school."

"Don't worry, Amber," the kidnapper would say. "Your mom and I have been friends for years."

"What are you doing, Triinu?"

"Get away from me!"

"It's Isabel." Someone turned on the overhead light in the car. I saw the familiar side ponytail. She wore a glittery green top and a shade of lipstick so bright it made my teeth ring. It *was* Isabel! "Get in. You're gonna freeze."

I stumbled out of the creek and sopped my way over to the passenger side.

Isabel turned up the heat. "What the hell are you doing out

here? I passed you, and I thought, 'That looks like Triinu, but we're in the middle of fucking nowhere.'"

"I …" I stared out the window at the dark fields now rushing past us. The heat from the car radiator was a miracle.

"There's an old sweatshirt in the backseat. Put it on. So, what were you doing?" Isabel asked again.

"I was hanging out with Ursula."

"And?"

"She wanted to make out with Jason Price."

"So you decided to walk home and go swimming in the gutter?"

"I thought you were a kidnapper."

"Do you know how far out you are? Town is that way. You were headed toward Eddiesville."

"Shit."

Isabel waited a beat. "Triinu?"

"It was just so rude. I mean, I was right there." I heard tears in my voice. "It was like I didn't exist, like I was supposed to be happy for her or something." I was aware of Isabel glancing in my direction. My story did not hold up.

"I mean, she just got back from France. I've hardly seen her. We're supposed to be hanging out, and she's making out with some guy."

Isabel snorted. "I never liked her."

"You don't even know her."

"She let you walk home in the dark because she was making out with some dude. What a bitch."

I still wanted to defend Ursula; perhaps I wanted to be the only one to hate her. But I just said, "What were you up to?"

"Molotov Squid was supposed to play this kid's fourteenth birthday party," she said. I could see her jaw tighten. Her grip on the wheel shifted from a gentle ten and two to an angry hand on the top of the wheel. Her other hand dropped to the gearshift. "The kid was this preppy little fucker, and his mom hired us because she thought we'd be 'hip.' After the first set, the kid grabs the mic and starts making fun of us to all his friends. He said we sounded like a train wreck hitting two cats in heat."

The description was not entirely inaccurate, but I said, "What an asshole!"

"Then, afterward, our drummer, Jug, said he didn't want me to do the song about my dad. He said it was too 'hippie-dippie.' He wanted to sub in this song he wrote called 'Anarchy is in Your Anus, Motherfuckers.'" I could only vaguely picture the drummer. He wore flannel and seemed somewhat greasy, like the last glass to be washed in an oily sink.

"You're the best thing about that band," I said, with conviction I truly felt. "They've got nothing without you."

"Thanks."

We rode in silence for a while, but eventually Isabel started humming, and I picked up the tune without realizing it. Then, as if we were still in youth choir and Pastor Brown had suddenly lifted his hands to signal the first note, Isabel shoved the car into fourth, revved the engine, hit eighty-five miles per hour, and we broke into a riotous harmony.

"Amazing grace, how sweet the sound, that saved a wretch like me." My mother always said the hymn was "overdone." My father complained that singers always held the note on "me" as though they could "eeeee" their way into heaven.

But I didn't care, and we sang it over and over again, all the way into town. "Through many dangers, toils, and snares I have already come; 'tis grace has brought me safe thus far, and grace will lead me home," we sang as we rushed headlong over Earth's convex surface, falling into a horizon of stars.

The Only Goth Dyke in the Grass Seed Capital of the World

I wandered into the kitchen the next morning and poured myself a cup of coffee. On the table, the newspaper lay in a pile with the comics on top. I read my favorites and then pushed them aside, revealing the front page. The headline stopped me: "Antigay Violence Hits Home." The photograph on the front page was just a mobile home in a field. It looked like any one of a hundred country homes, the white siding turning gray, the surface pocked by clods of dirt, an overturned lawn chair in the front yard, a pile of wood pallets sitting to one side. I read the first lines of the article. "On September 6, 1992, an unknown party opened fire on the home of James Grabble and Vince Propo, killing both men and injuring Propo's sister, who was visiting the couple."

I froze. I looked at the picture again. They weren't clods of dirt; they were bullet holes. The surface I had taken for window glass was in fact the absence of glass. I read on:

"Neighbor Allen Mater reports seeing a truck speed by shortly before the gunfire began. 'They were yelling, "Die fags, die fags,"' Allen said. 'My wife wanted to call the police. I told her we didn't have time. We had to get in the bathtub just in case any of the bullets struck our trailer and came through the walls.' A friend of the deceased, who prefers to remain anonymous, said, 'I always knew it was going to come to this. They were very open. They got a lot of threats, and they would not back down.'"

The article went on to describe the men's political activity, their pleas for help, the police chief's protestation that his department could not place a guard outside the house of every homosexual. The threats were coming in faster than the police could investigate them, and homosexuals who planted "No on Measure 9" signs in their yards could expect no less. They made themselves targets, plain and simple. "The easiest way for people to protect themselves is to keep their private lives private," the article quoted one police officer as saying. "If you leave valuables in your car, someone is going to steal them. If you put a target on our house, someone is going to shoot."

I ripped the paper in half, balled it up, and stuffed it in the garbage. I wished I could burn it on the porches of the men who did this and the police who shrugged it off and the wife who lay in a bathtub because her safety was more important than calling for help.

At school the next day, an enormous sophomore boy named Bobby Patch had taken over my spot in the front hall by the window.

"Get the fuck out of my way," I barked. "This is the senior hallway. I've been sitting here all year."

It was only September, but the rage I felt could have cleaved Israel in two.

"Somebody's PMSing." He laughed. "Smile if you're horny."

"What the fuck?"

"You're not smiling," he teased. "Smile if you're horny."

He yelled it at everyone, even Crystal, who had disappeared sometime in third or fourth grade and had now reappeared at our school, a teenager with tight jeans and the same horrifying topography of burns on her face. "Hey Crystal, smile if you're horny!"

A gaggle of girls with hair like bleach-blonde roadkill ran up to Bobby. One of them leapt onto his shoulders. From that vantage point, she flipped her friends off, yelling, "I'm not smiling! I'm not smiling!"

"This is my spot!" I didn't like to fight. It made my hands tremble and my sides sweat, but I couldn't take one more injustice. This was the only place in the hallway with natural light, the only place where I could look out at the hills and imagine my escape.

"Smile if you're horny," Bobby Patch yelled again.

Someone tapped my shoulder.

"Move along, Triinu." It was Principal Pinn. "These halls belong to everyone."

I marched past him and found my way back to Isabel. She had scoped out a bench near the language arts wing. I dropped into place beside her as though I had never abandoned her, as though she had not picked me up off the side of the road like a lost cat, as though we had been sitting here since ninth grade.

"How's it going?" I asked.

Isabel leaned the back of her head against the wall. A few yards down the hall, Ben Sprig spit into a trash can.

"Hey faggot," he yelled to a friend. "Check out this gnarly fuckin' loogie."

"He has a girlfriend." Isabel said. "There is actually a girl desperate enough to go out with Ben Sprig. Ugh."

Ben yelled, "Don't fuckin' throw any shit on it till you check out this gnarly motherfucker."

"I guess he's getting over Pip," I said.

"When you can hock a loogie like that, you can't just sit around grieving. You know, you've got shit to do."

"Did you see that article in the paper?" I asked.

The election was only weeks away. Every article in the paper was about Ballot Measure 9, but I knew Isabel would know which one I meant.

224

"Yeah," she said. "My mom was on the phone all night after it happened. It's like she's got some hippie disaster commission that calls her whenever there's a tragedy. I mean, what do they think they're going to *do* about it?"

"I feel like I should do something," I said.

"You go to all those awful Democracy Club meetings." Isabel produced a Red Vine from her pocket and chewed on it meditatively. "You could call my mom's friends and talk about how oppressed everyone is."

"They're doing their best!" I snapped.

"I know, I know." The Red Vine dangled out of her mouth. She looked like a cat that had eaten a licorice rat and gotten a scolding because of it. "I didn't mean anything. I'm just ..." She sighed. "My house is full of them. My mom doesn't have time to go grocery shopping, but she's got her hippie friends over every night to process their feelings about the election."

I stared down the hall. "I could write a poem," I said.

"That's a good idea," Isabel said, in the same way I had said Molotov Squid sounded really good.

I wasn't deterred. "I could write it and then leave it there, like an offering."

"Where?" Isabel looked over sharply, sucking the Red Vine into her mouth.

"At the trailer where they were killed."

"You can't do that."

"Why not?"

"What if someone sees you?"

"Would that be so bad?" I stood up. "I just want to pay my respects."

Isabel scrambled to her feet. "I mean, it might not be safe." She grabbed my arm. "Seriously! What if the guys with the rifles come back?"

I went nonetheless. I didn't have a poem. Love, loneliness, death, and fog were all in the valley that afternoon, but I thought poetry was supposed to be beautiful, and I did not have anything beautiful to say. Instead I drove the back roads for almost an hour trying not to find the trailer, but I knew those roads too well. I knew without knowing which unmarked turn to take.

Up close, the trailer didn't look like all the other homes. Broken glass lined the window frames like jagged teeth. The black bullet holes were clearly visible. A brownish stain ran down the side of the house beneath some of the holes, as though the house itself was bleeding. The lawn chairs in the front yard were shredded. A plaster gnome lay cracked on the front step. Above my head, the sky hung low and gray.

I pulled onto the shoulder of the road and parked. Cold rain spattered my face when I got out of the car. I looked around. The fields looked nothing like they had when my father had taught me how to drive. Gone was the golden stubble. Gone were the glowing clouds of dust. Gone, too, was the sense of space. Everything felt closed in now; even the sky was too close.

I shut my car door without latching it, afraid to slam it and disturb the silence. I thought there would be police tape or Do Not Enter signs, but the only sign was a large "No on 9" placard, punctured by bullet holes and knocked off its legs. The rain had pooled on its surface and in the potholes in the driveway and on the flat roof of the trailer.

I had imagined making a grand gesture, burning my poems, holding my hands up to the sky and crying, "Why?"

I inched forward, listening. Despite the lack of signage, I felt like a trespasser. I told myself it was just a driveway. It wasn't illegal to walk up a driveway. Maybe I was selling Mary Kay makeup or delivering the paper. Someone driving by wouldn't know. There was no one in the house. Isabel was silly to warn me of danger. The men were dead. The sister was in a coma. I wasn't hurting anything. There was no reason for the killer to come back.

I folded my hands and tried to say a prayer.

"Dear God." It felt strange, like hanging out with Isabel again after so many years. "I know I don't ... call." That wasn't the right word. "I mean pray. I know I'm not winning Acolyte of the Year." I whispered the words. "But how could you let this happen?"

Before I knew that I was going to cry, a sob broke from my lips so deep it seemed to come from the ground itself, swelling through my body and ripping from my lips like the cry of gulls over the ocean.

"You can't hate me!" I looked up at the sky as though God might be there, like a giant looking in on his little terrarium. "I loved you. And you left me. You just left me." I didn't know if I was talking to God or to Ursula. "Why did you leave me? Why did you let this happen?"

I wept on the inhale and on the exhale, great gasping cries, louder than I would ever have cried in my parents' house where they might have heard me. I cried until I doubled over and choked and spat up a mouthful of bile on the ground. I cried until the rain mixed with my tears and ran down my cheeks, into my mouth, down my neck.

I cried until I heard the sound of an engine in the distance. I wiped my eyes. The sound grew louder. At the end of the road, I saw a Jeep on oversized wheels. It was driving much too fast, even for the straight country road. As it roared past, a man stuck his head out the back window and yelled, "Fuck yeah!" The driver laid on the horn. It sounded like they were cheering.

I ran for my car, falling into the front seat and almost dropping my keys. In the rearview mirror, I saw the Jeep pull a

U-turn in a driveway about half a mile up the road. They were coming back. I kicked the gas and turned the key. The Blue Bird of Happiness sputtered.

"Come on, come on, come on," I breathed.

Fear had dried my tears. What if these were the men who had shot up the house? Criminals came back to the scene of the crime to gloat sometimes. I had read that somewhere. Isabel was right.

I offered another prayer to God as the engine turned over. I pressed the gas. The Blue Bird lumbered to life, but even with my foot plunging the accelerator to the floor, the car never went over fifty-five miles per hour. A second later, the Jeep was behind me. Men leaned out of both the back windows and the front passenger window. One of them threw an empty pop can. I heard it ping on the roof of my car.

They pulled alongside me, all of them screaming obscenities. "Fucking faggots!"

I kept my eyes on the road ahead.

"Die fag!"

I thought one of them might be peeing out the car window, but I did not look.

Finally, they honked a cheerful toot-toot-ta-toot-toot and pulled ahead of me. In a second, they were gone. My hands were shaking. I felt like my whole body had been deboned, as though I might slide into a puddle and disappear through the floor.

When I showed up at Isabel's house, she answered the door, her face dropping into worry. "What is it?" I said nothing as she ushered me in. Inside the woodstove was burning ferociously. Her family was elsewhere.

"Here, sit," she said. "You want a Dr Pepper?" I nodded. I didn't like cola, but I didn't care. "Stay here," Isabel said.

A moment later she appeared with a tiny airport bottle of gin. She poured a thimbleful into her glass and a thimbleful into mine, topping them both off with Dr Pepper. "You want to talk?" she asked.

I wanted Ursula. I wanted Ursula to cradle me in her arms. Wanted her lips to remind me why it was still worth fighting. If nothing else, I wanted our old friendship back. I wanted to rush to the Beanery and catch sight of her reading *Backlash* with a pencil in her hair. She would pat the seat beside her, loop her arm through mine, and pull me closer. "Try this coffee. Read this paragraph. Look at this bumper sticker." But Ursula hadn't called me since I walked out of the grass seed field.

"Not really," I said.

"That's okay," Isabel said. "That's what my mom's friends do. Talk, talk, talk. And what does it get them?"

"Nothing," I said mournfully.

"Nothing," Isabel concurred.

We sat in silence for a long time.

Finally Isabel said, "Speaking of my mom."

We weren't really.

"She says that I've led a 'privileged life.'" Isabel put the last part in ironic quotation marks. "She says I need to 'give back to the community.'"

"How?"

"I have to do volunteer work for the rest of the *year*! She says I can choose where I do it, but she wants me to work at this women's magazine publisher called WomynScript Press." She paused. "And I was thinking that you like poetry and all that goth stuff, and it wouldn't suck so completely if we could do it together, and it might look good on college applications. I mean, I know you're not interested, but ..."

"I'll do it," I said.

Isabel cocked her head, her ponytail bobbing to one side. "Yeah?" She raised her glass and clinked mine. "Right on."

WomynScript Press occupied three offices on the second story of a downtown building. The windows were partially obscured by a geometric latticework of wooden bars, an unfortunate decorative touch from the seventies. The offices themselves were an utter mess: books were piled in every corner, journals slid off overcrowded shelves, and posters of famous authors curled in the sun. Dusty philodendrons took root in empty coffee cups, defying the laws of photosynthesis. Everywhere, handwritten notes with unnamed phone numbers and urgent messages wafted around the feet of the WomynScript staff as they hurried from room to room, talking feverishly about Measure 9.

On our first day at WomynScript, Isabel and I were put to work shelving back issues of *Ploughshares* on a shelf so tightly packed with journals it seemed as though the employees were trying to create great literature by pressure, like pressing diamonds out of coal. I prodded the shelf ineffectually while Camilla, the matriarch of WomynScript, bustled about the room. When she left, I sat down on a box and rubbed at the dust that had smudged my velvet platform heels.

"These magazines will never fit," I said. "Why don't they just get rid of them?"

Isabel surveyed the shelf and removed a manila envelope stuffed with old receipts. In its place, she squeezed two *Ploughshares* and a *Glimmer Train*. She handed me the envelope. "Put this somewhere."

"Where?"

Isabel looked slowly around the room.

From the adjacent office, I heard someone say, "Chuck Garst is the most vicious person I have ever spoken with."

"Why were you speaking with Chuck Garst?"

"At the open forum ..."

There was a rattle of paper like the first rumblings of an avalanche and then a series of loud slaps and metallic snaps as though several binders had just leapt from a shelf to their death. I waited for the ensuing curse, but the women of WomynScript were used to that kind of thing. There was a shuffle of papers.

"Can you pass me that binder? Thanks. If the OCA gets a foothold in Oregon, it may get to a point where they can pass anything they want."

"Don't you think people will see it's just hatemongering?"

"I doubt it. People are in trouble. The logging industry is failing. Farms are going bankrupt. If the OCA pits the evil city of Sodom against the God-fearing people of rural Oregon, they've got support. People want someone to hate. There are a lot of people out there who have never met a gay person, never seen a photograph of a gay person, and the first thing they've ever heard about homosexuality is from the OCA: Gays are sexual deviants who turn children gay by molesting them."

"But even in eastern Oregon they can't be *that* isolated."

"Really? We live in the so-called 'liberal west.' Do you know how many lesbian movies they have at American Movie Rentals? Three. I asked the owner. And in two of those, the lesbian is a vampire and gets staked at the end."

"That's more a feminist issue than a lesbian issue. It's a penetration trope."

Isabel looked at me and rolled her eyes. "Do you want to get a coffee?" she whispered.

I nodded and dropped a stack of journals onto a cluttered table. We excused ourselves. As we descended to the street, I lifted the hem of my dress so that it wouldn't trail on the grungy linoleum.

"You are so gothic." Isabel glanced at me. "I wonder what the WomynScript ladies make of you. They've spent the last twenty years burning bras and here you are."

I shrugged.

"I wonder why they let us volunteer, anyway," I said as we emerged, relieved, onto the tidy street below. "They don't really have anything for us to do."

"Maybe they want to induct us into the lesbian conspiracy," Isabel said. She pushed open the Beanery's screen door. "Latte? Cappuccino?" She hummed to herself as we sidled up to the counter. "I'll have a triple Café Beanery."

"Me too."

"I can't believe my mom once said she felt a woman-spirit connection with Camilla," Isabel said. "God, if she said she was attracted to her …"

We moved away from the counter to wait for our coffee.

"What would Camilla think of that?"

"I don't know that she'd care. I mean, I think she's gay. Maybe she'd think my mom was a catch."

"Two triple Café Beaneries to go," the barista hollered in our direction.

Isabel picked up her coffee, but I had momentarily lost track of the coffee and the shop and the afternoon light filtering into the Beanery's dark interior. All I was thinking was, *Camilla's gay?*

"Here. Take your coffee. I remember when my mom tried to tell me that she wasn't a heterosexual person or a homosexual person. She was just a sexual being." Isabel wrinkled her nose. "That gave me the crawlies for a week. I mean, I just don't want to think about my mom that way. Ever. But she tells me these things. I tried to tell her I should never, ever, ever have to know about her sex life, but she said she wanted to share the revelation with me."

232

I was still thinking, *Camilla's gay?!*

That she might be gay would not have surprised a worldly person. Camilla was a strong woman in comfortable shoes, a no-trouble haircut, and a "Famous Suffragettes" T-shirt. The founder of a feminist publishing house, she was candid, political, and outspoken. She probably had a cat named Gertrude Stein. Of course she was gay.

However, I was not nearly as worldly as I liked to pretend I was, or perhaps I just wasn't good at math. I had read parts of the Kinsey report. I should have realized that if ten percent of the population was gay and thirty thousand people lived in my hometown, then there had to be at least three thousand queers. It was a simple story problem, but I thought that Ava was the only other lesbian who'd ever existed, and she was gone, making me the last dyke in the Grass Seed Capital of the World.

I was all alone until Isabel said, "I mean, I think she's gay. Maybe she'd think my mom was a catch." There were others like me. But this sudden realization didn't bring me comfort. I watched Camilla intently after that. She was a sturdy woman with muscular forearms, and she had a way of getting right to the point that made me uncomfortable. She was a good person, but she wore a fanny pack. I was seventeen and goth. I did not get things done at the expense of dirtying my fingernails. I did not squat in front of old file cabinets, lift up my arms, and say, "Whew, I'm sweating!" I wrote with a fountain pen, and if I could have found a quill, I would have used that instead. Convenience be damned, I was an orchid among women. If joining the lesbians meant letting even one wiry hair grow off my chin, then I would have to die alone.

Later I sat at a table addressing envelopes while Isabel wrestled with a ready-to-assemble desk and one rusty, ill-fitting screwdriver. I addressed the letters quickly so that I could go and help her. As I worked, another volunteer sat down next to me.

"Hi." She put a book on the table. "I just finished this book, and I thought you might like it." I picked it up. On the cover was a woman with masses of burgundy hair swirled in a mirage of coral and orange. "It's about Chicana *lesbians*," the woman said, stressing the word 'lesbian' as though it were a password. "I really liked it because I'm a Chicana *lesbian*, too. It talks about the lesbian identity and homophobia." She did everything but nudge me.

Part of me wanted to grab her arm and yell, "Me too!" I wanted to pound my fist on the table. I wanted to clench the book to my chest and say, "God damn it, yes!"

But I didn't. I was seventeen. I did not recognize those women as my own. What did they know about the seething clamor of the senior hallway? What did they know about loneliness? What did they know about grace?

They were tense, those crisp, hay-scented days before the November ballot decided our fates. "No on 9" campaign offices were ransacked around the state. Activists were routinely stalked. In the most liberal part of Portland, a gay man was beaten on his way out of a bar. His glasses shattered, and his attackers jabbed the shards of glass into his eyes, screaming, "Kill the faggots!"

In Salem, a black lesbian and her gay roommate were killed by a pipe bomb. Bystanders reported hearing the bomber yell, "I hope you pop like a hot dog in the microwave, you nigger fag."

Ursula called me that night.

"Did you see the news?" she said. "That's so awful. I just had to know that you're okay. Are you okay?"

I felt like my "no" would reverberate down through the center of the earth, so I said, "Yeah," instead.

"You sure?"

"Yes," I lied.

"Good," Ursula said, as though that ended the conversation. "I went to another town hall meeting today. You know what they said?" She went on for several minutes; I drifted in and out until I heard her asking, "Are you listening? Triinu?"

"Are you dating Jason now?" I blurted out.

"Jason? What?" Ursula giggled. "No. Maybe."

"You left me on the side of the road!"

Ursula paused, as though trying to remember what I was talking about. I pressed the phone to my ear with such force it made my ear numb.

Finally she said, "Oh, God, Triinu! We looked for you. We drove all the way back to town. Then we went back to the field and then back to town. Jason is such a nice guy. He said he would drive around all night looking for you if I wanted. Can you believe that? It's like he really cared."

"You could have called me."

"I was afraid you were mad at me."

"I could have been dead."

"I'm calling now. You said you were okay."

I didn't know what to say. I felt like the witness in the court drama we had watched in social studies. I had lied under oath, and now there was no way back to the truth.

Ursula said, "Come over. My folks are out of town. I'll cook you dinner. It'll be like we had our own place."

We slept together again that night—and several times thereafter. We never dated. We never held hands. She never kissed my forehead. I never said, "I love you," although I still did.

Once Ursula rolled off me with a satiated sigh and said, "Do you think Jason likes me or *likes* me likes me? He's just so cute; I can't stand it!" Often she talked about boys: Jason, Kent, Alex, Russ. There was a never-ending supply.

Frequently, we argued about virginity. Ursula held that she was still a virgin, and I argued that she was not. She did not get two virginities: a lesser one to squander on me and a greater, more important one to share with a man. Ursula pleaded, "I'm not saying that having sex with a woman isn't important. I'm just saying it's different."

"So if I never have sex with a man, I'm a virgin for life? My mother would like that."

"Maybe it's different for you. I'm just saying that when I have sex with a man, it's going to be something really special, and I want to wait until the right person and the right time. It's a big deal."

I actually agreed with Ursula. I did think that I would remain a kind of virgin forever. I thought there was something pure about women, about Ursula, about Ava beneath her ceiling of roses, about my body, as clean and spare as an anatomical drawing. In the naked dark, we guarded our secrets while men's dangled. I could imagine why Ursula wanted to find just the right man; I would not want to encounter those organs with a stranger.

Still, I argued vehemently, because every time Ursula jammed her fingers inside me, I felt like I lost something. I argued with her because she reached inside and touched me where I kept my rage. I argued with her because I had read about a seventeen-year-old girl who had drowned herself in the Willamette River, leaving a note that read, "I'm gay, but I'm not a sinner." The girl and I had been born on the exact same day.

The bitterness I felt spilled into my other lives. I ignored my parents. I snapped at Isabel. I sat in the windowless room that housed the books from my parents' college years and struggled through *Beowulf* with a hard determination that had nothing to do with the pleasure of reading.

On the night of the election, November 3rd, 1992, I picked Isabel up at her house so we could go get a piece of pizza. I did not mention the election, but I scanned the radio of the Blue Bird of Happiness for a news channel.

"God, the news!" Isabel said. "My mom's been listening to the radio all day with her crunchy friends. Every time Clinton gets another state they all yell 'Woo hoo!' I can't take it. I had to get out of the house."

"Do you think he'll win?"

I did not ask about Ballot Measure 9.

"I dunno," Isabel said. "My mom says people vote from 'the vantage point of fear.' What the hell does that mean?"

I shrugged.

The radio announcers clucked to each other. "Well Lonnie, what do you say to another twenty minutes of golden oldies, bringing you back to the way life used to be?"

"Well, I couldn't think of anything I'd like more, Ronald. Here's a fine ol' tune everyone will remember."

The radio cut to a song I had never heard before; it had something to do with a little shoeshine boy. The singer crooned. Isabel sang along, accentuating the word "little" in a way that made it sound dirty. Then she burst into a brief chorus of "Sex Dwarf."

I was thinking that maybe I could go to France, where it never rained. No one would know I was gay because my French was limited to textbook expressions like, "I go windsurfing on Tuesdays."

"So what do you think about Measure 9?" Isabel asked.

"I dunno." My face felt hot.

"You think it'll pass?"

"Of course it will pass."

In a world with Chuck Garst, Principal Pinn, Ben Sprig, and Jason Price fondling Ursula's breasts beneath the stars, in a world where the only justice was the death of Pip Weston—and that was just dumb luck and fifth of whiskey in the right place at the right time—how could it *not* pass?

"I don't think so," Isabel said. She turned up the radio.

I suddenly realized I had been driving the same loop for twenty minutes: through the university campus, past the Waremart Food plaza, past Forbearing Emmanuel, and back through campus again. The twenty minutes of golden oldies had ended. The voices of the station's announcers returned.

"Well Ronald, I think the votes are in."

"Democracy at work."

"I'd say it's poetry in motion, Ronald. Po-e-try!"

"So what is the verdict tonight, Lonnie?"

I held my breath. Our exact location on the street burned into my memory, like the shadows left by an atomic bomb. "Turn it off," I told Isabel.

She stopped my hand as I reached for the dial. "Hold on, Triinu."

"It looks like we have a Democrat for a president. Bill Clinton!"

"President Bill Clinton."

They ran through the senators and representatives for Oregon. I held my breath.

"And what about Measure 9? That sure stirred up a hornet's nest, didn't it, Ronald?"

"Sure did, Lonnie, and it looks like that one lost. Forty-three percent in favor. Fifty-seven percent opposed."

It failed! I felt like maybe I should stop the car. I thought that maybe everyone should stop, get out, shake hands, and walk down the center line of the road as my father and I had once walked along I-5 when a massive accident held up traffic for hours, the highway quiet and still. I had that same sense of disaster averted, of horror that had not happened to me.

"That's good," I whispered. "Did you hear that, Isabel?"

"Yeah." She reached over and squeezed my arm. "That's good." Then she added, "My mom is going to go crazy with all her hippie friends. You want to get that pizza, then go over to my house and see the madness?"

"Woo hoo!"

Inside the Avilas' house, the windows were fogged over and the woodstove had heated the room like a sweat lodge. On the table, Mrs. Avila had spread an array of oat bran brownies, pumpkin flatbread, and a bowl of nutritional yeast. The food was a bit more wholesome than I would have liked, but it had a rich cumin scent. Altogether, Mrs. Avila's house was looking brighter than it had for a long time after her husband's death. She had covered the walls with paintings of big-bellied women. A friend had made her a whimsical sculpture—an insect, or maybe it was a puppy—out of scrap metal, and it goggled at us from its seat by the fire. Blankets festooned the sofa. Small earthenware candleholders sat on end tables, casting a dancing glow on the guests, and everywhere women in T-shirts emblazoned with slogans lounged, their large breasts declaring: "Save the Rainforest," "Free Tibet," and "Every Child a Wanted Child." Camilla from WomynScript sat with her arm draped over the back of the sofa.

"Welcome!" she said as we came through the door.

"Oh! It's so good to have you here," Mrs. Avila enthused.

"This is a major moment in history. It's important that the generations meet on a night like this. Isabel, did you hear the news?" Isabel was trying not to roll her eyes.

"They lost," Camilla said. "Clinton won and Measure 9 lost!"

"Woo hoo!" a few women chorused.

"We heard it on the radio," I said.

"Oh, let me give you a hug." Mrs. Avila hoisted herself out of a rocking chair and wrapped her arms around me. "You too, Isabel." Over Mrs. Avila's shoulder I eyed the crowd. Those tough, plump, craggy feminists, those frank dykes with their rough noblesse. Those ladies. Those heroes.

Isabel and I retreated to the cold woodstove on her side of the house. Her brother was over at a friend's. Her little sister's door was closed, her chirpy voice soaring as she complained to someone on the other end of the phone. Isabel swung open the door to her bedroom, and we sat on her bed, our backs against the wall. A small reading lamp by the head of her bed was the only light.

"Thank God that's all over," she said. "I wonder how long they're going to bond out there. I guess it's their night, though." She paused. "Hey, I made you something." Isabel hopped off the bed and rustled around in the bottom drawer of her bureau. She pulled out a shoebox with "For Triinu" written in glittery script across the top. "Open it."

I took the box in my lap and admired the glitter work. The paint was still wet, and a bit of the glitter transferred to my hands, sparkling in the lamplight. I opened the box.

Inside was a Ken doll, very carefully dressed in hand-sewn clothing: a green velvet skirt, a silver bustier, and a gold lamé shrug with a tiny pink triangle pinned to it. Isabel had painted gothic makeup on his face and thigh-high stockings on his legs. Every detail was meticulously rendered.

"It's Transvestite Ken," Isabel said proudly.

"It is," I agreed. "I love it." I cradled the doll against my chest, then kissed his face. "I'll keep him forever. He can ride on the *Corazón Fiel.*"

"You know I lugged that goddamn boat all over Guatemala for you. You still have it, right?"

"Of course."

"You can never get rid of it."

"I know, and now I'll keep it with Ken." I paused a beat, searching the darkened window for the outline of the horizon. "I was going to tell you something."

Isabel waited.

"You know all that Ballot Measure 9 stuff?"

"Yeah."

I paused.

"You know I'm gay, right?"

Isabel glanced at me. She looked miffed.

"Well, duh." She bumped her shoulder against mine. "I'm not stupid. God! I've been your best friend since we were like, five. Was I not supposed to notice? You liked Jordan Knight from New Kids on the Block. He wears lipstick. He looks like a girl."

We said nothing more. Perhaps we had so much to say, we could not begin, or perhaps we had begun so long ago that we no longer needed words. We just stared into the dark beyond the window until the bedside clock clicked past midnight. Finally, I excused myself and drove home, beaming, repeating her benediction over and over in my mind: *Well, duh.*

At home that night, my parents were reading in the living room by the fire. Above them, the high ceiling rose up like a forest chapel. Outside the windows, the trees rustled in between us and the stars. Somewhere there were mountain lions, still and silent.

Put your arms out like you're flying.

"Mom? Dad?"

You look so beautiful in white.

"I have to tell you something."

I sat down. My mother smiled at me. My father put down his book.

It was harder than telling Isabel, perhaps because they were looking at me so intently. Perhaps because they loved me so much. I held their hearts in my palm, as fragile as hand-blown eggs. Perhaps because I had read about a gay rights attorney who had thrown her own daughter out of the house when she caught her in bed with another girl. "Just because we work for this cause doesn't mean we have people like that in *our* family," the lawyer had said.

I did not think that would happen to me, but I knew that if my parents disapproved, their silence would be impenetrable. There would be no breaking it and no escaping it. If my parents said, "No, not our daughter," what would I do?

"I don't always relate to the women at WomynScript. I mean, I'm not really like Camilla," I began.

My preamble went on. No preparation seemed adequate for the declaration, and I couldn't just sit down and say, "I see you're reading Auden, and by the way, I'm gay." I wasn't ready. My face flushed as I circled around and around the topic.

"It's part of why I didn't want to get confirmed, but I'm glad I did. I loved the dress you bought me. The election tonight showed that the world is changing. The church could change too."

I went on. It was an out-of-body experience. I saw myself talking, and I tried to stop, but I couldn't. It was like the dreams in which I tried to run from danger and couldn't, only in reverse: my mouth was running, and I was powerless to stop it. I told them every detail of Mrs. Avila's post-election potluck, right down to the bowl of nutritional yeast on the table.

"And I don't even know what that is," I said. "I mean, what is nutritional yeast? The Avilas put it on everything, but I asked Isabel, and she has no idea what's in it. It's just a powder ... or flakes. I think flakes are worse."

I had come to the end of the potluck items. I had nothing more to say about nutritional yeast. I paused. The world slowed on its axis to make the moment more unbearable. I took a deep breath. My parents nodded patiently.

"I'm a lesbian."

My mother said, "I see."

My father said, "Hmm."

I waited.

"I've been reading Auden," my father said finally. He flipped through his book. "Here's one for you. 'At last the secret is out, as it always must come in the end ... For the clear voice suddenly singing, high up in the convent wall, the scent of the elder bushes, the sporting prints in the hall ... the handshake, the cough, the kiss, there is always a wicked secret, a private reason for this.'"

My mother shook her head, but her disapproval seemed to be directed at my father. "Don't worry," she said. "You won't be lonely like Auden."

"Auden was gay," my father added, although I already knew. "And your mother is right. You have a gift for making friends. And you have us."

"We love you," my mother said. "We always will. Nothing you do will ever change that."

"And it's a new era," my father added. "People didn't fall for the OCA's gambit. They didn't bite. People say that's just because the ballot measure was poorly worded, but I think there is more to it than that. I think we'll see change in our lifetime."

"Maybe one day you could even get married," my mother added. "To someone of your choice. To a ..." Her voice faltered a little bit. "... a *woman* of your choice."

"Like a commitment ceremony," I said. I had heard the women at WomynScript talk about commitment ceremonies.

"Maybe even a real marriage. Is that too much to hope for?" My mother looked at my father as though he might know.

"Probably," he said in the apologetic tone he used for sad things that were not his fault.

Probably Forbearing Emmanuel would need a new roof.

Probably we would have freezing rain.

Probably I would never marry.

"But you never know," he added. "The Berlin Wall came down. People can't hold onto these old ideas forever."

I hugged them both and said goodnight as though it was any other night, but I lay in bed for a long time thinking. Ballot Measure 9 had failed, and my parents knew I was a lesbian, and they still loved me. And Isabel knew, which meant her mother knew. Probably all her mother's hippie friends knew, too. That was twenty people, at least. That was an army!

After that, I decided to call things off with Ursula. I wanted out. Out of the friendship. Out of the talks she insisted on having about boys. Out of the longing for her that I could not shake, no matter how angry I felt.

The following weekend, I met Ursula at her house.

"We have to talk," I said.

"I have to walk Scotch."

I sighed. It was a cold, wintery afternoon, and she was never ready when I arrived, as if my arrival meant nothing to her. I pulled my coat closer around my chest, and we headed toward the park in silence.

When we arrived, she let the dog off his leash to run. As he frolicked, we wandered toward the park's man-made lake. The shallow lake was nearly frozen, but at its center a few feet still remained liquid, and two errant ducks floated on this water.

"So how's Jason?" I asked, breaking the cold silence.

"He's good."

I took a few steps away from her. "I want to break up," I said.

"We're not going out," Ursula shot back. "I've been pretty clear about that."

Above us the sun had broken through the cloud cover, providing a slip of wan afternoon light.

"Yeah, you have." I turned to face her. "But that didn't stop you from fucking me."

"I didn't hear you complain."

I wanted to rip the pale sky and make it bleed.

"I want out."

"Okay. We won't fool around. I thought you liked it." Ursula wrapped her coat tighter around her. "You could just say no. It's not like I forced you or something."

"I loved you, and you knew it, and you still slept with me." My words came out as fast and sharp as Scotch's barks.

"You're beautiful." Ursula stepped toward me and tried to take my hands. I pulled away. "What we have is special." Her eyes had gone puffy. "It's cozy. It's different from all that dating stuff, you know? It's special because it's different."

I had never noticed how much taller I was than Ursula. She had reared up in my mind, a great broad-shouldered goddess, but I towered over her.

"You know what a real friend would do? You know what Chloe would do if she knew I was going to have sex with someone who didn't love me? You know what Aaron would do, or Isabel? If Isabel knew I loved someone, and they didn't love me, and I was going to sleep with them, she would tell me to stop. She would lock me in my own room. She would nail my door shut. She'd *protect* me."

Seeing the ducks in the center of the lake, Scotch barked and then set out across the ice, sending them squawking upward. We both glanced up, but I didn't stop. "Why didn't you protect me?"

Ursula shook her head vehemently. "You wanted to do it as much as I did."

"Because I was in love with you!"

"I never told you that I loved you like that. I never lied to you."

"You're such a fucking lawyer." The cold had gotten into my bones and left me feeling hard and raw. "That's not what it's about. You were supposed to be my *best friend*, and that's over now. I want out. I don't want to see you. I don't want to know you. I'm not your friend, and I'm not your lover."

Suddenly we heard a crash. Seeing the ducks rise, Scotch had leapt after them, and when he landed, he crashed through the ice. Now he howled as he sunk into the frigid water. He couldn't drown because the water was too low, but he was trapped shoulder-deep, unable to either break through the ice or clamber back up onto its slippery surface.

We stared at each other, then at Scotch. Even from my distant vantage on the bank, I could see him shaking. "We have to get help," I said.

Ursula was already taking off her Doc Marten boots. "He'll freeze by the time someone gets out here." She headed for the shallow lake, hesitating for only a moment before stomping on the ice, breaking the first step, treading on whatever rough, sinister vegetable matter coated the bottom.

"You hate that dog," I called after her.

She turned for a second. "Yeah."

Above her, the sky was like a summer sky with the wattage turned down. It was blue and clear with wispy clouds, but dim. Beside her stretched a tract of undeveloped suburb, populated with wild grass and rabbits. Behind her stood the office parks of Technology Lane. She broke a path through the ice with her stocking feet. She cracked her way to the dog, broke the ice around him, and led him back to shore. Then we walked home. There were no cars. No bikes. No pedestrians save for me and Ursula and her dog.

When we arrived at her house, she showered. I waited in her bedroom, although for what I did not know. When she returned, wearing a robe with her hair wrapped in a towel, she sat down at the far end of the bed. "Did you mean what you said? You don't want to be my friend?"

I had meant it. I had meant it in my bones. I looked away. I could still smell her shampoo. In my peripheral vision I saw her slippered feet: the same flat, pink slippers she had had since I met her in ninth grade, the kind of slippers my mother called a "tripping hazard." "They have no soles," my mother would say. In our family, slippers were rubber-shod. They were boots disguised. In our family we ate beets and cod and listened to Sibelius and owned a television that intercepted exactly zero channels.

By contrast, everything about Ursula's household was ordinary: mashed potatoes, siblings, football, the wide suburban street, the box hedge by the window, the stupid black lab she had rescued from the lake. How had I ever thought she was the rebel? Ursula, with her fawning preoccupation with boys? Asking, "Is he cute enough? Did he look at me?"

I could have died for my passion.

Ursula shivered. "Triinu?"

Ursula, my beast, my star. There is no love as cold and bright and angry as that first love. And yet I felt a story pulling me into the distance, like the gospels, like God lifting the soul out of the body upon death.

In half a year, you'll be in college.

How many days were left before we parted ways forever? I had waited so feverishly for her return, I forgot that I was leaving, too. We were all leaving. This moment, this childhood, this home with its patterned plates for Christmas, its American flag on a post by the front door, cheerful Mr. and Mrs. Benson waltzing to "Sweet Caroline" in the kitchen—so ordinary and so precious.

"I don't understand why you're always angry at me," Ursula pleaded.

"I love you."

"I didn't do that to you."

"I know."

Scotch waddled into the room, let out a piercing bark, and then laid his head on Ursula's knee. She patted him absently, her eyes fixed on me. "Is this the end, Triinu?"

"That's what high school is all about, right?" I didn't look at her. I only looked at Scotch's baleful eyes. "It's standardized testing and finding someone to crush your heart into a million little pieces."

"I'm sorry."

"And then it's ending everything. Leaving everything."

Outside, a few flakes of snow gusted across the driveway.

"He would have died," I said, nodding to Scotch. "If you hadn't gone after him."

"Yeah."

"If it had to happen, I'm glad it was you."

"Thanks," Ursula said bitterly.

"No. I mean this." I stood up and crossed the small space between us, then cupped the back of Ursula's wet hair. I breathed in the smell of her shampoo: cotton candy and strawberries. Then I kissed her gently on the lips.

I wanted to tell her what I had suddenly realized, instantly and utterly: that the first kiss held in it the sweet bitterness of the last, and that we were all whole in the mind of God. Even my sorrow was a pinprick in that starry sky, and I would choose her over all others for this, my first heartbreak.

This is Luxembourg.

This is the Loire.

This is Longueville.

This is mine.

Forgive me if I've told you this before.

I drove past the courthouse on my way home. The daylight was waning, and it had started to rain. In the glow of a street lamp, a cluster of shivering protestors held up their signs and waved to the passing cars. "Sin is still sin. God is the final judge," one sign read. Another bore the same sodomy cartoon that Pip Weston had taped to my locker. The words "still wrong" were spray painted across the bottom of the poster. A few of the passing cars honked. I pressed my middle finger to the window as I drove by. The newspapers all said that the Oregon Citizens Alliance was gearing up for the next election. A bigger campaign. A better measure. Critics said the new measure would pass. But for tonight, the protestors stood in the rain, and I was going home.

Wild Dogs and Lesbians

The second semester of senior year started the way all spring semesters had started for me: with the vague hope that somehow everything would have changed and the deeper certainty that it probably had not. Arriving at school, I saw that the front windows were still covered in lurid D.A.R.E. campaign posters, except now they were interspersed with signs encouraging me to vote for my favorite prom court couple. Someone had scrawled "no faggots or dykes allowed" on one of them. I wandered toward my locker. Bobby "Smile If You're Horny" Patch was still occupying my spot in the senior hall, careening in circles with a roadkill-blonde girl on his shoulders. Ben Sprig was still alive, which was a significant disappointment. Principal Pinn's morning announcement still encouraged us to embrace these precious days like they were our last, but when he saw me in the hall at passing time, he stopped me.

"I hope you aren't happy, Triinu. I hope you don't think your people won." He spoke through his big, corn-kernel teeth, a hiss moving through the cornfield. "Because your people never win."

I couldn't say anything. He was the principal. I was a senior. I couldn't risk a black mark on my transcript with college applications due in mere months. I turned away.

"Hey!" He grabbed my shoulder. "I'm talking to you." He leaned in, grinning. It was not a real smile. We both knew that. "Your type never wins, not in the long run." He pointed up at the ceiling, as though a wrathful God might be living behind the sheetrock, waiting to strike me down. "And not if I have anything to say about it."

I sighed. My first class of the new semester was Stream Biology. It was seven thirty in the morning, the sun was barely over the horizon, the principal had just told me I was going to hell, and I had elected to wade in the four-foot-deep creek that bisected the campus, collecting insects and drowning them in ethanol. It was basically the science class for illiterates, but I wanted to keep up my excellent GPA because everyone knew that the colleges checked on students' progress in the second semester to make sure they were "maintaining high academic standards throughout their senior year." With my miserable math skills, physics was out of the question, and I had already taken every language arts class available to me, so Stream Biology it was.

I took my seat in the back of the classroom. At the front of the room, Mr. Otto was chatting with two boys in dirty jeans and John Deere caps, explaining the primitive method of cartography that we would use to survey the creek. His red beard vibrated and his eyes opened wide as he drew an imaginary map in the air before him. The boys leaned in, apparently fascinated.

"Triinu!" Mr. Otto glanced up. "Grab a pair of hip waders from the box in the back. We're getting straight to business today."

I was surprised he knew my name.

I selected a pair of damp rubber waders. They were all about the same size, but some had a few inches of water left in their toes. They were definitely not goth, but I picked the driest pair. When I returned to my seat, Isabel had appeared at my table, her book bag slouching companionably next to mine on the black lab table. "Hey," she said.

"What are you doing here?" I asked. Isabel excelled in math and science.

She shrugged. "I already took AP Physics, AP Chemistry, and AP Biology. It was this or take another term of ceramics."

At the beginning of class, Mr. Otto assigned teams. Like always, the teams were fixed. There was no escape. "You *have* to get along with these people, whether you like them or not," Mr. Otto said. "Because that's what you're going to do when you graduate and get a real job."

He put me in a group with popular Tori Schmidt, a football player named Ted Grispy, and a boy named Mic Godwin. Then he winked at Isabel and me and said, "Let's add Miss Avila to that group, too." Isabel and I cast each other a questioning glance. Teachers never let students work with their friends.

"Spend some time getting to know each other," Mr. Otto said. "You've got a job to do, and you need to know your team." The other three joined our group.

"Want to see what I can do?" Mic said. Without waiting for an answer, he took his hand and bent it back at a sickening angle until it touched his arm. Then he let it snap back into place.

Tori squealed, "Oh my Gawd. Gag me!"

Mic and Ted leered at Tori. She had gained weight over the last year, and her breasts now swelled her sweater to extravagant proportions. "Monster knockers," Ted drawled.

Tori smacked her gum. "You guys are so dumb."

"Monster frickin' knockers," Ted shot back.

"You know, Ted," I started, "the phrase 'monster knockers' is incredibly demeaning to women ..."

Isabel rolled her eyes. "Losing battle, Triinu," she said. "You can't educate the apes."

"Monster Knockers doesn't care, do you, Monster?" Ted said.

Tori smiled tightly and rolled her eyes, as if to say "yes" and "no" simultaneously.

"It doesn't matter," I began, "Whether or not Tori is offended. It offends everyone. You say 'monster knockers' and that puts Tori down, that puts me down, that ..."

"Dude, you're such a feminazi," Ted said. "All I said was monster knockers. I didn't kill anyone."

Mic added, "Triinu should go to some girls' school like Smith College."

"Dude," Ted said. "I want to go to a girls' school and see a bunch of knockers."

"Heh heh. He said 'knockers.'" Mic did a quick Beavis and Butt-Head impersonation to keep the conversation on track. He then insinuated a finger behind his Adam's apple and showed Tori how he could waggle it back and forth beneath the skin.

Mr. Otto had given our team the creek quadrant closest to the road. In our section, the creek deepened before plunging into the culvert and disappearing into the adjacent wetlands. Isabel and I bragged that it was the only section where you could actually drown your teammates if you tried hard enough. We didn't, though.

One day Ted called Mic a "fudge-packing faggot," and I thought about plunging into the creek and knocking him down, but before I could process the whole scene in my mind, Mr. Otto appeared out of nowhere, his red beard bristling.

"Ted! Over here!" Ted waded out of the creek, and Mr. Otto hauled him by the arm until they were several paces away on the sidewalk above the small ravine. We couldn't hear their conversation, but Mr. Otto's face got redder, and Ted's broad shoulders slumped forward.

Eventually Principal Pinn caught sight of them and intervened. Mr. Otto sent Ted back to our group, but Mr. Otto and the principal stood on the sidewalk by the creek for a long time after that.

I thought I heard Principal Pinn say, "That girl ..." and point to me.

Mr. Otto said, "… a campus free from bullying."

"… those people!"

"Civil discourse …"

Their voices lowered. I saw the principal gesture angrily, like a boxer moving in for a punch. We all watched them. Finally, Mic asked Ted, "What was that all about?"

"He told me not to say 'faggots.'"

I was waiting for him to laugh and say, "Psych! He said I should say 'sodomite.' You have to call things by their scientific names," but he didn't.

"Otto said 'faggots' is the word for a bundle of sticks. They used to burn gays like witches, and the sticks they used to set the fires were faggots," Ted added.

"Dang," Mic said. "Heavy."

"I know. I told him it was just a word."

"Like 'nads,'" Mic said.

Ted imitated the Beavis and Butt-Head laugh. "Heh heh. He said ''nads.'"

"Is 'nigger' just a word?" Isabel interjected.

We all looked at her. No one at our all-white high school said the N-word.

"No." Ted hung his head.

"That's what I thought," Isabel said.

On the sidewalk above the creek basin, Principal Pinn raised his voice. "I don't like your tone, Mr. Otto."

"Listen to me right now, Rick. I will not back down. Not on this, not on any of your so-called 'morality initiatives.' There is no place for that kind of intolerance in this school."

"You don't understand the issue!" Principal Pinn shot back. "I think—"

Mr. Otto interrupted. "*I* think I have a class to teach, and *I* think that is more important than listening to your vitriol!"

254

Ted and Mic didn't use the word "faggot" after that. I doubted that they cared about gay rights, but we all saw the battle line drawn between Principal Pinn and Mr. Otto. In that war, we wanted to be on Mr. Otto's side.

We all grew a little kinder after that, too. Tori slipped on the muddy bank of the creek, and Ted cried, "Careful!" Mic stumbled in the sway of the water, and Isabel caught his arm. I plunged into the creek with an insect net and a pocket full of sample jars, and Mic came in with me to make sure I didn't fall. Meanwhile, Isabel, Ted, and Mic kept up a steady patter of Beavis and Butt-Head impressions that got funnier and funnier as the term went along.

When we weren't giggling over the word "balls," we talked mostly about college applications. One morning, while Isabel, Ted, and Tori were outside surveying the creek, Mic and I returned to the relative warmth of the lab to count insects in a jar. "So, you done with college apps?" he asked.

I pinched a tiny flea out of the water and placed it on a microscope slide. "I'm trying to decide between Reed and Lewis and Clark." Ever since I took the SATs, I had been deluged with college viewbooks, and, in truth, I could make little sense of them. They were like Ursula's European photographs, everything sunlit, everyone smiling, every school nestled in the foothills of Vermont's most beautiful mountain range.

"You applying to OSU or U of O or both?" Mic asked, still staring into the microscope.

I could not go to a state school. If the OCA got another measure on the ballot, and if it passed, they would ban gays from public universities. They had promised "no state funds for homosexuals."

"The state schools are lame," I said.

"Reed College has wild dogs," Mic said, skewering a beetle

and dropping it in a dish labeled "Misc. Beetles." He added, "There's a big pack of them and they run around the campus at night. You want to go there?"

"Are they dangerous?" I asked, tallying another beetle on our spreadsheet.

"No ..." Mic said slowly. "But people do a lot of drugs at Reed, so every once in a while someone overdoses and freaks out and the dogs chase 'em." He poked a pin under the wing of the beetle. "It doesn't happen a lot. But you know, I totally think you should go to some chick school like Smith. Seriously. You don't want to end up at a school with a bunch of guys like Grispy."

That evening I compared Reed's viewbook to Lewis and Clark's. Both schools were in Portland. From the viewbooks, it appeared that both schools were entirely populated by handsome men waving lacrosse sticks and pretty girls leaning over microscopes. I pondered: all else being equal, would I prefer wild dogs?

I liked them in concept. At rest, they would be silent, shadowy hummocks on the lawn, but when the nervous drug addict freaked out, as Mic put it, they would explode out of the darkness. A dense pack, purple lips slavering, spotted tongues lolling over ravening teeth. I could almost hear them breathing as I crossed the moonlit campus. I wasn't a drug addict, but what if I got in their way? Stumbled and fell too close to a friend like Pru-Ann, whose anxious smoking would surely smell like blood in their nostrils?

Blissfully free of wild dogs, Lewis and Clark seemed like a perfect fit. It had an English program, pretty girls with microscopes, and a reflecting pool. I had made my choice, and I set about dreaming.

It was the same daydream every time: in bed, on long walks

through the forest, in math class, and in biology, staring up at the rain until one of my teammates yelled for me to pass them the string. In some ways, it was the same daydream I had been dreaming since I was a little girl. "The gathering-in game," I had called it when I was little.

Before kindergarten, when I had no place in the world of things that must be done, I loved the gathering-in game most of all. I had a cardboard barn assembled from a kit. I set it on the living room carpet and populated it with a collection of plastic pigs. The pigs were safe in the barn, but they would stray into the wilderness of the carpet, and there they were threatened by an eclipse.

I had seen a solar eclipse when I was a child. Aware of the rarity of the phenomenon, my father had driven us to a place where we could witness it. He parked the car on the gravel shoulder of a country road. We stepped out as around us the day cooled, darkened, and grew windy. Suddenly night swooped down on us from behind the hills. I would have thought the world was ending had it not been for the calm presence of my father.

Playing my game back at home, I waved my hands over the pigs. "There's an eclipse!" Then I marched the pigs back to the barn. "Hurry, hurry. Come in. Come home." They gathered in a warm cluster, far from the barn's windows. "And they're all safe!" I cried.

That was the game. I played for hours.

The toys changed as I grew up; the pig farm was replaced by the Fisher-Price village, which in turn became the My Little Pony stable. The threat changed too, but that wasn't important. It was the gathering in that mattered: the warm barn, the safe village, the tidy stable, my mother, father, and I sitting before a fire while it rained outside. Come in. Come home. There was always room inside.

My game hadn't changed much by the time I sent away for my Lewis and Clark application. In sumptuous daydreams I imagined myself sitting on my bed in my dorm room late at night, waiting for my roommate to come back. In my dreams, she was in love with me, and I loved her too. But she didn't know that. She didn't know that I was gay. She didn't know that anyone else was besides her. She thought she was the only one to have experienced that strange unfurling of affection. Tormented by her secret love, she fled into the rainy night. She was lucky I hadn't picked Reed; otherwise, she would have had the wild dogs to contend with.

Eventually, soaked and exhausted, the roommate returned, her clothing wet, her cropped hair pressed to her forehead. "What's wrong?" I would ask. Then I would put my arms around her. I had not held enough girls to give much thought to how her body felt beneath my touch. Lean, angular, soft, or plump—it didn't really matter. It was less a romance, more an allegory. My arms were the opening doors of the barn.

"You'll hate me," she whispered. "I can't tell you." She always did, though, and every night I fell asleep dreaming of our requited love.

I could reimagine the scene for hours, but it was no more real than the shadowy threats that punctuated the lives of my plastic pigs. Only the paper that I printed my college application on was real. The rest was pure fantasy, so why not believe in wild dogs? Why not literary agents begging to publish my half-baked poems? Why not a college where the perfect woman was waiting for me?

I gathered the requisite letters of recommendation, joined

the yearbook staff so that I could brag about at least one extracurricular activity, and applied to Lewis and Clark. I wrote my application essay about how Vanaema Emi had shaped my view of the world.

I visited her nursing home, wincing at the smell of urine, and read the essay to her, although her chin rested on her chest and her eyes remained closed. "Do you think I'll get in?" I touched her hand. "Emi?"

She looked up, blurry eyed. "Zees are zee old people," she said, waving vaguely in the direction of the other residents.

"I know," I said.

"You're a good girl," Emi said. Then her chin drifted down again, and she was asleep.

A month later, I received an early acceptance to Lewis and Clark, contingent on my final grades, which I had secured by taking easy classes like Stream Biology.

However, the topic of college applications did not go away with my acceptance to Lewis and Clark. Every day in Stream Biology our group discussed the options. To my surprise, Tori had received early admittance into UC Berkeley. Ted had listed Lewis and Clark as his backup school. Mic had applied to several schools in Germany.

"Triinu's so smart, she could go anywhere," Isabel boasted to the group.

A faint blush rose in my cheeks. "Not really! You're the genius, with all of your AP classes."

"You really should look outside Oregon, Triinu," Mic chimed in. Ted and Tori nodded, as though this was something they had considered carefully.

"I might," I said, just to sound worldly. "After all, who wants to stay in Oregon?"

"Where else have you looked?" Isabel asked.

I searched through my memory. Where else had I considered? Harvard, Stanford, and Yale were too obvious. Everyone who lied about their college application said Harvard, Stanford, or Yale. In a flash of innovation, I thought, *Monster knockers*.

"I'm looking into Smith College," I said.

"That's great." Isabel said, punching me on the shoulder. "You're too good for Oregon. You should totally go there. If you go to Smith, and I go to UMass, we could visit on the weekends."

I had no intention of going to Smith, but people kept asking me where I was applying, and after that class I kept adding Smith to the list of schools. Eventually, I realized I would have to actually fill out the application or start telling people that I had been rejected.

"I don't really want to go," I told my mother as I sat at her electric typewriter and slowly typed my name onto the application. "But I'd like to see if I could get in."

Later, I received a letter from Smith College inviting me to set up an interview with an alumna in Portland.

The morning of my interview, I donned a long brown coatdress. Twenty-three tiny buttons ran the length of its well-ordered front; dressing that morning, I unbuttoned and rebuttoned every one. The formality of the occasion seemed to demand the effort. Then I fixed my makeup: pale, but not overly gothic. I gathered my purse, the directions my father had written for me, a sheaf of my poetry (love, loneliness, death, and fog), and the keys to the Blue Bird of Happiness and set off.

In Portland, the Smith College alumna took me to a restaurant in Old Town where each table occupied its own alcove and the walls were covered in velvet. The carpet on the floor and the fabric on the walls seemed to suck up noise. It was so quiet, as though the diners were whispering into woolen collars. I dropped a lump of sugar into my cup of Earl Grey tea. The clink of my spoon against the porcelain cup sounded sharp in the hush. I put the spoon down and rested my hands in my lap.

"The first time you considered Smith," the alumna asked, taking a sip from her teacup, "What inspired your interest?"

Monster knockers.

I said something intelligible about small classes and the feminist environment.

The woman nodded and reviewed a note in her small planner. "What do you hope to bring to the college?

"I would like to be a writer," I said. "I think I'm one of the best writers in my class. Of course, last week a boy in my class wrote a poem called 'Ode to Gatorade.' Not much competition there." The alumna nodded and made a note in her book. I wondered if I shouldn't have joked. I sat up straighter. "I brought you a poem." I handed her a piece of paper.

> Where my home is, the coyotes are singing about God
> because they have seen the galaxy frozen
> in the dark absolute of space.
> They have hung their fear on that sharp wheel
> and they have only songs now.

"Are you interested in conservation?" The alumna held a silver tray of shortbread toward me.

"Yes," I said, taking a cookie. "I am interested in conservation." I wasn't sure if I was or not, but I nibbled on my shortbread and told her about my mother's Sierra Club membership.

We carried on like this for a long time. My tea grew cold.

Through a small opening in the curtain that covered the front window, I could see that it was growing dark. I was used to adults fawning over me. I wasn't sure what to make of the alumna's calm questioning and her conservative suit.

Finally, she asked if I had any questions.

"No," I said. "Thank you." The check had come and gone and alumna's credit card slip rested, unsigned, between us. I straightened my shoulders and put my purse in my lap. "It was wonderful to meet you," I said. "Thank you for taking the time."

"There is something I would like to tell you," the alumna said. "I know you are genuinely interested in Smith College, and I'm not saying this to discourage you at all, but I think it's import-ant that you know." She lowered her voice. "There are a lot of wonderful things about the college, and there are also …" She folded her hands and tilted her head and looked up, as though searching for a phrase as proper as the last uneaten shortbread on the plate before us. "There are a lot of homosexual women at Smith College." She pronounced "homosexual" like three separate words—ho, mo, sexual—each one distasteful in its own unique way. "Like I said, I don't want to discourage you, but it's something you must be aware of."

I put my spoon in my cup and stirred the last bit of sugar. "That's good to know."

As I stepped out onto the Portland street, I knew I had to go to Smith. I would die if I did not get in.

That spring, Aaron and Chloe returned from their first year at Swarthmore College. They regaled me with stories from the East Coast. "It's wonderful," Aaron said, deftly cutting into the burrito he had ordered at the Beanery. "You can go anywhere. Just get on a train at some depot, and the next thing you know you're in Philadelphia, you're in New York, you're in Boston."

"What's it like? What do you do?" I asked.

"We live in a house called the Butcher Shop." Chloe chuckled.

"The Butcher Shop?"

"It's above a deli." Aaron hooked his long arms behind him, the fabric of his Joy Division T-shirt tightening across his chest as he stretched. "They always rent the apartment to students. Sometimes we take the school shuttle home from parties. You'd love it. The gay and lesbian group throws the best parties. Vodka martinis and dancing until two in the morning. Afterwards, we just flag down the shuttle and say, 'Take me to the Butcher Shop.'"

"And they know where that is?"

"Everyone does." Chloe brushed a bit of hair behind one ear. She had dyed her hair blue and matched it to a blue corset. We had passed Ursula on our way into the Beanery that evening. She had shot the corset a disapproving look and me a sad smile. Then she had disappeared with Jason Price.

"So are you going to Smith?" Aaron asked.

"Oh! Yes," I said. "I am. I mean I want to … if I get in."

"You'll get in," he said with the confidence of a real college student. "It's the perfect school for you."

Isabel said the same thing a week later. She caught me in the hall before Stream Biology. I leaned up against my locker, only half awake at seven in the morning, waiting for my class, waiting for my life to begin. She handed me a copy of one of her mother's local news magazines. On the cover the headline read, "Lesbians: If Not Oregon, Then Where?"

"Look, look!" she said. She opened to the main article. "Read this."

I took the magazine out of her hands. The magazine was printed in color on thin paper. The colors were slightly offset, so the red and the blue did not fully overlap, making it look like a 3-D poster. Mrs. Avila's house had always been littered with such publications, but I had never paid attention until now.

I read, "While many lesbians are determined to stay in Oregon to fight the Oregon Citizens Alliance, others seek more hospitable communities elsewhere. There is a place where lesbian mothers run the PTA, lesbian doctors staff the local clinic, and lesbian teens have their own prom. Lesbians have a promised land: it's Northampton, Massachusetts."

"That's where Smith is," Isabel said. "Now you have to go!"

I stared at the page. The photograph showed a street with little cafés, a bookstore, and a row of trees, leafy and sunlit. There was a place where lesbians went, and it looked a lot like home.

Later that day, Principal Pinn found me sitting by my locker. "Get up," he said.

Reluctantly I rose.

"Shouldn't you be in class?"

I didn't have class directly after lunch, and seniors were not required to spend their free periods in the study hall. "I'm just reading," I said.

He stepped closer. "The guidance office got your transcript request."

"That's good, right?" I grumbled. "They're always telling us to get our requests in early."

On the lapel of his jacket, he wore three small enamel pins: a cross, an American flag, and a football helmet bearing our school colors. "You think you're going to go to some highfalutin college?" Something in his voice reminded me of Pip Weston's singsong taunts.

I wanted to pull the pins out of his jacket and stick them in his eyes. Everyone at the school was going to some "highfalutin" college. That was the whole reason I had applied to Smith: peer pressure.

"You think they're going to pick you? Out of all these kids? Because let me tell you, they don't want your type."

I was tempted to tell him that Smith College had already admitted "my type" whether they wanted to or not. Instead, I stared at the pins. "I guess they can decide that for themselves," I mumbled finally.

Farther down the hall, a gaggle of freshman girls exploded out of the bathroom, giggling. One of them—I thought her name might be Cammie or Carrie—paused for a moment and watched us. I felt like a traffic accident. Everyone wanted to look and be glad they weren't the one being interrogated by Principal Pinn.

"Is that all?" I asked in a loud voice. "Can I go now?" I had nowhere to go except away, but that was good enough.

"No, it's not," Principal Pinn said. He smelled sweaty and stale, like something that had stayed in the refrigerator for too long. He leaned in even closer. "You better remember, young lady, I hold your transcripts. I release them. I tell the guidance counselors what to write in those letters of recommendation. I could call that fancy East Coast school and tell them exactly what you are, so you just watch yourself. This year isn't over yet."

"I already got into Lewis and Clark," I shot back, although my heart was pining for that treelined street where women ate at little cafés and bought books and loved each other.

"Don't think anything is set in stone," Principal Pinn said, then turned and strode off down the hallway while the freshman girls giggled about my fate.

I considered calling the Smith College admissions office and telling them that my principal was trying to ruin me. I wasn't a delinquent. I wasn't a Satanist. I wasn't even antisocial.

I wanted them to see me at work in the high school darkroom. I had joined the yearbook staff simply to have an extracurricular to mention in my college applications, but I had been promoted to photo editor, and besides, the other kids in the club respected me. As I bustled about the darkroom, other photographers came up to me with blurry snapshots. I wanted the Smith College admissions board to hear my quick, confident diagnoses. "Use a filter. Crop it below the feet. Let me see your proof sheet. Number ten is a better shot."

No one said, "Hey Triinu, do you like it in here because it's dark? Because you're a lezzie Satanist?" When the photographers sat down together to divide up tasks for the rest of the year, I agreed to take the senior prom. No one said, "Yeah, what else is she gonna do? Get a date?"

After the meeting, one of the younger photographers bounded up to me and breathed, "Thank you!" Her hair bounced in a ponytail on top of her head. "I was so afraid I'd have to wear a camera with my dress. I know I'm only a sophomore, but going to the prom with Colin means sooo much to me."

"It's no problem." I held up my hands to stop her from hugging me in excitement. "Prom is no big deal to me. Most of my friends are in college, anyway."

"That's so cool."

I shrugged. "I guess."

"God, you're lucky," the girl sighed. "And I'm glad you're taking the pictures. I know they're going to come out beautiful. Will you take a picture of me and Colin? Please?"

"I'll see what I can do," I said, although I wasn't sure she would like the pictures I planned on taking.

Tiresias at Prom

I studied the previous prom pictures housed in the yearbook archives. Only the hair changed, getting bigger or longer depending on the era, yet remaining consistently hideous—it was like nature had dictated that the more effort a girl put into her hair, the more she would look like a fancy dog. Two decades of guys placed their hands on the shoulders of two hundred matching girlfriends, each skewered with a sprig of baby's breath.

I wanted to immortalize the real prom. I would capture the sweat stains, the couples dry humping in the hall, the girls crying in the bathroom. I would give them a few beautiful moments: the developmentally disabled kids holding each other on the dance floor, a lone girl returning to her car with her dress trailing across the parking lot. But I would also show them Ben Sprig hocking a gnarly fuckin' loogie while attempting a ridiculous, groin-pumping dance.

I spent a lot of time planning all these photographs in my mind so I wouldn't have to admit that I, too, wanted something to mark this rite of passage, to make it mine. I would never get a date; I didn't even have any friends who were going to prom. Chloe and Aaron were in college. Pru-Ann was now in a teen rehabilitation camp in eastern Oregon. Ava was a globe away—did they even have prom in sixth form? I had disowned Ursula, not that she would have gone with me anyway. And I could not simply ask a pretty classmate the way the boys did.

Isabel said it didn't matter.

"My mom says prom is a 'capitalist trope,' anyway," she said. "It was probably invented by Hallmark." She chewed her lip, meditatively staring out of the window of American Dream Pizza. "Molotov Squid is going to play at a bar in Salem, and then we're all going camping. Greg said we're going to go someplace outside Eugene. There are hot springs. It's like a big, hot bucket of mud. You get in there naked with whatever creepy dudes are hanging out that night. I mean, if you want to memorialize high school, *that* is the way to do it."

I agreed.

"You should come. We won't make out in front of you like Ursula did. Greg's not that kind of guy. It'll be fun, and if it sucks we can sneak off and find some all-night diner and go in all covered in mud."

It was a nice invitation, but I declined. Just because I didn't want a boy to put his tongue in my mouth did not mean I was immune to the power of prom.

I found what I was looking for at the Goodwill. I hadn't meant to wander into the men's department, but it was Saturday afternoon and the day stretched on with nothing to do and nowhere to go. I leafed through the trousers, shirts, and sweaters, paying little attention. Then a shimmer of gray caught my eye. It was a three-piece suit with an Italian label, neatly pressed, barely worn. The fabric was almost incandescent, almost alive. I hurried to the dressing room and tried it on. It must have belonged to a tiny, narrow man, because it was a perfect fit for me.

I marveled at the woman before me in the mirror.

The only lesbians I knew were the staff of WomynScript, and they all seemed to be fashioned along the same model, a kind of woman farmer: baggy overalls, political T-shirts, and thick woolen socks peeking out of Birkenstocks. I had the vague sense that this was the only correct way to be a lesbian, an opinion supported by the latest release from WomynScript.

I had proofread several pages of the manuscript in which the author decried "the butch-femme paradigm." The author called it an *"oppressive construction that lures homosexual woman into heteronormative gender stereotypes, thus affirming the very system that excludes them."* Looking at my reflection in the mirror, I understood why that writer hated the idea of butches and femmes. She hated it for the same reason I hated prom, because despite everything we understood, both were still wonderful.

I held my hair back as I stared at the mirror. The woman before me was more than beautiful. At one glance, she was an antique photograph from a time when children grew up fast and men were as slim as the suit because their lives were hard. Look again and she was still ten years old, from an age before gender differentiated like cells dividing. I remembered that age, being half feral astride an imaginary horse, racing along the edges of the world.

I thought of my father stealing away to a dance in another town.

I thought of the Estonians, photographed in the refugee camps, still wearing their suits and their battered hats.

I was then, and I was now, and I was as big as the sky.

On the night of the prom, I accosted my father in the vanity and asked him to help me tie a tie.

"You're going to prom dressed like that? Oh, Triinu," he said.

"I'm dressed like a reporter," I said. I held up the old Leica camera that had belonged to my Uncle Paulus.

He grimaced. "Don't show your mother."

"Come on, Dad. It's just prom. It's a capitalist trope."

"She'll worry if she knows you've gone out dressed like that."

"Why?" Despite the adolescent whine that lifted my voice, I knew.

We looked at each other in the mirror. My tall, lean father. Me in the beautiful gray suit. We could have been father and son. We could have been the same man in two photographs, forty years apart. But we were father and daughter.

"It's not safe to be so obvious about things."

"Things?" I spat. I wasn't mad at him. I just didn't know how to tell him that I understood what he was saying. I had stared at the trailer shot full of holes. I had stood on the driveway along which the bodies of the two gay men had been carried. And prom still mattered to me. I wanted to go, and I had to go in that suit. I knew how foolish it would sound to my father, a man who had skipped all his graduations and eloped without a wedding.

"It means something because it's a symbol," I said.

"I thought it was a capitalist trope."

I ignored him. "It's like confirmation. You remember how you made me get confirmed?"

"That was your mother."

"But it meant more to her than what it was." I persisted. "Remember how we fought about it? That wasn't about me standing in a particular room in a particular church for two minutes wearing a dress she liked. That wasn't what confirmation was about."

I was ready to go on, but my father took the tie from my hand. He looped his long arms around me. "I understand." He held me in a loose embrace as he demonstrated the tie. "Go over. Around once. Around half more. Tuck and fold." He straightened the knot and released me. "I think you'll be fine, but call me if you need anything, and just … slip out before your mother sees you. She doesn't know that tonight is the prom."

What more can our parents do when we are so bent on our own designs?

He paused and looked at my reflection in the mirror. "You look like Paulus," he said, but I could not tell if he was proud or frightened.

Twenty minutes later, I parked the Blue Bird of Happiness in the school lot. Around me the pale daylight was fading to indigo. In the open fields behind the school, a few bales of hay crested over a sea of new grass like the shadows of whales. I could smell farmland and hear the creek rushing into the culvert in my Stream Biology quadrant.

I marched into the battlement of the school, my camera raised like a fighting arm. There I was: the only dyke in the Grass Seed Capital of the World—at least the only one under fifty. I was a gender warrior, a butch, a king. A man with the body of a girl, a girl with the feet of a mountain lion. My camera was the clear eye of reason in a world of conformists, but what I saw made me pause.

The janitors had swept the courtyard free of crushed French fries. They had swabbed the pale cement to a silver perfection. Parent volunteers had laid a path of lanterns from the far end of the quad, across its smooth surface, and into the dance. It looked like a temple. Not a temple to the Christian God, but a minor demigod: the god of suspended disbelief, the god of harmless regrets.

Ahead of me I saw Ted Grispy in a dark blue tuxedo. Held as tentatively as a rare bird in his meat patty of a hand were the tips of Tori Schmidt's fingers. They glided up the stairs and toward the glowing doors of the cafeteria. I lifted my camera and took a picture. I caught a faint whiff of marijuana. Then I heard someone say, "Not here, man. We'll party afterwards. This is the girls' big night. Don't be fucked up."

Inside, the lunchroom had been decorated with candles, white tablecloths, and a banner reading, "The Glow of

Enchantment Prom 1993. Remember This Night Forever." An innocuous love song hung in the air. Plump, cheery-faced Julie Cotswold turned an elegant circle beneath the arm of her date. Mic Godwin bowed in front of a girl with daisies in her hair and asked, "May I have this dance?"

The girls fixing their makeup in the bathroom looked pretty. No one was crying. No one was ripping off fake fingernails, tossing them in the industrial-grade sink, and sobbing, "I don't know why I even try." The girls parted to allow me in. They watched me out of the corners of their eyes and smiled shyly as I took a picture of their reflections.

As they left the bathroom, they complimented each other tenderly.

"That chignon turned out very well."

"Maybe next time I'll put flowers in it."

But there wouldn't be a next time. They must have known that. We had been raised on *Pretty in Pink*. We knew—hate it or love it—there was only one senior prom.

So, despite myself, I was grateful when several hours later, Brent Macintosh tapped me on the shoulder. "You want to dance?"

I did want to dance. It was June. A hundred parents had conspired to make this the night upon which we hung our nostalgia. Brent led me to the middle of the dance floor and steered me gently around in a circular motion that passed for dancing.

"Did you get some good pictures?" he asked the air behind my head.

"The lighting is a little tricky."

"How do you remember all those dials? I took photo class. I could never focus."

"Sometimes you don't need to focus," I said, although I prided myself on my sharp pictures.

"Really?"

I hadn't thought about it, but I said, "Sometimes the good pictures aren't the *good* pictures. Sometimes it's what's in the corner of a bad picture that you really care about."

"That's kind of deep."

I warmed to the topic. "Take the prom pictures, for example. I looked at twenty years of prom pictures, and they all looked the same. Boy, girl, dress, tuxedo, flowers, bad hair. And you know what?" As if to prove my point, the music cut into a rendition of "Save the Last Dance for Me." "You couldn't tell them apart. I mean, I presume they weren't all clones from some alien planet sent to brainwash us. Some of those people must have had real personalities …"

I was feeling very clever, discoursing on the aesthetics of prom photography, so it took me a moment to notice that Brent had stopped circumnavigating the cafeteria floor. His arms had stiffened. His shuffle had lost its fluidity.

"This isn't the last dance, is it?" he asked.

"I don't know. They're playing that stupid 'Save the Last Dance' song."

He stopped moving entirely, looking anxiously around the cafeteria. "It's really the last dance? I thought they announced the last dance. I thought they always announced the last dance before it began."

A girl stood on the side of the dance floor, her neck like a swan's, as she watched Brent.

"There's someone you should be dancing with, isn't there?" I asked.

"I … yeah … kind of."

"You had better go find her."

"I'm sorry," he mumbled as he rushed off, leaving me alone in the middle of the dance floor, trapped in a maze of tender embraces.

Ted and Tori floated past me, like Beauty and the Beast twirling gracefully on top of a music box. To my left, the sophomore photographer clasped a chubby boy, presumably Colin, while he stroked one stray curl of her hair like a child comforting itself to sleep.

Bobby Patch was not dancing with any of the bleach-blondes who persistently climbed on his shoulders. He danced with Crystal, the girl who had been so badly burned in a house fire when we were just children. She stood very straight and very gracefully. Bobby placed his hand on her back above the drape of her dress, and they danced.

In the distance, haloed by a net of white Christmas lights, I glimpsed a girl resting her head on Ben Sprig's shoulder, apparently insensitive to the fact that it was he—not I—who was Satan.

There was nothing to do but walk off the dance floor, obvious and ashamed. At the City Nightclub, even walking was a kind of dance, and the lines between the dancers and the watchers and the dreamers were tenuous. Here, there were winners and losers.

I caught the eye of another loser, a girl sitting alone at a circular table, a red rose pinned to her dress. It was the girl who had watched Principal Pinn interrogate me. I suddenly remembered her name: Carrie. I recognized her from the halls. A freshman. I wondered which upperclassman had invited her to prom and then left her, conspicuous and alone in her fluffy black dress. Although she was arguably a greater loser than I—at least I was a senior—she stared at me with disbelief in her wide eyes. Her mouth formed a shocked O.

"What?" I mouthed as I walked past her.

"Nothing," she whispered, but she kept staring.

I stopped and stood in front of her, looking down on her.

All of the Pro-9 literature painted homosexuals as preda-tors; I could see their warnings reflected in her dark eyes. She thought I was going to drag her behind the gymnasium. She thought I was going to leap on top of her in a fit of lust and perform unspeakable acts. I would probably pee on her.

"You've never seen a girl wearing a suit before?"

The girl shook her head.

"You want to dance?" I sneered, waiting for her to tear up or flee.

I stuck my hand out. A threat. I knew she would be humili-ated. All her friends would talk about it. She would be suspect just because I had looked at her. "Why'd that girl pick Carrie?" they would ask each other behind her back. "Why wasn't Carrie dancing with a boy?"

Carrie's version of Pip Weston would call her a dyke. She would hope that he'd forget the incident over the summer, but at the start of her sophomore year, he'd be waiting for her out-side the bathroom. "You eat any pussy this summer? You gonna go to any lezzie dances?"

I didn't really hate her, but she was there.

I left my hand out, so everyone could see. "Well?" I said. "You scared? It's just a dance."

Then very slowly, she lifted her hand from her lap, and she rested the tips of her fingers in my palm. She smiled, and it was not horror that filled her eyes. It was awe. For a moment, I had no idea what to do. Then I closed my hand, very gently around hers, and lifted her to her feet. "Would you like to dance?" I asked again, gently this time. "For real?"

"I was hoping you would ask me," the girl said and blushed to match her rose corsage.

It seemed as though the room expanded as we walked toward the dance floor. The straight couples swayed in their mismatched pairs: boy, girl, boy, girl. A few people whispered. One girl pulled her boyfriend aside. I wasn't sure if I dared move into the center of the dancers, but I felt exposed on the edge where everyone could see us. The girl tightened her grip on my hand. I could not turn back now. What if I was her Deidre Thom?

I placed a hand on the back of her dress. She was sweating through her crinoline, but it was a sweet dampness that spoke of summer. Her perfume smelled like violets. She looked up at me. "I … I watched you all year," she whispered. "How do you do it? I mean, for *four years*."

Looking at her now, I saw something familiar behind the baby-fat cheeks and the pink makeup. A hardness. A story. I knew what she was asking.

"You just do."

I wanted to say more. I wanted to tell her that there would be an Ursula Benson to break her heart, and that that was still better than being Ben Sprig's girlfriend. I wanted to tell her that Ava had touched me, and that God had been in our bed, no matter what anyone said. And I wanted to tell her how Isabel had rescued me again and again without my even noticing, and that she had a friend like that, too. Probably.

Suddenly, I felt a hand clamp down on my shoulder. For a second, I thought it was a boy, perhaps the girl's date who had come to cut in on the dance. I turned. Principal Pinn's face was inches from mine.

"I've had about enough of you," he said. "This behavior is unacceptable." A fleck of spit hit my face.

The girl dropped my hand. Principal Pinn eyed her. "Did she force you?" he asked.

The girl shook her head.

"Well, you'd better rethink your answer before I call your

parents and tell them what you were doing." He looked back at me. "Her father is on the school board!"

"It was just a dance," I stammered. "I'm on yearbook."

"I don't care what you're on." He tightened his grip on my shoulder. "Come this way, Hoffman."

I kind of liked the way it sounded: Hoffman. Not Triinu, not Triinu-Wiinu, not even Katariina, but *Hoffman*.

"Why?" I shrugged out of his grasp.

"Because I've had enough of this filth," Principal Pinn hissed in my ear. "You're in a room with *normal* kids, *corrupting* them."

The dancers had slowed. Some had stopped with their arms still around each other. Everyone was looking at us.

"I'm not corrupting anything." I pulled away from him.

"Right. That's it. I'm calling your parents, and then we'll settle this once and for all." He grabbed me again. This time his grasp was inescapable. He marched me down the nearest hallway, unlocked an empty classroom, and pushed me in. It was the biology lab; I couldn't help but think back to junior year and remember the look on Pip's face as he sliced into the frog he was dissecting. I heard the door lock as Principal Pinn closed me in.

There was a lot to think about locked in a biology lab, after hours, with only pinned, pickled, and taxidermied animals for company. It was almost midnight. Ursula would be riding home with her date. He would probably kiss her, and she would kiss him back. It was prom night. That's what a girl did.

Someone would lose their virginity tonight.

Someone would get pregnant.

Someone would have the night of their life, which was sad, too, because prom was nothing more than the cafeteria lit by tea lights, made special by the sense that it was all suddenly over.

I took out my camera and snapped a few photographs of the stuffed owl.

Smith College was still deliberating over my application. If I got suspended, Principal Pinn would definitely call them. I had read in the viewbook that Smith received thousands of applications every year but accepted only a small fraction of the most talented and upstanding. I thought of the Smith alumna I had met for coffee. *There are a lot of wonderful things about the college, and there are also a lot of homosexual women.*

I perched on a lab stool and sunk my head in my hands. I wasn't Hoffman the gender warrior anymore. I wished I had a pink sweater to wrap around my chest, or, better yet, the soft yellow blanket from my childhood. I would throw it over my head, and the world would disappear. It was late. I was tired.

I had just wanted this to be my special night, too. I was sick of being bold all alone. I was sick of hating nice things so that it wouldn't matter that they weren't mine. But that was my role in life, and I had wanted to play it in my magical, iridescent suit. In that suit, I could imagine that I was a part of something bigger. In that suit, I could imagine that somewhere there was another girl alone at her prom, dreaming of me. We would meet at the Smith College gates—except that now Principal Pinn was going to call the admissions office and tell them I was a deviant and they wouldn't admit me—and share our prom pictures. She would have said, *"The first time I heard a love story I started looking for you."* In that suit, I could almost taste her kiss.

I sat for a long time. Eventually, the door opened again. Principal Pinn stood before me with a wad of fabric in his hand. He closed the door behind him. "Put it on." He threw the garment at me. It unfurled in my hands, a paisley jumper about six sizes too big.

"No," I said. "Let me out. Let me go home."

"I won't have you walking around this school dressed like a pervert. There are parents out there."

"I'm not going to put this on. It won't even fit me." The jumper looked like it had been sitting in the locker room for a very long time.

"You'll do what I tell you." Suddenly, he lunged at me. I stumbled back against a lab table. He grabbed my suit jacket, ripped it open, sending one of the buttons skittering across the floor. "Take it off!"

"No!"

His fingernails raked my arm as he pulled at the sleeve of the jacket. His face was pinched, his teeth clamped in a snarl. "You will. You fucking will!" He slipped two hot fingers into the front of my shirt and pulled. Another button popped.

"Rape!" I yelled, as Miss Lopez had told us to do if a stranger tried to touch us.

"I wouldn't touch you," Principal Pinn hissed, even though one of his hands was on my arm and the other was ripping at my shirt. "I just want you to be decent."

"You're not decent!" I dropped to my knees and slipped beneath his grasp, leaving the jacket in his hands like a lizard's tail. I was panting.

He picked up the jumper and came after me, one hand raised in a fist. For a moment I thought he was going to hit me. "Come on," I said. "Do it." It would be worth the black eye. It did not matter what I had done; if he struck a student his life would be over.

"Do you think this is funny, Hoffman?" He stepped toward me. I backed up until I felt my back against one of the coolers.

"You wearing that suit! I let it slide, because I didn't want all those liberal parents breathing down my neck about self expression and women's rights. But you went too far with that girl. Carrie Hunter is a good student. She's on JV soccer. She's just a kid, and if you think you can go in there and lure her into your sick little world, if you think I'm going to let some punk kid mess with her …"

I could have pointed out that I was clearly not a punk. Please! Where were my safety pins? Where was the leather jacket, the spikes, the Mohawk? You would think a principal would know the species that lived under his roof. However, I had more important clarifications to make.

"I'm not a punk. I'm a dyke!" I shot back.

Principal Pinn spoke through his big closed teeth. "It's kids like you …"

"There aren't any other kids like me," I said. "Maybe if there were, this school wouldn't suck so much. But when I got a death threat from your precious Pip Weston, you thought it was funny!"

"Pip was a good boy!"

"Pip was a bully and bigot!"

"If you kept your private life private, no one would bother you, but you want to flaunt it."

"I'm just trying to get out of this school before you let my classmates kill me."

"No one is trying to kill you." Principal Pinn looked like he could kill me. I held my ground. He moved closer. "You make me sick," he said.

"I hate you." I felt tears in the back of my throat, but they weren't cool and sad. They were the kind of hot tears that made a quiet Lutheran girl suddenly unafraid to die. "Isn't there something in your job description that says you're not supposed to be an asshole?"

"You don't get special rights, young lady!"

"Young lady, special rights," I mimicked in a singsong voice. "Is that all? Is that all you're afraid of? You're so worried that I might get something you don't have, that I might be happy for two minutes. I'm not even asking you to like me. I just want you to leave me the fuck alone."

Principal Pinn's eyes looked like they might pop right out of his head. He would have to be careful. Mr. Litel might just put them in the cooler and use them for biology class. I glanced at the cooler behind me.

"It's like the frog." It dawned on me in a flash. "And the fetal pig and that stupid lung in a jar. That's what education is to you. You take something that's fine, then you peel the skin off it, cut it up, and have everyone stand around and say how awful it is. But you know what? In a couple of weeks, I won't be here. I'm going somewhere far away, and I'm going to fuck whoever I want, and you're going to be stuck here chaperoning the prom for the rest of your pathetic life."

Principal Pinn's eyes narrowed. His breath was hot on my face. I wondered if I could outrun him.

"Go ahead. Hit me," I said.

Then I heard voices at the door. Principal Pinn stepped back and straightened his tie.

Led by a weary-looking secretary, my parents stood in the green glow of the hallway's security lighting: two sweet, gray-haired people in loose-fitting clothes. They were older than other parents; I saw that now. Their faces showed the terror of a late-night phone call. When the phone rang, there had been a moment—one Pip's mother knew too well—when they thought, *She's been killed.* I read that in my mother's eyes.

"What have you done to her?" My mother's accent grew thick with fear. "You have locked her in a lab! You have torn her clothing?"

My father lunged forward. "If you laid a hand on her—"

"I think you'd better hear what she told me," Principal Pinn said.

"What happened to your shirt?" My mother rushed to my side and enfolded me in her arms.

"Mr. Pinn!" my father exclaimed.

I glanced back and forth between Principal Pinn and my father. My father was a much bigger man. I remembered the story about his childhood bullies: *I realized I was bigger than they were, so I sat on their heads.*

"I don't care what Triinu told you!" I had never heard my father yell before. "I don't care what she did. Why do you have her in here? How long have you ... Triinu, did he touch you?"

"He tried to make me wear a dress," I said.

"Are you going to tell your parents what you told me?" Principal Pinn smirked. He thought he had the ace up his sleeve. "A *dyke*, Mr. Hoffman. That's what she said she was. She wasn't even ashamed. She said she was a ho-mo-sexual."

"Why do you people always have to say it like it's three separate words?" I spat out.

Principal Pinn looked at my father expectantly.

"Are you okay?" My father looked at me.

I nodded, still cradled in my mother's embrace.

"*Really?*"

"Yes."

I could see my father steady himself, release his breath, release his fists.

"Ask her," Principal Pinn said. "She probably doesn't have the decency to lie to you."

"Why *do* you say it like it's three separate words?" my father asked.

Principal Pinn shook his head as though a fly had landed on him. "She's a homosexual. Look at her outfit."

282

"Is there a dress code?" my father asked.

"She was dancing with a girl."

"Well, that will cut down on teen pregnancy, won't it?"

"People were taking photographs, photographs that were supposed to last a lifetime, treasured memories, and there she is, flaunting herself."

My father looked at me. "Principal Pinn thinks you're a lesbian." I thought I caught a wink in my father's eye. "He finds this very shocking."

"It's a sin!" Principal Pinn's face was red. "Don't think that all of a sudden it's okay to act like that just because Measure 9 failed."

"Sweetie." My mother squeezed me tighter.

My father turned to Principal Pinn. "Of course, you will have heard the story of Tiresias."

Principal Pinn shrugged with irritation. "I guess. Did he go here?"

"The stories vary." My father had a sonorous voice, perfect for church readings. Anger made it even deeper. "Some say he lived a hundred years as a man and a hundred years as a woman, and for the wisdom of those years, he was struck blind by the gods."

Principal Pinn's mouth formed the word "What," but no sound came out.

"Of course, the first mention of homosexuality is arguably in the *Symposium*," my father added.

My mother wiped her eye with the back of her hand. "'A handful of such men, fighting side by side, would defeat the whole world.'"

My father glanced at Principal Pinn as if he were an uninspired student. "That was Phaedrus, discussing the love between male soldiers. It's erotic love. Eros is the oldest of the gods and the one without parents. That is why Eros is so powerful. Now, Aristophanes says that we were once two-faced and four-armed. The bodies that held two men were born of the sun, the bodies that held two women of the earth, and the bodies that held a man and a woman of the moon. But now we are cursed by the gods to live separately, and we spend our lives chasing our other half. It is meant to be a comic story."

"But it's so sad." My mother released me and stepped toward Principal Pinn. Her voice shook. "We're supposed to mock Aristophanes, but isn't he the one we all remember?"

I could tell by the shade of crimson spreading across Principal Pinn's cheeks that he did not feel the pathos of the story. "I need to know what you're going to do about her," he said. "She has been blatantly disrespectful and insubordinate …"

"I told him he was going to have to spend the rest of his life chaperoning the prom," I said quietly. "Like Sisyphus. It's his curse."

My father chuckled.

"I could have her expelled," Principal Pinn said. "This is not an acceptable situation. I need to know what you're going to *do*."

"'Make me a willow cabin at your gate,'" my mother said. "'And call upon my soul within the house.'"

"*Twelfth Night*," my father said.

"Full marks, Roger."

"A male actor playing a woman disguised as a man who woos another woman into passionate love," my father added, as if for Principal Pinn's benefit.

A vein had appeared in Principal Pinn's neck, bulging like a fat, red snake. "I realize some families do not share the same values as the rest of this school." He hissed like a snake, too. "But we have expectations. I will not be mocked. I want her out of here. Right now! Take her home and make sure she comes back next week in *decent clothing*."

I suddenly realized that Principal Pinn had lost. He was like the dog owner who yells at his recalcitrant mutt, "Don't sit!" Of course my parents would take me home. They weren't going to leave me locked in the biology lab all night. We weren't going to stage some kind of protest in which we camped out with the stuffed owl, reciting poetry.

"Get her out of here," he said again.

"'Come, I pray thee, now too, and release me from cruel cares,'" my father added, conversationally, as though these phrases just rolled off his tongue.

My mother finished with him, "'And all that my heart desires to accomplish, accomplish thou, and be thyself my ally.'"

"Sappho," I said.

"Wharton's translation," my father said.

"I like Mary Barnard's translation better." I shrugged.

"Of course," my father said. "Wharton is too lush. Barnard is so sparing with her words. She says less, so it's truer." He held out his hand to shake Principal Pinn's hand. "Everyone knows that."

My mother cried on the way home, then hugged me in the foyer of our house, holding me tightly in the soft lamplight.

"I just want you to be safe." She spoke into my hair. "I love you."

My father patted me on the back. "She'll be okay."

When my mother released me, my father took me by the shoulders and turned me toward the light. "Who does she look like, Katariina?"

My mother cocked her head. "I don't know."

My father took the camera I had slung over my shoulder and adjusted it so it hung in front of me. "Now?"

My mother covered her mouth.

"Paulus."

After that, I came out to all my friends. The story was simply too good to keep to myself. I had been locked in a biology lab with Principal Pinn, told him he was a loser and sworn at him, and gotten away with it. For a week, I was the center of every conversation at the Beanery.

The barista gave me a free espresso. "I heard about you," he said. "That was hardcore."

Chloe and Aaron, back from school, both congratulated me on standing up to Pinn. Chloe told me she had been waiting for me to come out so that she could talk to me about Ava, because Ava had written to her about everything. Aaron said the girls at Smith would love me. He just knew it.

Ursula approached me shyly, as I sat surrounded by my friends. "I heard about what happened. I'm glad you're okay," she said, and her downcast eyes were a knock on the door, an invitation that I knew I was not going to answer.

"Yeah," I shrugged. "You know, no biggie."

Then Pru-Ann barged through the door of the coffee shop and past Ursula, knocking her out of the way. "Holy fucking *shit*! I go away for a while and look what happens." Pru-Ann had recently returned from her rehabilitation program. "My little Triinu-Wiinu is all grown up, and you've kissed a girl. Have you gotten laid yet?" Then she told me about a party she had been to the night before where someone drank beer out of a boot.

Isabel lounged in her booth at the Beanery, watching me bask in the glow of my newfound fame. "My mom is so glad you're gay," she said when there was a break in the crowd. "I mean, someone like *my mom* with four heterosexual children! What is she going to tell Camilla? I swear, if my dad was still alive, she'd have another kid just so she'd get a gay one. She'll probably want to have a 'womyn' to 'womyn' talk with you, so

286

be prepared." Isabel pronounced it "Wo-meeen" so that I would hear the "y."

One evening a girl with short, spiky black hair stopped by my table and said, "You're the dyke who told off the principal." Then, before I knew what she was doing, she had slipped into the booth behind me, thrown her arm around my shoulders, and taken our picture with a little point-and-shoot camera. I never saw her again after that, but her visit hinted at another life.

The letter from Smith came a few days later. It was a beautiful Sunday, one of the first unambiguously warm days of the season. After my parents returned from church, we went out to lunch and then took the long way home, admiring everything. The sky was a huge blue, as though God had lifted His dome to make room for the cumulous clouds that drifted above us. On all sides of the car, the grass seed fields glowed. It was like the shoots of grass, first dragged out of the ground in April, had been glutted with light and now released their excess into the cumulative brightness of the day. I wanted to breathe it in until every cell in my body was as clean and deliberate as the air between the green fields, the white-bottomed clouds, and the blue, blue sky. The world was so big and perfect, and I was heading out into it.

We had forgotten to pick up Saturday's mail, so I strolled down the driveway toward the mailbox, dreaming of big skies and grand departures. "I'm going to Smith," I said out loud, and then added, "The prom doesn't even matter to me." I liked the way the phrases slid off my tongue, as certain as if they had been true.

I pictured Tori, Ted, Ben, Colin, and the sophomore photographer all at Smith College. We were at a dance—the last song of the last dance of the year—and their hands were on their cameras. Meanwhile, I swirled across the floor in a tailcoat and a top hat with the girl from my fantasies anchoring me to the ground, lest my happiness lifted me up and carry me into the clouds.

I was so immersed in the fantasy that I took the mail out of the mailbox and shuffled through it once without seeing the letter. It wasn't until I turned to walk back that I glimpsed the envelope peeking out from between catalogues. I withdrew it and traced the Smith College emblem embossed on the left hand corner. It was a very small envelope.

Everyone knew what the small envelope meant. A single sheet of college letterhead reading, "Dear Applicant … regret to inform you … not among those … sincerely …" Accepted students got a big, fat manila envelope stuffed with forms and brochures.

I felt like the sunlight had been let out of the day like air released from a balloon. Principal Pinn had called Smith. It wasn't fair. It wasn't fair that my fantasies, so vivid and inevitable, should culminate in this one, noxious, cream-colored envelope, the result of a single phone call from a man with no more wit or soul than Pip Weston—probably less, since Pip at least had the decency to die young and Principal Pinn would go along ruining high school for generations of students. It was not fair that I had seen the viewbook photographs—the campus hung with lanterns, the buildings garlanded with green ivy—and now would never actually be there. Now that I thought of it, it wasn't fair that I had to spend hours developing prom pictures when the one sweet dance of my high school life lasted barely a minute before being cut short by Principal Pinn. I would never be allowed to dance with anyone but Brent Macintosh, and even Brent wouldn't dance the last dance with me. And neither would Ava. And neither would Ursula, who left me for eleven miserable months and wrote only one postcard. It didn't seem fair. I had written to her so many times that I could price an airmail stamp just by holding the envelope: forty-three cents, fifty-two cents, ninety-eight cents, a dollar ten.

I flipped the envelope over and examined the crisp seam on the back, weighing it in my hand. Three sheets and maybe a small cardstock insert, a little postcard. Twenty-five cents, regular post. A breeze blew through the trees, parting the new leaves, letting another tablespoon of dancing sunlight into the forest. It never took three sheets and a postcard to send a rejection!

I ripped open the envelope and pulled out the letter with shaking hands. It read,

> Dear Ms. Hoffman,
> While the applicant pool this year was highly competitive, your application rose to the top as one of the finest candidates for admission to Smith College. You would make a wonderful addition to our campus. While we expect you will receive many college acceptances, we hope that you choose Smith College for your under-graduate education.

I was in!

What You Carried for Me

I packed with a vengeance.

"I'm not keeping anything," I told Isabel, who was sitting on the foot of my bed, surveying the boxes destined for Goodwill. I wasn't just "going away to college." I was leaving, making my grand exit. Farewell, close the curtains, cut scene. Fuck you, bitches!

"You better have kept the *Corazón Fiel*," she said.

Her Spanish had gotten quite good, and I did not recognize the name through the accent. "The what?"

"Don't tell me you got rid of it."

It clicked into place: the hand-carved model ship from Guatemala. Where was it? I cast my eyes around the room. My shelves were empty. The Goodwill boxes were tightly packed. I had not seen the boat for years. "Of course I still have it," I said.

Isabel's raised eyebrow said, "You better."

Ursula Benson always accused Chloe Lombardi of being boy crazy. But it wasn't Chloe who was boy crazy; it was me. I wasn't crazy about boys, of course, but I was crazy for love. There was something about the pang of romance that made me feel closer to God. Perhaps it was all that poetry, or the secret of being gay, or the dearth of people saying, "Oh, snap out of it. Let's get a burger." I thought no one had loved before me. I thought love was a sacred fire I kindled with my tragedies. I was its acolyte, and my lovers and I were the most important people in the world.

In reality, it was Isabel all along. Along with my parents, it was Isabel who was the most important person in my life. She understood me. She knew my childhood. Isabel stood behind me in a recycled bridesmaid's dress and recited the creed before the congregation. "God from God, Light from Light …" She raced me to Fred Meyer Grocery to buy candy. She took me to church camp, and we lived under the stars.

I had abandoned her for Pru-Ann, and then I had fallen in love with Ursula, whom I had loved so much. Then Ursula would mention a boy she liked, and I would drive out into the rainy countryside, park on a bluff, and weep. When Ava had appeared in her stead, I momentarily forget about Ursula. Ava and I had lain together only a few times, but I filled pages of my diary with musings about noble love. Nothing Isabel had ever done had ever elicited this kind of response in me, so my diary never recorded this memory:

It was a Saturday in the winter of our senior year. Isabel and I had nothing to do, so we walked to the ramshackle mini-mart three miles from her house and bought pockets full of cheap, old-fashioned candy: Lemonheads and grape gum in boxes shaped like miniature milk cartons.

We stepped outside, trading the smell of hot dogs and burnt coffee for the smell of rain and gasoline. Everything was gray. The peeling painted wall of the mini-mart was gray. On the two-lane highway, every car was made gray by a thin layer of mud. Even Isabel's red cheeks looked gray in the fading afternoon light. It started to rain. Across the road, between the market and Isabel's house, stretched a large acreage of grass seed fields, cut to stubble and muddy.

"Let's cut across the fields," Isabel said. "It's half the distance."

The rain rolled down our necks as we crossed the highway

and walked into the field. As we trudged across the muddy furrows, the sky lifted a little bit. The rain slowed to a heavy mist. After a while, I turned around and looked back. Behind us, the world looked as distant and flawless as a model railroad. The little trees looked perfectly treelike, the little barns perfectly barnlike, and the little market would not be improved by a new coat of paint. On the highway, tiny, perfect cars passed by, filled with people who were almost certainly good. I pulled the grape gum out of my pocket and put a piece in my mouth. I tasted the surge of sugar and felt the whole expanse of gray sky wash over me.

I thought, *I am perfectly happy*. For a few minutes, in the middle of a muddy field, tasting grape gum underneath the gray sky, I was perfectly happy. It was a happiness without cause and without objective. No preconditions, no stipulations, no hidden clauses. I was happy because I was alive, because the world was real, because I had a friend. Happiness at the heart of friendship is not a thing of wringing hands and midnight anguish.

"You know we've been friends for thirteen years," Isabel said.

A beam of sunlight slipped past my bedroom curtain, illuminating the carpet and casting shadows among my boxes. We were silent for a moment. I thought about grace, so often extolled at Forbearing Emmanuel. Grace: the unmerited favor of God. The gift that you are given, that you do not deserve, that you did not earn. I thought, *I am happy*. I thought, or perhaps simply felt, *My happiness is a golden thread that ties me to Isabel and to our childhood, so that as time moves forward, I will never be lost*. I thought, *I am perfectly happy, and I am filled with the honor of her friendship*.

Then I thought, *Shit, shit, shit, where is that fucking boat?*

Isabel leaned across my bed to the wooden chest that my

father had built into the space between the bed and the sloping wall. She opened it. "Ah," she said. "I knew you would keep it." She lifted up the boat and blew a bit of dust off it. "Are you going to take it with you?"

I took it from her hands and touched the sails. I turned it over and examined the rough, planed bottom. I traced the name with my finger: *Corazón Fiel*. "No. I'll leave it at home, and then I'll always know where it is." I placed it back inside the chest, the boat Isabel carried for me across Guatemala in her arms when we were only children. Isabel: my faithful friend.

My friends left one by one as their chosen colleges called them to summer prep courses, new student orientations, and ultimately on to fall. Smith College figured I could handle the rest of my life without inordinate orientation, so I was the last to leave.

On the night before I left, my parents and I sat on the back porch in the twilight. An evening fog lingered in the forest garden, collecting wherever the ground dipped. The sun lowered its head toward the horizon and cast thin strips of light through the trees, catching in the fog and turning it gold.

I talked incessantly, telling stories about my friends and classmates, philosophizing about life, love, death, and God. It occurred to me that I missed the church. I missed the Sunday services: the wedding at Cana, the story of Christmas, and all the stories where angels arrive and announce themselves, saying, "Do not be afraid," because they are so terrifying. And there was something else I wanted to say, something bigger.

"In World History," I began, "We learned that some Native Americans think God is a raven. Some people in India think God has three eyes and wears a garland of snakes or that he laughed, and when he laughed he gave birth to a son with the head of an elephant."

"That's a lovely image," my mother said.

"Maybe He did, you know? Or He could. Maybe we don't have all the answers."

"Of course we don't," my mother said.

"I've always had this other picture of God."

"Oh?"

"When we look up at the night sky, I think we're looking at the inside of a dome, and that's the dome of God. We think we're looking at stars, but we're really looking at *other people* looking at God." I leaned forward, eager because it seemed so true. "When the Muslims look into the dome they see Mecca, and when the Jews look, they see Elijah. The Christians see Jesus. But I think … I think I see Isabel. She's leaning on her porch railing eating that stupid nutritional yeast, and she's sad because her father died, and we can't talk about it, because we're just not that kind of friends, but I see her, and I know she's part of God." I hesitated. "And I see Ava." I remembered her face as she disappeared into the airport terminal. "And Ursula. And Chloe and Aaron. But most of all … I see you." I looked back and forth between them.

The twilight had faded to black, and the forest filled with the mystery of nighttime creatures. It struck me that the whole, perfect scene—the fog, the night owl, the smell of the forest—had made me terribly sad. I stopped talking. When my mother asked me what was wrong, I blurted out a clutter of mournful clichés. "We only live once. We'll never have this day back again. I feel time slipping through my fingers."

My mother smiled, then looked at my father, as though deferring to him in a matter that was still a man's responsibility.

"*Lacrimae rerum*," my father said. "There are tears for passing things. Did I ever tell you the story of Aeneas?"

"I don't think so."

"Aeneas was a Trojan, a hero and the son of a prince and a goddess. When Troy was conquered, he fled the city, carrying his father and his gods on his back. His wife was lost, stumbling behind him. Later, in a distant land, Aeneas saw the story of his own lost home painted on a wall, and he said, 'There are tears for passing things. Here, too, things mortal touch the mind.'"

Having said this, my father picked up his glass and toasted the summer with a little swirl of Gewürztraminer. I raised the drop of wine he had poured for me, no more than a communion serving, and clinked his glass, realizing only dimly how the world comes to an end and is reborn again—like the ocean, ever breaking and rising to meet the shore.

Later, beneath a bedside lamp, I took out my diary and tried to find words for the night. I scratched and scraped away at the blue-lined notebook, but the truth seemed irretrievable. There were no words wide enough for the dark sky, no words tender enough for my father's tousled hair, no words for the elegant crescents of white on my mother's fingernails as she raised her wine glass and said, "To us!"

Forgive me if I've told you this before.

MIXTAPE PLAYLIST

Step by Step • New Kids On The Block

Summer of '69 • Bryan Adams

Like a Prayer • Madonna

West End Girls • Pet Shop Boys

Love Will Tear Us Apart • Joy Division

The Last of the Famous International Playboys • Morrissey

'Til I Gain Control Again • This Mortal Coil

Troy • Sinéad O'Connor

A Little Respect • Erasure

The Passion of Lovers • Bauhaus

Sex Dwarf • Soft Cell

Everybody Knows • Leonard Cohen

Sweet Dreams (Are Made of This) • Eurythmics

Vision Thing • The Sisters Of Mercy

Worlock • Skinny Puppy

Head Like a Hole • Nine Inch Nails

Driven Like the Snow • The Sisters Of Mercy

Every Day Is Halloween • Ministry

There Is a Light That Never Goes Out • The Smiths

Acknowledgments

Thank you to the English department, especially Terrance Millet, for the many lifetimes we've shared; Chris Riseley, for being such a top-ten friend; Robin Havenick, for seeing the light in everything; Paul Hawkwood, for your insightful advice; Rob Priewe, for giving me the What Would Rob Do test; Jane Walker, for your kind presence; and Matt Usner, for your wonderful dry sense of humor. And thank you to all my friends and colleagues at Linn-Benton Community College, especially Liz Pearce, who never leaves anyone out, and Scott McAleer, the sanest person alive.

Thank you to Maria Isabel Rodriguez for over twenty-five years of seasonal candy, glamour photos, gothic Valentines, Venetian bar fights, and so much more.

Thank you also to all the people who made my adolescence fun despite it all, especially Amanda Gallo; Shannon Sedell; K8 Darling; Erik Henriksen; Summer Boslaugh; Mr. Sherwin; Ms. Eberman; Mr. Madar; Pastor Paulson; the Rodriguez clan, including Juanita, Nita, Edilberto, and Marguerite; and the Parrott family, including Wanda, Keith, Kim, and Jeff.

Thank you to Shannon Parrott for all the late-night conversations we hoped would never end and for the many, many years you have been such a fervent supporter of my writing, starting with the first half-baked poems.

Thank you to the Smith girls. Thank you to Kim Pippin for your steadfast friendship; Jen Nery for keeping the good times alive; and Myava Escamilla for getting me out of my shell.

Thank you to all the other friends who have read my work, supported my dreams, and otherwise made my life brighter, including Lori Major, the Bennet Family, the Mishra/Kerekes family, Linda Kay Silva, James Norlie and the folks at Luther House, the women of the Flattail/Stash softball team, and the women of Sapphire Books.

Thank you to all the people at Ooligan, especially my editors McKenzie Workman, Drew Lazzara, Sarah Currin-Moles, and Sarah Soards. Thank you, Mary Breaden, for inviting me into the PDXX Collective.

Thank you to all the activists who fought against Measure 9 and continue to fight for equality in Oregon and beyond. Thank you to Margarita Donnelly and Calyx Press for supporting women's writing.

Thank you to all the poets quoted in this book and to all the writers who shaped me, especially Jeanette Winterson, W. H. Auden, and T. S. Eliot. Thank you to celebrities like Ellen and Macklemore and Ryan Lewis for providing inspiration from afar.

An especially big thank you to my parents, Elin and Albert Stetz, for giving me a castle in the woods, a home filled with all the books, cats, frogs, and dreams a girl could possibly want. I grew in good soil because of you.

And finally a big, big thank you to my wife, Fay Stetz-Waters, for making the sun shine and the music sound better. Happily ever after began the day I met you.

Credits

Karelia Stetz-Waters is the author of the novel *The Admirer* and the serial novel *The Eastbank Killer*; her work has also appeared in *Calyx* and *First Time: An Anthology of Lost Virginity*. She holds a master's degree in English from the University of Oregon and a bachelor's degree in Comparative Literature from Smith College. A member of Willamette Writers and the Gold Crown Literary Society, Karelia teaches technical writing and English composition at Linn-Benton Community College. She lives in Albany, Oregon, with her wife, Fay; their pug, Lord Byron; and their cat, Cyrus the Disembowler.

Ooligan Press

Ooligan Press is a general trade publisher rooted in the rich literary tradition of the Pacific Northwest. Ooligan strives to discover works that reflect the diverse values and rich cultures that inspire so many to call the region their home. Founded in 2001, the press is a vibrant and integral part of Portland's publishing community, operating within the Department of English at Portland State University. Ooligan Press is staffed by graduate students working under the guidance of a core faculty of publishing professionals.

Project Managers
Sarah Soards
Ryan Kauffman
Stephanie Podmore

Editing
Sarah Currin-Moles (manager)
Katey Trnka (manager)
Drew Lazzara
Monica Rudolph-Ruiz
Geoff Wallace
McKenzie Workman

Design
Riley Kennysmith (manager)
Erika Schnatz (manager)
Robyn Best
Stephanie Podmore

Digital
Meaghan Corwin (manager)

Marketing and Promotions
Adam Salazar (manager)
Ariana Vives (manager)
Laurel Boruck
Emily Goldman
Kate Marshall
Tyler Mathieson
Lydia Morlan
Tenaya Mulvihill
Paige O'Rourke
Ellie Piper
Stephanie Podmore
Tiffany Shelton
Katey Trnka
Theresa Tyree
Caitlin Waite
William York

Forgive Me If I've Told You This Before is set in Cantoria MT Std, designed by Ron Carpenter. The cover title is set in Adamas Regular, designed by Octavian Belintan. Chapter art is based on Adamas Regular.

CPSIA information can be obtained at www.ICGtesting.com
Printed in the USA
BVOW07s1218111214

378229BV00002B/3/P